GAME
SLAVES

GAME SLAVES

. . . by Gard Skinner . . .

Houghton Mifflin Harcourt

Boston   New York

www.hmhbooks.com

Text set in Adobe Garamond
Character illustrations by Cameron Davis

Library of Congress Cataloging-in-Publication Data

Skinner, Gard. Game slaves / by Gard Skinner.
pages cm
Summary: "A highly intelligent group of video game enemy non-player characters (NPC) begins to doubt they are merely codes in a machine. Their search for answers leads them to a gruesome discovery."—Provided by publisher.
ISBN 978-0-547-97259-6
[1. Video games—Fiction. 2. Science fiction.] I. Title.
PZ7.S62812Gam 2013
[Fic]—dc23
2012045057

Manufactured in the United States of America
DOC 10 9 8 7 6 5 4 3 2 1
4500449572

. . .

To my three lovely women: each of you—
just like *rock paper scissors*—is funnier,
smarter, and more beautiful than the last

. . .

TAG: DAKOTA
LEVEL: 60+
CONFIRMED KILLS: 2,635,445
ACCURACY: 63%
HEADSHOTS: 28%
PREFERRED LOAD: SNIPER,
COMBAT RIFLE
UNIT AGE: UNKNOWN

TAG: PHOENIX
LEVEL: 60+
CONFIRMED KILLS: 96,598,322
ACCURACY: 67%
HEADSHOTS: 22%
PREFERRED LOAD: SHOTGUN,
MACHINE PISTOL
UNIT AGE: CLASSIFIED

TAG: RENO
LEVEL: 60+
CONFIRMED KILLS: 89,996,899
ACCURACY: 68%
HEADSHOTS: 37%
PREFERRED LOAD: LASER
MACHETE, SNIPER CANNON
UNIT AGE: CLASSIFIED

TAG: YORK
LEVEL: 60+
CONFIRMED KILLS: 92,135,698
ACCURACY: 59%
HEADSHOTS: 21%
PREFERRED LOAD: ROCKET
LAUNCHER, KNIVES
UNIT AGE: CLASSIFIED

TAG: MI ["ME"]
LEVEL: 60+
CONFIRMED KILLS: 86,002,354
ACCURACY: 74%
HEADSHOTS: 39%
PREFERRED LOAD: RANGED
WEAPONS, EXPLOSIVE
ORDNANCE
UNIT AGE: CLASSIFIED

TAG: JEVO
LEVEL: 60+
CONFIRMED KILLS: 56,021,888
ACCURACY: 48%
HEADSHOTS: 44%
PREFERRED LOAD: MELEE,
FISTS, TEETH
UNIT AGE: CLASSIFIED

. . .

. . .

. . . LOADING . . .

. . .

. . .

Level 1

Our first war with Dakota she was wetting her pants, pinned down by laser-machine-gun fire, explosions everywhere, missiles screaming, star fighters diving, cannons thumping . . . The girl was terrified, spouting gibberish, but, OK, not *really* condition yellow.

Sure, she was redlining. We all were. It was an inferno out there. But to be fair, her army-issue trousers were not pee-stained. Or two-stained.

Was she brave that day? Not a bit. All huddled in a ball, a teddy-bear clutch on her weapon, cringing at every blast as Planet LB-427 was reduced to ash.

A seven-hour battle. She didn't fire a single shot at the enemy. But at least she could still move and speak, which counts for something when you're dropped dead center in the most intense firefight ever spawned by bloodsucking alien invaders.

In the distance a chrome skyscraper erupted in flames and toppled over, crushing half our regiment. Two orbiting star destroyers collided and rained razor-sharp chunks into our foxhole. Smoke billowed from a crashed troop crawler while a monstrous spider-bot lost three legs and rolled on its back, squirming, helpless, just a countdown away from its atomic core going auto-destruct.

It wasn't a totally unusual situation—another day on the front lines, another hopeless battle. Our side was defending the last bridge to the Lair of Ultimate Doom as the enemy advanced on our position and tried to wipe us out. Before night fell, they hoped to storm the fortress gates and have it out with our boss, King Necramoid.

Typical intergalactic war. The noise. The smoke. The burn. The death.

Pure slaughter. Blood frosted the ruins. Severed body parts entangled our feet as we struggled to move. There were just a few dozen of us left, all wearing the slime-green Nec uniform, armed with single-burst blasters, and while we had the numbers, the gamer out there was mowing us down like he was cutting grass. This one was a good shot. Quick with his weapon switches. Flawless ammo management. Relentless power-ups.

Over to my right, by the concrete barriers, Third Platoon caught a full wave of Dicer fire. They were sliced neatly in two, all right at the waist. A med-bot tried to revive the top halves but lost both arms to a frag grenade for the effort. All the dying bodies squirmed, bled, and finally went still.

But that day, Dakota—man, she was *not* with the program.

"I don't wanna die!" she screamed, cradling her cold rifle, all curled up in a spot where the gamer had no angle to snipe her in the helmet or toss a betty in her lap.

"It's your *job* to die!" I argued. "Now get out there, expose yourself, fire off a few random shots, and let the enemy rip you to pieces! At least we can use you as a distraction so the rest of us can take him out!"

"Why can't we *reason* with him? I'm sure he's just a normal person like the rest of us! Let's wave a white flag and sit down to discuss a peace treaty!"

KABOOOOOOM! The gamer blew up our force field generator with a Quasi-Burst Rocket Launcher. Those babies are lethal. Downside: they take forever to reload.

Dakota jumped to her feet. Out there in the clearing, the gamer was reaching for another shell for his QBRL. She had a moment to do *some*thing. *Any*thing. She might have even taken him out with her weapon, but instead, she waved and screamed, "Hey! You!"

The gamer looked up. Wow, they never look up. Not even when one of us emits a truly beautiful death howl or dying scream or some kind of agonized shriek. Gamers refuse to pay attention to the NPC hordes. They just kill us over and over and over again.

But this one did pause. He stopped loading. He looked right at Dakota as she hopped over the low wall, tossing her weapon aside.

"I'm not going to hurt you!" she promised, removing her battle helmet, blond locks tumbling out. "Really! Trust me! I just want to talk. You look like a reasonable person . . ."

The gamer shrugged.

She rambled on. "So have you ever stopped to ask yourself *why* we have to fight and *why* we have to die and what's the *point* of—"

The gamer holstered the rocket launcher and quickly drew a pair of hand cannons. *KERPOWWWWW!* They looked to be the .46-caliber upgrades. Both glowed gold and packed armor-piercing ammo. Bad spot for Dakota to be in, but she dove quickly into a bomb crater, her hands still stretched up in surrender.

"You don't have to kill me!" she yelled. "And we don't have to kill you either! There can be *peace* between our species!"

Strange moment. The gamer paused. Why would he pause? He had a lot of work to do before finally reaching Necramoid's war chamber. These guys don't stop for anything when a boss battle is so close they can smell it on their progress bar.

But Dakota was having an effect. There was no doubt. The gamer lifted his weapons, taking harmless aim at a blank wall in the distance.

Dakota peeked her head over the edge of the crater. Realizing the gamer was not going to sizzle it off, she clambered across the bloodstained dirt.

"Who are you?" she asked him. "What's your name?"

The gamer pointed to a readout over his head. His tag, God_of_Destruktion glowed green.

Then she let him have it, like a dozen questions all at once. "So, how old are you? Where are you from? How did you get here? And who am I? How did I get here? What time is it? What day is it? What year is it? What is this place? Why all the anger and hostility? What did *I* ever do to *you?*"

God_of_Destruktion tilted his head. He looked confused. Heavy metal armor shrugged again, the dents and scars moving like skin over a massive frame. His facemask, dark as a sith helmet, began to pan around.

He sensed something. It made him nervous. But he wasn't sure what it was.

Dakota pressed, moving forward a bit, "Really, tell me, who *am* I?" she pleaded. "Why am I *here?* Part of this madness? Help me, G-O-D, *please* . . ."

But something set God_of_Destruktion off. He jumped back a step, boot rockets popping on, catapulting him a dozen yards away from the approaching girl. A trap! That must be it! He seemed to puzzle it out very quickly . . . Had the NPCs in this level sent a pretty girl as a . . .

"Suicide bomber," I heard him mutter over the radio. "Nice work. Clever game."

Yes. That had to be why this enemy soldier had approached him. Unarmed. So gorgeous. So vulnerable . . .

Dakota froze, and I watched the whole thing unfold. Honestly, I'd never seen anything like it in all my years in the muck. Nothing even close. And I've sent *millions* to die. Maybe the gamer was right to be afraid. What if Dakota was some kind of self-destruct bomb? I'd only met her that morning while getting suited up. For all I knew, she might be the next generation of NPC soldier.

God_of_Destruktion wasn't taking any chances. He wanted to live just as bad as Dakota.

The guy pulled a fusion grenade and slapped it to a sticky pad —another nice move. I could see what was coming. That guy knew war—then he threw the thing neatly at Dakota in a long arc. There was a *SPLAT!*

She turned to look back at us, the blinking device stuck squarely to her forehead; one great toss, if you ask me.

The gamer dove behind cover. What could the rest of us do?

We all dove too. Reno, York, Mi, Jevo, all of us.

Dakota erupted in a shower of red mist and electrical backlash.

When the battle resumed, there wasn't a piece of her left that was larger than a raindrop.

Level 2

"OOOOOOOWWWWWWWW!" Dakota moaned. I could tell the reassimilation was hurting, but that's usually the way it goes the first few times. Some soldiers can take it. Others have to let you know they don't like pain. That second kind is also prone to all sorts of other whining. I'll get back to that later.

She was lying on the operating table, the arms and beams from the giant machine quickly knitting her back together. A foot here. A leg there. Two hands. The organs and glands and blood vessels. Arteries were strung, sealed, and pressure-tested. Veins were filled with fresh blood. Eyeballs plopped into sockets, a synaptic wand stabbing in the side and neatly stitching the neurons to her oblongata.

"OH, man, this *HURTS!*" she cried.

"Of course it does," I agreed, grabbing her left fingers to see if the feeling had returned. "You took a fusion grenade to the forehead, dummy. It isn't supposed to feel *good.*"

"They didn't tell me about that in training," she spat, obviously angry that her drill sergeant had left out a few key facts.

"They assume you understand that getting shot or blown up or run over or disintegrated all the time isn't going to be a walk in the freakin' park." The words came out of my mouth a little mean. Not sure why I lashed out like that; I really didn't have a reason. I kinda liked her so far. She must pack a different kind of guts to face a gamer without a weapon like that.

I noticed I was still holding her wrist. Not sure why about that, either. It looked different. Strong, tough, but . . . different.

"You're Phoenix." She said it flat, like repeating a fact for a test. At the same time I saw her start massaging the ink around her hand.

"No one told me I was getting another body."

And what a body too. You can't imagine. Some artist pulled out all the stops for this one. Built for war. Just plain built.

She'd taken her paw away, was making a fist. I wanted it back. Something along the palm . . .

Dakota sneered. "I do not plan to end up on this table. Not *ever* again."

"I like the attitude, Dakota. Staying alive *is* the game. You sound like a winner."

"I just don't like getting pulverized."

"None of us do. Hop up, kid, let me show you around."

The machine finished sewing her back together. She zipped her jumper but was wobbly as both boots hit the floor. Typical. Something about the first few times you go double-z. As in 00, when you die, no hit points or health left. Your equilibrium gets all messed up for a while. Anyway, she stumbled into me. Man, she was stacked, for war, for pinup photos, you name it. Head to toe, not a muscle or bulge out of place.

I could see her weaving as we walked. Didn't mind when she leaned against me, not one little bit. Just doing my duty for my team, right?

The inside of Central Ops was, you guessed it, constructed just like you'd want a cost-is-no-object top-secret military installation to be. Steel grates for walkways. Sliding doors. Cold gray walls and thick windows. Everything burly and tough and top of the line. Very little wasted space. Hall after hall with closely spaced cabins. Deck upon deck of them. You'd get completely lost if the coordinates of your location weren't painted every few steps on the floor.

At CO, no one gets lost because there's nowhere to go. You're totally enclosed except for the out-portals in mission control. Incoming mail goes straight to Re-Sim.

The place seems huge your first day, and then you realize how small it is.

"Where are my quarters?" Dakota asked, and of course this was my choice. I was team commander, and I'd planned to put her down below with the other new grunts, but on a whim, I changed my mind. We were on my deck now, and one of my corporals had just been promoted to Boss, so what the heck, I gave her his cube. That put her about five doors down from me, and again, why do that? She already seemed like a whiner.

Maybe it was that hand. We've all got the company tat, you know. Around the palm. Have had it as long as any of us can remember. But hers . . . now it hit me . . . hers was off somehow.

Dakota was an interesting addition to my squad, no doubt about it. That blond hair. Around the same age as the rest of us, which was in the prime of our fighting lives. But she wasn't built like a teenage girl. No, she walked like an athlete and moved like a warrior. You probably know the mold. You know it for all of us.

I was way over six feet, about 250, and all of it ripped muscle. I made the Hulk look like he should do a sit-up or two.

Wire hair. Block steel for a skull, iron girders for bones. And here's the kicker: none of us could legally join any military we'd ever heard of. Years-wise, we were too young. But it was all about combat experience, right? My squad was ten times as battle-hardened as any puss gray-haired general on any planet. We'd seen more, shot more, and suffered more than entire armies. Some days, we *were* entire armies.

Our whole regiment was the same way. You've seen us in games, in comics—we're the biggest of the big and the best of the best. Looking for a steamroller in combat boots? A truck in pants? A wrecking ball wearing army-green?

You found us. *And* you found a world of hurt.

But Dakota, the closer I got to her, the more time we spent together, there was something else. Something extra. A blackened core in those dark eyes. A gaze that made you shake a bit.

Strong, yes. Confident, absolutely.

But no one would forget her on the battlefield earlier. She sure hadn't shown much in the way of common sense when hot metal began tearing through soft flesh.

So I told her where to find things. The mess, where she could grab whatever she wanted to eat. The gym, where she could work out if she felt like it, clear the cobwebs or whatever. We had a library and a game room and a bunch of other spots to gather during off-hours, but interest in those really came and went.

Up ahead, my buddies, who'd been here almost as long as I'd been at CO, were just coming out of the section lounge. Drinks, games, chatter. It had a monitor for the latest outgoing missions, something we checked all the time. Like any military, we lived our lives on call. Long periods of boredom punctuated by intense moments of sheer terror.

"What's the drill?" I shouted to Reno. The boy just shook his big head, neck tendons rippling. He was always first to check for action. First to go over a hill or through a door. I trusted him with my life every single day of my life.

"Nothin'."

"Nothin'," York echoed. He was always doing that. Going with the flow. Never a complaint. Dude was a monster, skin dark as shadow, the kind of bald beast you don't want to run into unless you've got a lot of friends around the corner.

Mi—full name Miami—was right behind them. Of course it had occurred to us all long ago that we'd each been named after some city or state or something in the United Zones of whatever they were calling it these days. Who really knew what was going on outside CO? Our information came straight through the propaganda channels. And even the little stuff we could glean from our enemies, from their chatter, from their habits . . . well, at least *we* had a safe place to sleep every night. Didn't seem like that was a common luxury these days.

You might have seen Mi around. She was a hottie. But in a complete-opposite-of-a-weak-supermodel kind of way. Body, brains, and brawn. Not to mention those eyes. If you ran into her on the front lines, trust me, you didn't forget. Something about when you mix radioactive green peering through coal-black locks. Her gaze was the last thing, the very last thing, a lot of gamers ever saw.

So, more about our names: I was probably from Arizona originally, Mi from the Orange State . . . New York, Nevada, Sarajevo, and so on. You'd have to be a complete moron not to have picked that up right away.

So of course the next question is, why not just go by our real names?

And that was the thing. The central point. None of us could remember our real name. None of us had any solid memories at all of where we were before we joined up. That part of our lives — how we got here, why we were here, where we came from — it was all a big blank in our heads. It was as if someone had kidnapped us, opened our skulls, and melon-balled out all the memory stuff. The only things they'd left behind were the training and the encrypted tattoos. We got blank slates, serial codes on our hands, and the ability to get blown to a million bits in insane battles day in and day out. Then they gathered up the debris and pieced us together again.

What a life.

Or was it even life?

It might have been death. None of us really had a clue. None of us really cared, either.

Not until Dakota started asking hard questions.

Level 3

Our shift came up, like it always did, at around 1600. That's about when day workers come home from their slog and begin a lifelong quest to avoid reality and live inside video games instead. God bless 'em.

From four till about dinner, then for much of the night, those were prime duty hours. And that was when my regiment was on duty. Team Phoenix. Not to brag—OK, to brag—we're the best. We're the next-generation, cutting-edge, biggest, baddest group of kickass NPC AI mother-crushers that ever played game. We've got game. No, we *are* the game. We're the top team.

There were others. A vet named Rio ran a solid crew, kind of like us, but focused on previous-generation servers. She was tough. Two-dimensional attack strategies, but tough nonetheless.

Another guy, Lima, had a tight squad. Great at hand-to-hand, melee, the up-close-and-personal wetwork. Syd, Dub, Scow . . . I knew most of them, but *my* team topped every stat.

We played prime hours, the newest games, on the toughest settings, and we won more than most. Not all the time, obviously, but we won.

You wanted to be a real gamer? You had to beat my crew, day in and day out, across all the platforms, across all the games, and then, maybe then, you'd be pretty good.

There'd been a new release of SLAUGHTER RACE EXTREME! the day before, so it was no surprise we spent most of the shift in the cockpit of cross-country war machines, blasting our way from one coast to the next. The open scenery was great, city after city, all postnuclear, of course. No closed-in walls of an orbiting prison or abandoned outpost tonight. Freedom to speed. We were the band of evil slavers that had to be defeated by the Democratic Resistance.

Every vehicle had weapons. Some had rocket launchers. On the back of mine, Mi was manning—ha ha, womanning—a minigun from a rotating turret. We had a good run. The only real problem was she kept kicking me in the back of the head every time she spun to shoot cars on our six.

Side note here: Mi's hit rate was *over 90 percent* that day. She was popping gamer heads and kneecaps like they were water balloons filled with red dye.

Because of her accuracy alone, we lasted all the way to Vegas before someone laid a trap and we ran over a huge IED. *BOOM!* The concussion sent us a mile into the air, splitting our rig clean in two.

Mi's half tumbled away from the blast, back in the direction we'd come. And when I landed, I actually hit pretty soft, spun a 180, and limped my battered machine toward where she'd cratered in.

Bet you never saw game villains do that, right? Go back for one of their own?

"You should have left me here to bleed out," Mi moaned, red goop pouring through broken teeth like drool from a baby's mouth.

"I wouldn't leave you." I smiled, knowing that she'd played her last level today. "I'll always come back for someone who, well . . . shoots as dead straight as you."

We could both see a heat seeker approaching from the south, arcing over, locked on, smoke trail a long curve and coming down to end it for us. Nice and quick. No way to run, nowhere to hide.

Flash of light. Then the explosion.

Woke up in reassimilation . . . Re-Sim . . . Like always, got a drink of water, quick bite to eat, and back on the road. Lots of miles to cover. Didn't seem like the gamers, whoever they were, had a curfew to worry about.

Late night, most of the younger gamers go to bed—we can tell because the voices change—so you'd think the violent gaming would die down. Think again. Those tend to be grownup hours. The language, the brutality . . . we really get to see what evil lurks in the hearts of men. Women. Grandparents. We see some cold, cold stuff.

So late night, new orders: SAVAGE SEWERS. We were back to the desolate wasteland, assigned to mutant duty in the radioactive tunnels below Old Denver. At least as *intelligent* monsters we could coordinate an attack on the Peacekeepers. (As usual, our minions — the zombie undead — had to just shamble from tunnel to tunnel, eating gamer bullets one after another. Sucked to be them.)

Mutant York had the idea of using our zombie horde as a diversion. Good call. York's what we call a "Stop 'n' Thinker." Always takes an extra microsecond to analyze before he hacks 'n' slashes. That's a good quality to have on any team.

While ma-and-pa video-game addicts were shooting York's decoys, we got Mi and Reno in behind their position. There were six gamers playing co-op over their controllers — from the voice chatter I caught that they were all part of the same hoity-toity country club during the day — and we took them out quite a few times before they figured out our strategy.

Then, the last run, those tennis moms and squash dads figured out where our hidey-hole was and went to the locker to switch up weapons. Flamethrowers. Ouch. They cooked us good.

As we were all roasting, skin peeling away like sheets sliding off a bed, we could pick up their cross talk:

"Burn those mutants, Sally! Burn 'em all!"

"Hoo ha ha ha ha ha!"

"*Shhhh!* Don't wake up the kids."

"It's so *real!*"

"Look at 'em twitch! I can almost smell the flesh!"

"Hey, speaking of the undead, don't we have that PTA thing tomorrow?"

"Toast 'em! Light those creeps up! Extra crispy!"

"The PTA?"

"No! More zombies are shuffling in!"

Sometimes the parents of teenage gamers are even more twisted than the teenage gamers themselves.

Next to me, as we lay there smoking, flames roasting our bones, I could hear Dakota groaning. "Owwwwwwww. Owwwwwwwww. This place just *sucks . . .*"

Level 4

She was right, to a point. Getting burned and shot and blown up a dozen times a day has its drawbacks. On the positive side, our health plan is great. The BlackStar Re-Sim machines run without a hitch. They *always* put all the parts back in the right place.

BlackStar owns video gaming. You know that. They're the planet's largest manufacturer. It's what they do. It's all they do. On every continent, in every home. Hundreds — no, *thousands* of titles. Everything from sims to MMO to RPG to puzzle to football to hockey to sweet little games for sweet little kids to big open-world butcher-fests for anyone who can legally buy the discs.

Legally buy the discs . . . Ha ha. Good one.

So that was our day. Every day. Between eight and sixteen hours on, playing the most advanced, CPU-intensive games as the bad guys, getting blown to smithereens. Then eight hours off. But we never worked more than sixteen a day. Not once in all the years I'd been running this regiment.

It makes sense to me. We had a job to do, but we need a break from time to time. You can't just surround yourself with all that mayhem 24-7 and not have it twist you all up, even if it is graphically generated. No brain can take that kind of intensity.

"I hate it," Dakota was saying that night. Man, she'd been pushing my buttons ever since she was assigned.

Reno, I think, was also fed up with her moaning. It was an honor to be on our team. Why not act like it?

He told her, "You know, you could be a thousand other places, Dakota. You could be a mischievous frog in FAIRYLAND ADVENTURES or a banana peel in BARBIE KART or even just a lowly ghost in ULTRA PACMAN. How boring is that? Floating the same pattern in the same maze over and over again throughout eternity? You should be *proud* to be up here with us."

"*I* am," Mi said, squeezing my arm. She likes me a lot, by the way. She likes this team. Good fighter. Follows orders. Zero whining.

I like Mi too. What's not to like? She's a stud athlete, hot from head to toe, and did I mention the ZERO WHINING part?

"Plus," York added, "we get to play the *fun* games. Best weapons. Best tech. Best worlds. And we get to wipe out the gamers almost as often as they incinerate us. We send them back to their checkpoints with their tails tucked tight!"

"Right on!" Reno agreed, fist-bumping his buddy.

"Dead straight," York continued. "Do other teams get to play next-gen games? None that I know of. They give *us* the most wicked bombs and vehicles and let us try to outsmart and outgun the best players on the net."

"*That there's* a fact," Reno said.

"But"—Dakota was used to standing up for herself, *that there* was obvious—"you idiots just don't get it, do you?"

Idiots? I started to smirk but caught myself. I should keep a straight face. They all look up to me and act like I act. After all, I'm senior guy around here. I've got a role to play, same as them. Usually it's combat leader. Other times it's more like father to squabbling kids.

"Idiots?" Reno howled at Dakota.

"Right, *idiots*," she repeated. "Are you too much of a meathead to be aware of what's going on?"

"Aware?"

"They're *using* you! BlackStar's making a fortune off us dying every few minutes or hours, then patching us up, then tearing us apart again!"

"So?" York asked.

"Yeah, so?" Reno echoed again. "This job's a whole lot more fun than flipping dog burgers or asking if people want fries with their chicken parts."

"I couldn't do that," York said.

"Me neither," Mi agreed, still clutching my arm. "By the way, anyone check the stats lately? See whose accuracy rating now leads all BlackStar NPCs *and* gamers worldwide?"

I'd checked.

Mi rocked, no doubt about it.

That's my girl.

There, I said it.

'Cuz she is.

Do I love Mi? Well, I sure love *me*.

But Miami . . . I don't know if I can call it love. It might not be in my programming.

Ah, WTH? Why quibble over code?

Yeah, maybe I do love her. What's not to love? Brains, body, those eyes . . . plus, she's got great stats.

Welcome to BATTLEGROUND 7: THE SPAWNICIDE. Team Phoenix playing the part of the shipwrecked extraterrestrial tribal horde. Mostly human, we had big insect parasites embedded in our bleeding eyes. Mi still looked totally hot, even with the antennae coming through both nostrils and thorax deforming her freckled cheeks.

The asteroid mining colony was all burned out. The only things left were their abandoned machinery, settlements, and drilling rigs. As bad bugs, we were supposed to also have mind-control powers, but so far, none of them had worked. No matter what spell we chanted or fierce stare of cranial dominance we tried, the enemy would not just put down their weapons and let us bite off their heads.

The gamers, well, they were next-gen human infantry with superior weapons and hypersonic hovercycles. Their laser-sighted smart bullets could curve around walls, barricades, and cruise right into our basement headquarters.

It'd been hard to escape that opening-scene bloodbath, but we got out. Through the alleyways. Across the molten river. There we found a couple of half tracks and motored across open asteroid to our next rendezvous point.

Right now, about eight of us were holed up on an oil derrick platform in the center of a rock plateau. Bad place to be, but at least we had hostages.

That's right. *Live captives.* What a game element. Along one wall, we'd come across a dozen of the gamers' squad. Sure, they might just have been foot soldiers, but they were ours now. Some other NPCs had trapped them, disarmed the whole bunch, and then gotten creative. The jailers were long gone, but they'd left us bargaining chips.

We'd found the men up here, suffering. Still kicking. They were strapped to the wall with heavy chains, and someone had obviously been asking hard questions. Evidence of torture was everywhere. As soon as the gamers on our trail found this place, well, we knew they'd blame us. We'd take the rap for this little house o' horrors.

All of the captive men were still in their issue gear. Flak jackets. Some had helmets. Some wore their boots, while a few had scorched bare feet. The only consistent feature was that each of them, one after another, had had his right hand hacked off just above the wrist.

And it was not a messy job. No, the cuts were clean, like sliced with big teeth. Then someone had used barbed wire to form a tourniquet. Still, whether the amputations had been for information or snack purposes, the neat wounds matched each other.

Man, in this heat, those must have hurt.

There wasn't much we could do. Put a bullet in each of them? No, not yet. We could use the collateral. The gamers were no more than a click or two away.

Mi wasn't fazed a bit. She'd seen worse. If anything, she didn't much like the prisoners being underfoot as we strung up our defenses. Claymores guarded the entryways. Tripwires crisscrossed approach gaps. It was all about covering weak areas and finding ways to whittle down the odds.

At one point, though, she was back at my side. Felt just right under my arm. Like our bodies had been carved as puzzle pieces that were a flush-perfect fit. Not only our bodies, you know, but our minds. The way we thought. The way we fought.

Her fingers came up, picked off a piece of scrap or something that had stuck to my forehead. I saw it again, like I always did—she didn't opt for shooting gloves in desert environments—I saw the branding tattoo that wrapped around her palm and the back of her hand. An artistic loop. The string of holographic slashes and dashes.

Blue ink that was etched into her skin. Like a bar code, only with curved lines. Different thicknesses. Swirling and dancing, woven in a 3-D helix. A striking mark. Maybe ten thousand swipes of the tattoo gun, glowing that faint blue, beautiful as LED-powered holiday decorations.

And that's when Dakota walked into the holding room dragging a burlap bag. A drippy burlap bag.

"I found 'em," she told us all.

"The gamer attack team?" Mi asked, turning to the window, hoisting her sniper rifle.

"No, Mi. For the *stumps.* I found their *hands.*"

"From our prisoners? So what?"

"I think we can still match 'em back up."

"What? *Why?*"

There was a grate, a trapdoor, in the center of the room that opened onto the asteroid surface thirty feet below. Dakota started kicking debris down there, making space to work. Then, one by one, she pulled the severed paws from the bag and lined them up so that she could look at each, then up at the string of men who were chained to the wall.

A pile of right hands. A dozen handless men. It was almost like one of those draw-a-line sheets where you match the chicken or the cow with the house it lives in.

She moved the palest limb to position three. It matched the third guy's skin tone.

The bigger one with the tribal ink probably belonged to number ten. That left a freckled one. She put that over in front of the redhead.

We all watched her. What on this barren world was she doing? Why?

No one moved as Dakota just kept at it. Trying to put the correct hand back in line with the correct mangled limb.

I finally walked over. It looked like the gamers had hit PAUSE or something, so we had a few minutes, but this was not the way to spend it. This was useless.

We heard a scratch at the door, then a slight whimper. There was an animal out there on the railings. Reno moved over to look through the hatch.

"Dog," he said.

"Duh," Mi needled him.

But Dakota kept going. I picked up one of the hands, and you know what I saw. It was so near-perfect that it was almost as human as the hand in front of your face right now. Still, you could *tell*. If they could someday make these environments indistinguishable from reality? Who knew what they'd do? Still, there are *always* minute glitches. Take these hands. Sure, they *looked* exactly right, but maybe the weight was off a little or the skin tone was too perfect. Was the blood running after it should have dried? Did the bone shards feel as sharp as bone actually feels? What about the hairs, or the texture? Sticky? Not dry enough? It can be tough to tell, but you can still tell.

Dakota put the darkest-skinned hand in front of the black man. A tanned one was placed with a guy who looked like a surfer; he had long, shaggy hair under his helmet.

One after another. The men moaned. They moved. The pain was still intense. None really acknowledged her work, though.

She scraped her fingers in the bottom of the bag. "I'm missing one," she announced.

No matter. Nothing she could do. Then, one at a time—and we all watched, still wondering why waste her effort—she took a matched hand and walked it over. With a gentle shove, she tried to work it back in place on the soldier's arm.

Of course it didn't stick. Or weld. Or melt on. C'mon, these wars are realistic to the last detail. All it did was make the soldier jerk back in pain. What could she have been thinking? Certainly not about our mission.

Scratch, scratch, that dog really wanted in.

Reno opened the door. The animal trotted in, a mangy black cur that probably hadn't eaten in a week. Which was why, we knew, that final missing hand in his mouth was a fine catch.

He had the last limb. And he went over into one corner, sat down, and began licking and gnawing on it.

"Nice detail," York snarked. "There's always a mangy dog licking the wrong thing."

But Dakota would have none of that. No, that hand seemed to belong to her.

She jumped at the dog. It growled, and I wondered what would come next. Along that far wall, twelve men—eleven with their hands back at their sides, one without—also watched her every move.

It wasn't like she could cure the combatants, right? The mission profile had nothing to do with playing *medic.* None ever did. We were probably going to kill them all when the next attack came anyway. Those gamers weren't going to leave it on PAUSE forever. They wouldn't let all these low-level online combatants stay captive. The game had to move along. Objectives had to be met.

The dog growled again. Dakota growled back. She reached for the hand suddenly, trying to catch the dog off guard, but the beast coiled and snapped. It crawled deeper into the corner with its fangs between its tasty meal and Dakota's approach.

"Gimme some food," she said. "I'll distract it with some food."

"It already *has* something to eat," Mi corrected her, shrugging. "Damn, girl, what is up with you?"

Then Mi did what we'd all thought of doing first. Well, not Dakota.

Mi walked over, chambered a shotgun shell, and blew the dog's head off.

Brains spattered the wall, but she didn't even break stride, reaching down for the hand. Casually, she tossed the thing at Dakota.

"There, OK? You better get it together, D. Keep this up and you'll get sent down for sure."

Dakota, the sagging appendage in her hand, just stared back. Then she went over and placed it by the final hostage.

And that's when the gamers attacked.

Rocket shells flew through the windows. Grenades bounced up through the trapdoor. Over our heads, an Apache space chopper rained hell in the form of 34mm mini-gun tracers.

My team was quick, returning fire. Even Dakota.

Reno, York, me, Jevo, the rest of the crew: we poured lead down on the exposed gamers. We had position, and they had a rescue mission to complete.

All except Mi. Through the smoke I caught a glimpse of her walking along the soldiers, kicking their reclaimed hands one by one at the hole. She watched them drop and bounce off the rocks below.

An hour later, traps exhausted, caught in multiple crossfires, we lost our rear wall. After that, they cleaned us up pretty quick.

I took a bullet in one ear. On its way out, it cleaned wax from my other ear as well. But we all went down fighting, 'cuz that's what we do.

I woke up with a headache like you could not believe. At first I thought the Re-Sim blades had forgotten to close a door on my skull plate or something, but when I ran my fingers over my head, everything was intact.

The pain, though, was intense. It was just over my right eye, to the side, in that soft gap where it feels like you can push in and touch the edge of your cornea. The temple is a tender spot. Trust me, you don't ever want to get punched there.

If only this felt like just a punch. But no, it was burning, more like a cyst or growth, pulsing and cheesing and building up explosive pus. It throbbed as if it might pop.

Then, right in the corner of that eye. I saw it. But I knew I *didn't* see it. Ever get an eyelash stuck and it looks like a shadow? This was no shadow, it was a sign. A road sign. Like a memory or glimpse, but even as clear as it got, I knew it wasn't really there. When I turned my head, it turned too. It was just something stuck in my field of vision.

In the rest of my line of sight was Dakota, bouncing off her table. Mi was getting up too, and it didn't escape me that her hand went to the same side of her head. Clutching the spot. As if someone had driven a heated knitting needle as deep as they could push it in.

Reno, York, Jevo, the others. Wincing. Like bright lights had pierced a dark sleep.

I tried to focus.

I tried to see what was on that sign, but it was fading. It was probably just a leftover image from the mission. Maybe the name of the oil derrick or the colony or . . .

No. It wasn't that.

Not at all. This was something new. Something I'd never seen online before.

What it read, I realized as the image and the pain quickly faded, was:

ENTERING PHOENIX, ARIZONA

TAKE ANOTHER STEP AND YOU WILL BE SHOT

Level 5

Dawn broke through some low-lying clouds, and that was exactly the last thing we wanted. Now, with the sun up, the pack that was hunting us could use their spotter scopes to keep track of our movements.

THE HILLS HAVE TEETH IV. We, of course, were the hills. Or the teeth. Whatever. Me and Mi and York and Reno and Dakota and about a dozen more were dressed in rags and looked like inbred hillbillies. Jevo was the huge behemoth country hick who bit stuff. He did look the part. All bulk, no brain, jaws of rusty brass. There always be a-one them in those-there backwoods gigs, ain't I right, y'all?

According to the cutscenes, the story line, we'd kidnapped and —get this—*eaten* the gamers' kids or something sicko like that. Can you believe this crap? Cannibalism as a story line for kids, adults, whoever? BlackStar was one twisted company. They stopped at nothing. If rock beats scissor and paper covers rock, you can bet that for a corporation profit crushes morality. Anything for a buck.

For a billion bucks? Total perversion.

Anyway, so my friends and I, according to the intro movie, were the so-called *flesh-eating fiends with nasty teeth and bulging eyes and yellow claws for fingernails!* Oh, brother, how stupid can it get? Anyway, we'd done some atrocious thing to the gamers' children, so now they just *had* to hunt us down and get their sweet, sweet revenge.

Dakota was right. While the gaming parts might have been fun . . . the running and jumping and shooting . . . why did BlackStar designers have to wrap it all up in grosser and grosser story lines? My team didn't care one bit if we were wearing denim rags, like now, or driving futuristic mech-bots. We just wanted a challenge—an athletic combat puzzle. We wanted to win a few and lose a few. We wanted to try different strategies. We wanted a couple of laughs and surprises along the way.

Revolting story elements had nothing to do with the quality of the actual gaming experience.

Still, there we were, just coming out of the low foothills, getting chased by four gamers who were maybe an hour behind. During the night, while the—oh, brother, here it came again—*vampire werewolves* were out (yeah, they actually had those in this game)—we'd taken a chance and moved early. It'd paid off, and now we'd put a little gap between us and our pursuers.

"We can't cross the open plain." Jevo was pointing ahead, his torn flannel shirt drooping off dirty muscles.

"They'll spot us," Mi agreed, panning around, a hand up for shade, searching for a new route. Reno handed her some binocs. Those two always moved like a team. Made my job easy.

"What're they on now?" York asked, watching our six, making sure we didn't get sniped from behind.

"I heard motorcycles late last night," Dakota offered. So far, she was actually being a big help. Maybe she did belong here with us after all.

"Then they got attacked by the undead dogs. Big fight. But I think they also found another ammo dump and rearmed."

"We've got nowhere to set up an ambush." York kicked the dirt.

"There's a ghost town over near that tree line." Mi pointed. She was right. It was a ways off but was a much better option than crossing open ground.

We humped along the ridge for a while. Once, we heard barking, but that was probably just random background noise. While we villains were often given vicious guard dogs or attack beasts to use, the gamers almost never had trained animals in their inventory. They did, however, get night-vision goggles, radar, and all kinds of maps, clues, and hints along the way. So if we'd found this town, chances were good they knew about it too.

"It's a trap," Dakota warned as we neared the edge of the settlement. Cracked pavement stretched ahead. Abandoned gas stations, dark homes, wood rot, fallen signs, rusting cars: the detail was exquisite. I was pretty sure one of the circling buzzards actually rained poop on a broken windshield. Some designer had spent time on this town.

"What're you looking for?" I asked York. He had a spotter scope out.

"The diseased house dog licking a dead corpse. Apocalyptic scenarios always open with one. Then I kick it. And it scampers away, howling."

That made me chuckle. York.

"I don't think they could've circled ahead of us." York countered Dakota's theory that it was a trap. "Chief," he said to me, "let's set up our own front here. Best place for it."

"No other place for one," Reno agreed, already hoisting his shotgun.

"That's exactly the point," Dakota snarled at them. "They've been hunting forever. This is the only destination for us. They need to wipe us out to get revenge or satisfaction or whatever, and everything points to *this* place."

"But how could they have gotten here first?" Mi challenged her, also wanting to set up and fight it out with our alpha crew. "Transporter device? Unlikely."

"Helicopter," Dakota suggested, looking around.

"No way," York argued. "There are no military vehicles in this game. It's been very straightforward: supposedly, we ate something we weren't supposed to eat. A simple revenge plot line followed . . . they came looking for us in our cave complex. Big battle. We lost most of our minions. Jevo snuck around and dined on their remaining infants."

"Which were way undercooked," Jevo tossed in there.

York continued, "We moved to the trailer park. More battle. Then we went through the abandoned research facility where evil scientists did secret experiments and the virus got out of hand."

Reno sneered. "There's *always* an abandoned research facility where the secret experiments run amok and the virus gets out of hand . . ."

"Anyway, from there it was a straight shot to the gorge. Then to the dam. Then through the high mountains. Some vamp wolves. Fight-fight-fight. Big cliff. Raging river. Now to the plains and the abandoned ghost town."

"Right, very predictable," Mi said. "Theoretically, they might have found jetpacks or something back at the research labs, but it's doubtful. We're here *first*. So let's set up a couple sniper positions on top of the creepy library and the haunted grain silo."

Reno helped out. "I'll position the mortar over there behind the deserted police station, and, Dakota, how about if you place the machine gun in that convenient machine-gun nest? The one on top of the fully filled aboveground gasoline containers at the corner gas station?"

"Gee, how *surprising*," she replied. "What are the chances the gamers will shoot the clearly marked explosive tanks?"

"Very funny, Dakota."

"Wasn't making a joke, Reno."

"How's your ammo?"

"Unlimited," she told him with another face, sticking out her tongue. That's, like, the oldest one in the book. AI, NPCs, we *always* have unlimited ammo.

"So that's our plan, chief?" Reno asked me.

I nodded, but didn't tell him it just didn't feel right. Yeah, games are predictable. Environments are predictable. And this title was creepy, to be sure, but still, something didn't add up.

After all we'd been through, had the designer really just led us—and the gamers—to this abandoned town to have it out in another run-of-the-mill gunfight?

Maybe.

Although . . . it sure didn't feel much like a final boss battle. Nope, it still felt like we were working our way through the maze.

We saw them coming from a good way off, but the strange part was how long it'd taken. I'd sat there most of the day with Mi in her sniper position and waited for the enemy to appear. Quiet.

Thoughtful. Comfortable. We didn't really talk much out here without a reason. That was kind of the way it had gotten between us. Can't explain it, but when you live with someone you also go to war with, a lot of the operational details can go unspoken. Makes it nice. Efficient. Reduces the background noise.

And, no doubt, it helps in battle to know what the others are thinking. We had that, all the team did, and Mi had it with Reno, too. Put those two in a bunker together and they'd be *tough* to dig out. Make him or her defend that same bunker with Dakota? Who knew what freak-show event would happen next?

I knew how Mi fought just as well as I knew how long it took her to get ready in the morning. I understood her strategy about when to shoot and when to hide and when to move just as easily as I could predict what she'd eat each night for chow.

We'd been together for lifetimes. That was the rhythm of our days. One death after another. I'd seen her get blown away so often it just didn't hurt that much anymore. I knew she'd get put back together, more beautiful each time, a new nick or scar, perhaps—and there we'd be, laughing, joking, slugging each other back at base, waiting for our next assignment. For a new challenge. For more good times.

So there we sat, on the grain silo, for way too long. I took a minute to look at the tattoo that ran around her palm. It was beautiful, changing color in the light, nothing like the plain tribal ink you usually saw. And mine, well, so similar in color, swirls, and code. We were made for each other.

So I asked, I had to ask. "When we came out of Re-Sim last time, did you get something stuck in your eye? Some pain there?"

She turned—it looked like the memory was there—then nodded.

"Some kind of bird, I think. Big one."

"Hawk? Eagle? Raptor?"

"Sorry, *war* bird, more like a bomber," she clarified. "Not a bird bird. A plane. Raining acid from wing sprayers. Sort of a crop duster, only one the size of a superjet."

"Wow."

"I don't think I've ever fought one like it before."

"Acid, huh?"

"Old people melting like butter underneath. Alligators turning into highway puddles. Strong stuff."

"Was it real?" I pushed her. "I mean, had you seen it in any game before? Like a ghost memory?"

She shook her head.

I told her about the sign. The Shoot on Sight sign with my name on it.

She smiled. "Maybe like a premonition, or a preview? Of something we get to play soon? I kinda like it already. I hope *our* side gets a few of those aerial supersoakers."

I laughed a bit. That's my girl. Big guns made her happy.

"Might not be a game preview," I muttered. "Something stuck in the system."

"It's not my first one," she suddenly admitted. "Been getting them ever since Dakota . . ."

Then she stopped.

"Since Dakota showed up?" I finished. I thought back. Was that when my first weird memory happened too? I thought it was.

Not a memory, though. More like a glitch. Something we weren't supposed to see.

But really . . . what was to fear, a few ghost images? With all we went through? Hell, maybe they *were* just clues for an upcoming mission.

Our town was still quiet. We owned it. I thought I should maybe make a run and repaint the sign on the edge to read NEW PHOENIX, but didn't want to give away my position. Or Mi's. We had a good spot.

So where were the gamers? Strange they weren't just rushing in. Most of you gamers play a pure hack 'n' slash game. Your kind relies on brute force, overwhelming firepower, and plenty of health packs or shield regenerators to wade through my NPC team. Very few of you are truly strategic. Some of you are outright stupid, and it takes you dozens of tries to figure out how to defeat us. You just blunder around over and over again until you eventually stumble on the correct tactical solution.

But again, this was a bit odd. This *game* was odd. Most of the time, for us, it's deep space and alien monsters and super-high-powered weaponry. This place, though: regular shotguns and Uzis and pistols. Most of us even had bats or machetes as melee weapons. Very unimaginative at our level of play, and it was puzzling why my team would be assigned to second-rate programming like this. It just didn't make sense.

The first thing we heard was the crunch of big rubber on gravel. Nothing in nature makes that noise. And these tires were huge.

On a distant hill, a vehicle appeared, rolling easily over the boulders in the scree field surrounding the town. It was a monster jeep, and from the looks of it, the gamers had spent time piecing it together from the scrap remains found back at the research lab.

Six huge tires. A massive roll cage on top. Each corner had a gunner with some kind of harpoon launcher. And behind the buggy —very strange—it was towing a trailer that looked like a circus cage, only the top was left wide open.

What was going on here? Wasn't this just another first-person shooter? Why all the machinery? Why give the gamers the option to stop and make new vehicles? Why not just give them bigger guns and some kind of prefab tank?

"Should I pick one off?" Mi asked, hoisting her sniper rifle, laying the crosshairs over the closest gamer's head.

"You'll give away our position."

"I think I can get two of them before they fire back," she muttered. "Wanna bet?"

I believed she could pull off the shots, even at this distance, even with the targets bouncing and moving. She was that good.

I radioed York and Reno to ask if they had clear lines of fire yet. Nope. But Dakota, over on the gasoline tanks, promised she could also open up. That helped. See, if you ambush an enemy from a single firing position, it's easy for them to spot you and get to cover. When you catch them in a crossfire unexpectedly, it's completely different. They have very little opportunity to spot either position or find a place that's safe from both vantage points.

"OK," I announced, "when the vehicle reaches the second stop sign, Dakota and Mi, take out the front corner gunners. You two coordinate your targets. The dual gunners behind them have limited visibility. Reno, can you get a grenade or Molotov on top of their RV while they're still trying to pin down our positions?"

"I can try."

"That's the plan, then. I'm going on foot. Once they're occupied with you, I'm going to flank left. Let's end this weird session once and for all."

"Roger that."

"Jevo, get ready for dessert."

"Here comes my morning bacon."

Little did we know.

Level 6

It got ugly. It got ugly very quickly.

Mi was true to her word and her aim. As soon as the nose of the massive buggy was even with the second stop sign, the front gunner's helmet exploded into crimson spray. Chunks of brain splattered the roof of an abandoned minivan. On cue, Dakota took out the other, and it looked like we'd gotten the upper hand.

A vehicle that size, especially towing a trailer, could never turn around and scoot for cover. It was a sitting duck, and the only way to go was right into the teeth of our ambush.

The enemy's back gunners opened fire, but fortunately, Dakota and Mi had planned their shots perfectly. The gamers were spraying wildly. The idiots had no clue.

I pulled up my scope, was off at a 90 to the enemy's right, and surveyed the remaining force. The front two players were dead and useless. Gone from this world. I panned over the back two gunners, looking for their tags floating over their heads. I'd take any advantage to try to isolate a target.

But that's when I saw the bad news.

The big buggy wasn't just a big objective. It was a moving screen.

Behind the rig were four gamers, and I knew they were the shot callers by the gold lettering floating over their helmets. Gold is the prime color. That's the highest level you can achieve online. And they were waiting, like a second wave. True veterans. Thousands of hours playing vids between 'em. Mad skills, to be sure.

Each was throttling a modded dirt bike with machine guns where the headlights should have been. The tires were rimmed with razor-sharp spikes. On the back, where another passenger might sit, a robot gunner added even more firepower to the arsenal.

The big buggy had been used to get the cycles in close. A mobile diversion. Nice move. We'd been so focused on the strange contraption and taking out the easy targets that we'd never realized those were just sacrificial offerings to our snipers.

I'd blown it. Now, unfortunately, they'd had a chance to narrow in on our positions. *And* get close.

Clever jerks. Gamers just have to show off, don't they?

Two of the riders broke left and the other two went right. That was a small mistake; they didn't know it yet, but I was to their right.

I hoisted an AK-47 on one arm and a giant revolver in my other hand. I'd only get one chance, but they had no idea I was hiding over here. A good spot too. Down behind a rusting mailbox. They split up to move around it, zipping past me on either side.

One motorcycle raced by, then the second, the riders' backs fully exposed. I stood, steadied my legs, and opened fire. The AK was full auto and cut the rider on my left in half; he died, tumbling like a rag doll into a low wall.

But on the right, my hand-cannon's first shell bounced off the mechanized soldier in the passenger seat. No damage. Still, the rider felt the impact or heard the ricochet: he ripped a neat cookie in the street and zeroed in on my spot.

Bummer for *me* now. Before, I'd had perfect cover. Now I was just a guy in the open with a machine gun that needed another clip and a mailbox behind me that was of no use whatsoever.

I dropped the AK and tried to sight down the barrel of the nickel-plated handgun. I had five shells remaining, but this next shot would have to be *perfect*.

If I hit the charging rider in the body, it wouldn't do enough damage. Anyone who games knows that *only* head shots are any guarantee of a fatal blow.

The bike's front-mounted guns started peppering bullets, but they were wild, hitting my legs, arms, shoulder, nothing vital. Sure, it hurt, and it knocked down my health a lot, but he too would need a head shot to guarantee a kill.

The notch on my gun centered right over his facemask. That was the most vulnerable point. Any revolver these days, in any game, packs a massive damage rating. The downside? Slow rate of fire. Slow reload. Only six bullets in the chamber. Each bullet does a good job, you just have to make sure every shell counts.

KABOOM! I fired. I missed. It did occur to me, so you know, that Mi would have picked him right off.

But he was, after all, on a motorcycle, speeding and weaving. A tough shot. You try to make it.

KERPOWWW! The third bullet glanced off his temple. Not a direct hit. No solid damage at all.

His machine guns kept up their chatter — *RAT-A-TAT! RAT-A-TAT!* — the bullets stinging off my knees, elbows, making it almost impossible to line up a fourth shot.

Still, that's what they pay me for. I make my living putting up a good fight, right to the very end.

The sights finally found a home. Right over the middle of his helmet. It would be a nose shot. Nice splat on impact. Nothing left inside but cerebral soup.

I win.

I pulled the trigger.

CLICK!

What?

Out of bullets?

I began counting. One when he passed. It hit the robot.

Two more at him after he spun around to take me out? Had I gotten trigger-happy and emptied the cannon by spraying fire . . . ?

Wait! No! I'd only fired *one* at the bike as it passed. Then two. I should have had three left.

Had I forgotten to reload earlier? Yesterday? Had I been packing a half-full gun all this time? No way. Not a chance. I never forgot to reload. And the weight of the gun would've felt funny.

CLICK! I tried it again.

CLICK.

Click.

What was the use? I was a sitting duck. No shots left. So much for unlimited ammo . . . What kind of crap game was this where the NPC *ran out of bullets?* Or was loaded with duds? How could that be fun?

"Go shoot hillbillies whose weapons are empty or jammed!"

It'd never sell.

So I waited for the guy on the motorcycle to finish me off. Or run me over with those spiked tires. Or rope me with a steel cable and drag me to my death all over that scraggy landscape.

But he didn't. The rider fishtailed to a stop right at my feet. We were almost nose to nose, but I still couldn't see a face behind the smoked helmet visor. Nor could I pick out any skin behind his full-body riding armor. Bullet marks and skids were all over him, including a big dent where my last bullet had very narrowly missed center-skull.

"Gotcha!" he yelled.

Funny. When those guys spoke into their wireless headsets, we usually picked up the chatter. Now this one was talking to *me*. Directly?

What the . . . ? OK. Why not talk back?

"I ran out of shells," I told him, popping open the chamber to show him six spent cartridges.

"Lucky for me," he responded. "You're Phoenix, right? *The* Phoenix? Your scores are off the charts."

Scores? Charts?

Not me. I have no tag. I'm an NPC. I have no rating he could access. I die for a living. How could he have known?

He lifted a hand-cannon of his own. At least this time, for me, the end would come quickly.

In just a few digital seconds, I'd be back home. Climbing out of the Re-Sim. Good thing, too. This had been a really long session. I was starving.

"You win . . ." I smiled at him through my gnarled, inbred teeth.

He nodded.

". . . *this* time," I added. "Next time, who knows?"

He shrugged too, taking his time with the mercy kill. Why? Behind him, I could see his crew laying waste to the rest of my team.

And still he waited. Why not shoot? He just sat there on his bike, pointing the massive barrel at my forehead, in no hurry at all. What kind of juvenile, violence-crazed, prepubescent carnage machine *was* he? Get on with it, already! I was hungry!

"Game's over," I finally told him. "Finish it. You've been chasing us for days, I'm starved."

"Starved?" He cocked his head.

Then I heard the crunch behind me. That unmistakable crunch. You already know nothing in nature sounds like that. Tires on gravel.

The buggy. It had driven up.

And then the gamer said one last thing, and it completely gave me the creeps.

"It's not over yet, cannibal."

A harpoon fired and a shaft of metal as big as a baseball bat sliced clean through my leg. It hurt, it hurt bad, but that wasn't the death blow.

No death blow would come. The gamer was right; the contest was not nearly over yet.

The harpoon was attached to a steel cable that hoisted me up, over the buggy. The arm of the crane then swung me like a sack of dirt. At the last moment, the hook released and I was tossed, very roughly, in the back cage. Into the circus trailer.

Quickly, the whole craft lurched forward. On with the mission.

These guys weren't killing.

They were *hunting*.

What kind of game was this?

They moved in to try to capture Mi, but she got shot down. York and Reno were fried to a crisp when the gas tanks went up. The rest of my team, unfortunately, was wiped out soon after by mortar fire.

I watched them try to do the same thing to Jevo. They cornered him, put a spear through his neck, then stood there and watched him bleed.

That same rider, I believed, was over there talking to him. Then he was talking to his buddies. For some reason, Jevo wasn't the right catch. A bigger guy knocked my bigger guy to the ground, sat his rear motorcycle tire on our goon's head, twisted the throttle, and ground the skull down to the pavement. Jevo died. Mercilessly. Never saw the big man again, either. Not like that, anyway.

Then, as it always happens in war, everything went from pure chaos to dead silence.

Nothing marred that perfect quiet. Even the tires had stopped rolling.

And that's when I heard her voice.

Dakota.

She was lying in a heap on the other side of the cage, pinned down under some concrete debris. Her leg, too, was sporting the shaft of one of their whaling harpoons.

"I really, really do *not* like your world." She grimaced my way, covered in dirt.

I helped her up, brushed off the dust, but by now, the monstrous craft was leaving town. Heading off across the barren desert. Wherever we were pointed, it looked to be a long journey. At least the sun was finally going down.

"What kind of game is this?" she asked with a lot of menace in her voice.

It was exactly the same feeling I was having. Gamers never take prisoners. Why would they? They get no points, no thrill, no "delightful" death graphics like spurting blood or exploding rib cages or careening body parts. Those guys live for rag-doll physics. Not for building a zoo.

There was no point in capturing even one of the enemy.

"I don't know," I told her honestly. "But this is by far the longest session I've ever been assigned to."

"You're sure it's a *game?*" she asked softly. The sun had just reached the distant horizon. We had maybe five minutes of light left. And we'd been in here twenty-four hours, easy.

Sure it's a game? I just shook my head. I really didn't know. I had no clue where we were headed. Or why. From the gamers' perspective, those guys on the motorcycles, why would they ever want to play anything that lasted so many hours and *didn't* end with the thrill of killing a disgusting enemy like us? What was the point?

We rolled across desert. Yard after yard. Mile upon mile. Answers seemed a long way off.

"Did you see their tags?" Dakota asked.

She seemed to be getting a second wind. And her wounds, like mine, were healing up. Limb damage was never permanent for us.

"Their tags?"

"Gamer tags."

"I know what tags are." I laughed at her.

"But did you *read* them?"

I thought back. No. I never did anymore. They're always something stupid like God_of_Destruktion or Apocalypse_Cow or Killin_Machine_666 or Im_da_Bomb! Whatever. Most are ridiculous. You go blind to them after a while.

"The rider who captured me was called BlackStar_2."

I just stared at her. That short a tag? That, well, nonviolent?

I had to clarify. "*BlackStar_2?* That's it?"

She nodded.

"Where's the evil mischief? Where's the dastardly, juvenile-stupid name in *that?*"

She shrugged, then added, "The one who had that gun pointed at you was BlackStar_3."

"You've got to be kidding."

She shook her head. "The first motorcyclist you shot in half was BlackStar_1."

Whoa.

Weirder and weirder.

Maybe this wasn't a game after all.

Level 7

They dumped us in a cell and, well, since you're familiar with video games, you know it could only go two ways.

One kind of cell is like the dirtiest, scummiest, most rodent-ridden pit ever created by graphic artists. Old skeletons, rats eating rib meat, spiders the size of a principal's butt, the works.

The other kind can be even more frightening, as it inevitably leads only to cruel medical experiments performed by insane scientists.

Unfortunately, *the other kind* was where we were stuffed.

The walls were clean, the table immaculate, and the bunks looked as if they'd never been used. Maybe they hadn't. We are, as you remember, the cutting edge of gaming NPCs. This might have been an entirely new environment. Unsoiled and untouched. Maybe something made for a top-secret military training game. Or a test arena for the next generation of combat.

⊕   ⊕   ⊕

What were our captors waiting for? What kind of game has long breaks in the action where you do nothing?

The boring kind, I guess.

Dakota and I got cleaned up. Robots removed all the hillbilly clothing and makeup, and they rinsed us off in four-nozzle showers. Any nonfatal wounds, as usual, were healing quickly. The water was hot and felt great. My thick arms and legs finally relaxed after that marathon on the run. The smell washed down the drain along with about a pound of the barren landscape we'd been tromping across.

Crazy, the water, it was nice and warm. Not freezing. Not boiling. Just perfect.

Then they fed us. Now, this was also strange—consuming food in a video game? Not once in all the years I'd been running the team had we stopped in the middle of a session to eat. Recharge, whether it was a meal or sleep or just some time off, always came *after* the session. Back at Central Ops. After we died or the gamer saved and let us go home. At no point did the actual gaming platform include fried chicken and gravy and big bottles of Coke and a huge mound of mashed potatoes.

It tasted great. Absolutely great.

"We're not in the HILLS HAVE TEETH world anymore," Dakota slurred to me through a mouthful of spuds. "Not a chance. We got pulled or pushed to another environment."

I didn't agree. The two were linked. Some kind of door or portal. Maybe this was just the next level, but still, the main question, *why* capture us? It wasn't like we knew anything . . .

Or did we?

I didn't know squat.

But Dakota had been grabbed too. And nothing had been the same since that day on LB-427.

How long would it take, really, before gaming environments mirrored real-world challenges even more realistically? What if this was the next generation? Instead of the gamer having to decimate every enemy, what if now, in this new arena, the NPC had information you had to extract in order to continue to level up through the game?

Interesting twist. And innovative game tech always sells.

One thing backed that theory up: our gaming worlds *never* sat still. Those designers out there were always trying new things. This might just have been one of those tests. A trial environment. Made some sense. Introduce a torture chamber or an interrogation challenge. Still, what could we possibly *know?* Or have seen? Why imprison us? Why feed us? Why not just get to the information extraction part of the session?

"Think it's a game glitch?" Dakota asked me, stuffing calories in as fast as her hands could shovel.

"It's new to me," I admitted, then took some time to really look at Dakota. She was still so fresh. We'd had a couple of weeks together. And it was true that over the years my team kind of came and went. Lately, we'd been pretty solid. Mi and I had been partners the longest. York and Reno, eons together. There were a dozen other NPCs in the system whose moves I knew as well as my own; guys like Jevo, or this other one, Deke, who ran his own team now.

But Dakota, she was a wild card.

Sure, teammates moved. It happened. They got burned out, they lost a step, they took too many frag grenades to the chin. Most of the time they'd be assigned to a less stressful team. Maybe driving computer-controlled cars in GREED FOR SPEED. Or playing Bowser or Luigi or Clank or Ratchet or Jak or that rat-thing he carries around on his shoulder. There were plenty of jobs out there.

Then, of course, we'd get a replacement.

And that's how we got Dakota. She just appeared one day. She looked the part, like Mi, with blond hair instead of Mi's black. Both were about the same size with the same athletic build. Both could run, jump, fight, shoot, and hold their own day in and day out. Both ate when hungry, went to sleep when tired, and rolled with the punches as well as any other stud on my team.

But Dakota, she was off a bit. I thought back to that first battle. That day she was pinned down, not fighting, and thinking she could *talk* her way out of the carnage?

Didn't work then. Wasn't going to work now.

The door clanked open and four very serious men strode in, clamped huge restraints on our arms, and dragged us out of our cell.

I looked this time. I took notice. They had no overhead tags. This was all programmed; these guys were the same as the robots, sent to manage the NPC leaders.

Still we had no clue why.

Level 8

I was bolted to an upright board and leaned back at about sixty degrees. Bright lights. Probes on weird machines. An EKG machine or whatever was attached to one arm over my holo-tattoo, beeping away, telling me or them or whoever that I had a pulse, and it was going off like a trip hammer.

I gotta admit, I was pretty scared. These freaks had no intention of letting us go. We were alone. Mi was . . . well, wherever. Not at my side, that's for sure. And I couldn't watch her back, either.

My team was toast. For all I knew, this might be the end of the road. No more CO. No more missions, no more gaming. No more life. Just a blank cell and no idea why I'd lost everything I ever had. A life sentence. But for what crime? Had we lost one too many times?

Dakota was right next to me, and I could hear her machine buzzing away. They say it takes intelligence to feel fear, so on that scale, she was a lot more intelligent than I'll ever be. Her heart rate was off the charts, pinging like a pinball machine.

"Shut off the lights," a voice from out there, behind the apparatus, told someone.

The lamps died. Now we could see better. A big room. An operating theater. Faces pressed up against glass in the overhead viewing area. Four or five men on the floor with us, checking the readouts, making adjustments, pointing data out to each other.

"No spots?" one of the techs asked.

"Don't you think bright interrogation lights are way overdone?" another guy answered. I got a good look at him: Long hair, tied back. Glasses. Lab coat. He even had a clipboard. How cute.

The man stared at me and I made a point of glancing over his head. There it was, his tag, BlackStar_1.

Around the room, the others from the desert town were there: BlackStar_2, 3, and so on.

The whole gang was back together again.

"So you respawned?" I said to BlackStar_1. "That's a cheese-dick way to keep playing, if you ask me."

No response.

"I got you good," I boasted. Empty words, to be sure. He wasn't the one about to get cut open.

He smiled. Maybe he liked to banter with the toys. "I didn't see you behind that mailbox, Phoenix. Good spot. Good move. But I guess that's why we give you all the tough gigs, huh?"

My turn to smile. "Let's play that scene again, bro. I'll come up with a better angle to counter a rigged gun."

"Clever." He nodded, then turned to a buddy. "Hand him a pistol."

BlackStar_8 stood up, a redheaded guy with bad teeth, and pulled a nice chrome-plated Desert Eagle off a table. He walked over, freed my arm, and slapped the semiauto into my hand.

"Now," BlackStar_1 said to me, "you can either shoot yourself in the head—and as soon as you do you go right back to Re-Sim and Mi and your home base—or you can use that huge thing to punch holes in me and everyone else in the room."

I didn't think twice. I raised the gun right to his forehead and pulled the trigger.

CLICK!

Darn!

CLICK!

CLICK!

Empty! How many times were they going to pull *that?*

BlackStar_1 smiled. Seemed like I'd given him the right response.

"See!" he barked at one of the other techs. "*Great* reaction time. No hesitation. I just don't see the issue here. Our numbers are still at an all-time high and growing steadily. Sales through the roof. Corporate loves *our* product. Phoenix, and every NPC like him, they're performing *flawlessly,* just like I predicted."

"You don't get it yet, Max," BlackStar_4 spat back at him. "The issue is not with *that* generation. The issue is with the new recruit."

"Her?"

"Her."

"Dakota?"

"I told you before what happened. About the anomaly."

"Sam, she's been fighting just fine for weeks," BlackStar_1 countered. "One inventive episode? Don't we *want* that? And it could have been a scratch on a disc. A bad relay cable. Anything. One little power surge and you all lose it."

"But if it re-creates itself, if there's a virus or a bug of some kind crawling around in there, think about *that.* We could have a systems crash. What if all of our NPCs simply want to stop fighting? Our customers don't want to *talk* things out. They want to *shoot* things out. The whole thing would fold over-freakin'-*night* if we lose our edge."

BlackStar_1 — I'd gathered his actual name was Max — was nodding but seemed unconvinced. He asked, "Think you can replicate the error?"

"Even if we could, it's not like we could do anything about it other than erase that whole batch file. Once they're spiked, none of the units can be retroactively altered."

I was starting to catch on. And it was some scary stuff. I liked Dakota. A lot. Good team member. Fun to watch fight. So what if she kooked out every now and then?

I hoped she was catching on too, because I was pretty sure the next couple of moments were going to determine the rest of her life. Or whether she'd have a rest of her life.

A bunch of the guys started punching buttons, configuring things, and generally acting like they were about to launch a space station.

"What do you want to do for an environment?" a tech asked. "Return her to the original landscape? That Nec war? Replicate every last battle condition?"

More voices:

"Do we have to go that far?"

"How about dropping her in the middle of imminent danger and seeing if that triggers the irrational response?"

"Didn't we just try that?"

I turned my head to look at Dakota, to see if she realized this whole thing was centered on her. All of it. From getting dropped into the HILLS environment to the chase to the fiery town battle to the long ride in the cage.

Even, I thought, giving us all that food and those hot showers.

The whole time, they'd been trying to elicit a particular response.

Did she get it?

Because they hadn't gotten that response yet.

Did she understand the way she was turning our universe upside down? The way she could, if she acted incorrectly, end my life? Her life? The team's lives? Mi and Reno and York, if they were back home at CO, might not even realize they were dying as the whole base was simply shut down.

Did Dakota *know?*

She watched them all move. One tech was talking about the weather that day, the day of the error. The others were searching for the random gamers who'd played in our session. Another was pulling up a schematic of the actual concrete debris she'd hidden behind.

I got it. I knew. It all made sense now.

At the time, we'd just thought she was chicken. But in the real world, somewhere, somehow, word of her actions, or her *inaction,* had gotten back to BlackStar and gone all the way up the chain to the company president, Mr. BlackStar_1 himself.

BlackStar_1.

Max . . . something.

His last name escaped me. But it was there, somewhere, in my memory. Maybe a game title. Something. From a long time ago. It just wouldn't cipher itself out right this minute.

Max was watching his team work to try to re-create the conditions that had led to that particular game systems failure on that particular day. Finally, after listening to them bicker about ambient music and gore settings and if the y-axis needed to be inverted . . . finally, he'd had enough.

Wherever that guy was out there in the real world playing this game, this scene, this level, whatever he actually looked like, his body did the same thing it did in here.

He strode purposefully over to my table. I could see the anger in his eyes, could read the fear that was beginning to build. I could almost smell it. And why not? This was where I lived. This was my world. I was a permanent resident. They were only tourists. The weekend warriors. They dropped in and out like it was some kind of digital vacation.

Max picked up the gun. I let him have it. He yanked out the magazine, inserted a full load, cocked the slide as expertly as any SWAT commando on the planet, and turned to Dakota.

He removed her shackles.

All of them.

And we watched as she tipped off the examination table and stood eye to eye with the BlackStar company founder.

She was equal in height. Stronger. Muscle tone and obsidian eyes. Standing there confidently, almost daring anyone in the room to suggest that she was no more than some kind of two-dimensional gaming enemy.

Max offered her the gun. She took it with her left hand, then tossed the heavy metal into her right, fingers and palm landing on the trigger and grip as easily as if she were brushing back a strand of hair.

BlackStar_1 grinned at her.

"This is not a similar set of conditions for the experiment, Max," the guy named Sam snarled.

"It's loaded," Max told Dakota.

"Something like this would punch a hole in your head as big as a fist." She grinned as she said it.

"Use it." He waved around to his team and to the observers overhead. "You could finish us all off and we'll send you right back to your base. Him too." He waved at me. "You can both go home."

Dakota's smile left quick. "That's not my home, and *you* know it."

Max didn't answer. He didn't even try.

She continued, "Why do we have to fight? Why can't we just try to get along? What's the point in all that killing?"

The room was silent, other than a smart-mouth in the back who muttered, "Corporate dominance. Food on my table. Quarterly bonuses . . ."

"Shut up," Max said to him, then looked at the one he'd called Sam. "See? We don't need the battlefield. It wasn't *fear* that made her not want to fight that day."

"Not fear?" Sam asked, incredulous. "Then what?"

No one said a thing.

"What now?" he asked. "What do we do with an NPC who's not going to get with the program? She's not a freakin' medic. No more hand surgeries. She needs to *fight*."

"We'll go back to the original versions," another tech suggested.

"Impossible," a third replied. "Gamers are used to smarter enemies. They don't want to go back to eating a bunch of yellow dots or battling a monkey who throws barrels one after another."

Another suggestion. "We could shut down for a week and hunt the virus . . ."

"It's not a virus, it's a *systemic* infection . . ."

"You're crazy, it's biological. Talking too much has to do with Dakota's gender."

"Menstrual? Ha! Don't be an *idiot*. These systems are not male or female dependent. We have plenty of female NPCs who are even more merciless than the males."

"Now *you're* being an idiot. Of course the subject has a sex. Look at her! They also have an age and preferences and tendencies just like we need them to have to be unique. It's *all* in there."

A moment of silence, then it started back up again.

"So we erase the Dakota version? Keep the Phoenix series? And never let a word of this out."

Now it quieted down. All the techs, all the observers, they began to glance over at Max. He was the one who had to make the decision.

Finally, he spat out a breath of air.

He panned around. "I don't think it's as bad as it seems. So one of the NPCs wants to *reason* with gamers? We have no proof it's systemic. We have no indication that her series will all develop this fault. So what if, every now and then, in some game, in some online arena, one of the enemy throws up her hands and wants to talk things out?"

"It's just, well, unnatural," Sam moaned. "At least, in there it is."

"I agree," Max decided, "but it's not a deal killer like you all had me thinking. In fact, it might be an interesting twist. Maybe we can profit off her. The team might secretly strap her with remote control explosives, and when she lures the gamers in for a peace talk with the seductive blond NPC, she blows them up!"

Some mumblings spread; ideas began to form.

"She could be the *unwilling* kamikaze pilot . . . ?"

"The world's first superhottie suicide bomber?"

"No, better yet: *the devious second-in-command who disobeys boss orders . . .*"

"That's *great!*" Sam agreed, getting with the program. "No game has *different levels* of evil in their enemy AI. Then, what if, eventually, the gamer could actually *convert* enemy lieutenants at some time? Like, make them into double agents?"

"Not a bad idea. Interesting twist. Would it sell?"

"Set up a market test," Max ordered. "But for now, with revenue where it is, we simply cannot retire that entire series just because one of the units tried to surrender. You don't need me to tell you there's no time. Too much is at stake to back down."

Nods all around the room. It was decided.

One minute later, Dakota and I woke up back at base.

Level 9

I don't know what I expected after that. Dakota and I had shared something, something really weird, but the last thing she seemed to want to do was talk about it.

The very next night we got assigned jungle duty in NAZI HATEFEST: THE JUPITER MISSION, the story of Hitler as a respawned alien trying to take over the universe. His goal, this time, was to control the outer-rim mining district and put all those hardworking Plutonians in gas-cloud concentration camps.

Yeah, I know, *stupid* premise, but Adolf always sells copies.

So here's how the whole thing works.

As soon as you plug that game into your console, the call goes out to my crew. A mission hits our board, we report to the briefing room, and the uniforms and weapons are in our lockers.

We dress quickly. Those loading screens you get don't last forever. There's usually some chatter now between us . . . what to do later, maybe set up a date, maybe hope that your gamer characters are good-looking cheerleaders or swimsuit models this time. Just empty blabber as the carnage is about to begin.

Then I walk over to the console and put my hand inside the

register, and it reads my holo-tat string. That is how it knows my team and where to send us.

Simple enough. Into the portal, through an open door, and out the other side, where we join the fray.

That day I was a Nazi general. York was SS. Mi was a Luftwaffe pilot. Reno mounted up as her tail gunner. Jevo . . . ? Hadn't seen muscle-head since that last town, when he was getting a motocross-tire haircut. He never came back out. But honestly, not a big loss. Jevo was never the quickest circuit on the board. Plus, you know, his diet was questionable.

Dakota's gig was to run a concentration camp, complete with boxcars full of children and wards packed with human experimentation. She didn't really say much, fought halfheartedly, got shot and knocked into a holding pond, drowned quickly, and that was that.

Same thing the next night, when we were dressed up as time-traveling mummy terrorists. And after that, when we had to play the role of satanic dinosaurs armed with exploding pterodactyl launchers. And a day later, when they turned us into great black sharks, which were a lot like the great white ones, only we also had laser guns and torpedo rays and could run across land at the speed of sound.

The missions kept coming. Fight after fight, race after race. Some of them fun, some of them spectacular, and all of them painful. Death begat death. Do you gamers feel much of a twang when we hit you? The same as we feel when you snipe us?

I don't know. I've never played from your side.

We can hear you, though. What you say to each other when you play games together. The crosstalk . . .

"Shoot that Nazi." "Kill that mummy." "Oh, no, I'm late for work."

It's interesting to pick that stuff up. Most of the time it's game-related. Strategy or profanity or threats. Other times we gain an edge. HINT: You might not want to yell into your mic that your buddy is sneaking around behind us, especially when I'm right on the other side of a door with huge bullet holes in it. I heard you too. Now I know where *both* of you are. And I will react. I will counter.

So maybe it was a week, finally, when we were all together again in the main lounge. York and Reno came out of Re-Sim looking a bit more haggard than I remembered. Maybe some of the light scars looked a little deeper, maybe their eyes just said tired. That happened. I could get them a break and figured I would; it had been months since the action had slowed down.

Mi was there, as usual, on my right, just as happy as normal. She seemed to like the time off—not that she wasn't always ready to pick a fight, but these periods of inactivity recharged her a bit more easily than the rest of us.

The food was good. The mood was pretty good too. Whatever the panic had been from our employers before, it seemed to have passed. Dakota was fighting, not great, but we all had off days. Sometimes we sent a gamer back to his checkpoint every single time they handed us a weapon. Other times we stumbled around and barely put up much resistance. Like sports, war can be 90 percent luck and 10 percent is just plain chance.

And that's when I saw her, out of the corner of my eye, walking purposefully toward our table. I could tell before Dakota reached my seat that everything was about to get weird.

She looked at Mi, very directly, and asked—OK, told her—"Mi, give me a minute with Phoenix. Now."

Mi was startled, but only for a second. Remember, this was a girl who kicked serious butt day in and day out, so the look she returned to Dakota was in no way one of fear. It was more of "OK, I'll *let* you." As in "Remember that I'm the one doing the allowing here."

Kind of cute, if you ask me.

It got less cute.

Dakota straddled her chair and stared right in my eyes. Something was eating her, I could see it, and it'd been gnawing away for the better part of that week.

"Phoenix," she whispered, but good luck keeping this quiet. I could already feel the rest of the team circling.

"I've wanted to talk to you," I said back, "ever since they returned us from the BlackStar base."

"Me too," she continued, "but I didn't know where to begin."

I waited. You'll run into this as a leader. Sometimes you let people work things out on their own. They don't always need to be told the answers up front. Trust your soldiers to chew their own meat.

Her eyes met mine, and I could almost predict the questions that were stirring in there. I knew they were coming and was positive she was going to hate the answers.

Out on the edge of my vision, I saw York and Reno lean in. Mi didn't. She was moving the other way but keeping a watchful eye on the two of us. Crazy moment, until . . .

Dakota asked simply, "Tell me. Tell me straight. Don't lie. What *am* I?"

I never looked away, even though the answer was going to really hurt. And like I said before, I liked her. Loved her, in fact. Like a brother. Like a sister. Even more deeply, though, because I had shared things with her that very few ever share with anyone: death, pain, survival.

Reliance, conquest, peace.

Trust. More trust.

"What *are* you?" I repeated, hoping she would begin to figure it out for herself.

"Really, Phoenix, am I just a disposable enemy? A kind of highly trained worker for some big industrial gaming company? Why do I have to live *here,* in this complex? I want a real home. Why do I have to fight every day? It makes no sense. Really. None of it adds up. I don't remember making this choice."

I let her go on. I knew she would.

Her voice had come up a bit, and everyone else in the room was starting to follow along. A lot of it probably sounded pretty familiar to some of them. If they too had begun to wonder what *it* was all about.

"I mean"—she was stumbling a bit as the chain began to form—"I can think. I can feel pain. I need to eat and sleep and have time off. But every other indicator points to me just being another cog in the industry. I'm the enemy. The gamer kills me and blows me up. But I can adapt. I can learn. I can adjust. But then I'm the enemy again. And again . . ."

York and Reno, I saw, kind of knocked fists. Not like when you celebrate, but more like when something is getting shared that you both hold inside. That you also keep deep down. Memories so painful or ideas so hard that they really shouldn't surface all too often.

Dakota, though, she was on the verge. She was about to tip over . . .

"All this time I thought maybe this is like a camp of some kind. Perhaps I'm enrolled in some kind of army or military and this just has to be my everyday life for a while. Until I get the rest of my memories back. But, Phoenix, really, that makes *no* sense. I have . . . conscience, right? 'Cuz I also wanted to heal? This isn't *all* there is . . ."

She was looking around. The steel walls. The charm-free tables and chairs and rooms and cabins and everything—from forks to spoons to pillows—all sporting that BlackStar logo.

"There's *more*," Dakota said firmly, trying to convince herself.

But she was wrong, of course. This was all there was. This was all we got.

"There has to be more. This cannot be all . . ."

Then, like she'd discovered some kind of perfect argument, she yipped, "What happened to Jevo? Why didn't he ever come out of Re-Sim that day? Is he free?"

I shrugged. No, not free. Jevo was gone. It happened. We burned out sometimes. Sometimes we didn't reboot. Everything eventually becomes obsolete.

I put my hand on her arm, very softly, and gave it a squeeze. I could feel the sharp tendons in her arm, the triceps. And I had a chance to do something I'd always wanted to do.

I turned her hand over. The holo-tattoo was picking up the overhead light. Her brand was a shale blue with little specks and dots of green sparkling out. But the lettering, the series of bars and dashes that labeled her BlackStar property, I wanted to see them up close. The same way I had studied Mi's.

I'd suspected it, really, since the first day, when Dakota had seemed so afraid. That her tattoo would be different. That on there, somewhere, was a different slash or character.

A bit of syntax. A string of new commands. An upgrade.

But it wasn't in the characters. There *was* a difference. Was it brighter? Did it glow a bit more than ours?

Not really. It was the color. So slight. But hers was indeed darker.

I put my own hand next to it just to make sure—that's when she pulled away.

That was all meaningless to her. She was quivering. Shaking in small spurts. So strange for what she is—essentially, just a long string of 1s and 0s stored in some supercomputer database somewhere.

"I'm *not* just a program," she whispered. "I know there's more, Phoenix. I have memories. Real, live, actual memories."

I shook my head. "I don't think you do, Dakota. I'm sorry, but they're just part of the code."

One half of her hadn't accepted it. The other half had but didn't want to. But it was tipping.

Mi—and I never heard her coming—sat on the other side of our teammate. She put a caring arm around Dakota's shoulders, and the two of them broke into slight sobs. Tears came from their eyes, perhaps the first tears that weren't caused by the real pain we found every day and every night on a thousand different battlefields across programmers' warlike imaginations.

"There's *more* to me," Dakota was saying. "I know there's more than just *this*."

Mi was shaking her head no, holding Dakota tightly now, helping our friend let it all out. The sobbing got heavier and heavier.

I took my hands off Dakota. I sure didn't want to hurt her, but is it worse to not know a painful truth than to know it, face it, and learn to live with it?

Because we all have something we live with. Some hard fact. Some inconceivable notion. So take it on. Headfirst, right?

Remember, we hear chatter from you in the outer world. You have a short life span. You get sixty years, maybe. You fight disease and crime and poverty and a thousand other things. If you fail out there, you don't return to the checkpoint. If you get hurt, you might not heal.

Not us. If we get hurt, BlackStar puts us right back together.

If we get hungry, they program a meal. If we get tired, they recharge our batteries.

So we have our own painful truth to deal with. And Dakota had just figured it out.

"I can't just be a computer program." Dakota was still crying. "I'm real. I have feelings. I think and act independently and have needs and frailties and fears and . . ." But her voice was already fading.

Because sure, she *thought* she had all those things. The same way I *thought* I had a girlfriend and the loyalty of my team and a plate of biscuits and gravy in front of me on the table.

But it was illusion. It was *all* 1s and 0s.

Mi explained. She told Dakota, very caringly, what the rest of us already knew.

"You're *not* just a computer program, Dakota, please remember that. You're the most advanced program written by any human, ever. You *do* think. You *do* feel. You react and strategize and provide the highest-quality opponent ever produced. Please, if nothing else, take pride in that. You are actually, of course, some kind of *mega*computer, sitting in a bank of perfect computers somewhere, so outstanding and amazing and unique that you're a shining star. You've got an unlimited life span. You'll never get sick. Never go without nourishment or companionship."

"But I don't want to be an NPC," Dakota said, sniffling. "I don't *choose* to be artificial intelligence."

"And some gamers probably don't want to be mortal." York

tried to help. "Ever play? It could not possibly get any more boring than it is out there. Drama, work, school, bills, work, school, no joy. No thrills. *Nothing.*"

Reno added, "And the bare truth is, we can't change who we are."

"You all know this already?" Dakota asked, looking around.

I nodded. York and Reno did too. Most of the room was trying to help. To empathize. For some reason this realization was coming hard to Dakota, harder than it had to any of us.

"I'm sorry." Mi was also sniffling.

"Me too, Dakota," Reno offered.

"So I'm just some box in some server bank?" the girl moaned. "Nothing but a set of commands and reactions? Everything preprogrammed to serve the needs of a bunch of video game addicts?"

"I don't think anyone has any more guarantee that they're not the same thing," Mi assured her. "Who really knows *what* they are or where they came from? Not a single being, ever, has figured that out."

"And which is better?" I asked. "For us, in here, we have each other. Our needs are met. We do our duty and we do it better than anyone ever has. It kind of *has* to be enough."

"But this is all so real." She knocked the table. It made a perfect *CLANG.*

She knocked it again.

The same perfect, recorded *CLANG.*

"I just can't get used to the idea that someone might trip over a power cord and my life would be over."

"Well, I'm sure there are backup generators," York said.

"And backup files," Reno added. "Battery packs too. They can't take chances."

"If you think about it, we're probably so valuable they pay more attention to us than they do to a lot of people on machines in the hospitals."

"It still makes no sense. There are holes everywhere." Now Dakota was just arguing.

"Really?" Mi asked.

"Really," the girl assured her, trying to convince herself that she was indeed flesh and blood somehow. That she did actually breathe air and digest food and feel emotion rather than exhibit predetermined reactions to everything.

Her mind was searching so randomly now. "Or maybe I'm dead? I remember falling from a really high place, a wall of rock zooming down. It's so vivid. Am I hallucinating *all this* before I hit?"

No one answered. We'd all been tossed off cliffs before. Hundreds of times.

"When I was maybe four or five I liked to play cowgirl," she continued. "When I was around twelve I could reprogram satellites. No, that's *not* fake information. I remember things. Summer camp. Maybe a soccer game? Swim lessons. Yes, swim lessons for sure. From that, uh, guy? Girl. What was her name? In a pool. No, a lake. The water was too cold or something."

"NPCs can't swim," Mi reminded her.

"I had friends. I had a *life*."

"Can you name them?" York asked.

"There's more. Your explanation doesn't add up."

York leaned over. "Or, admit this, it could be that you're programmed to think it doesn't add up?"

Dakota glared at him. Real hatred. "It does *not* answer everything," she stressed. "I feel more for some of you than others. Some

I don't like at all, York. The point is, I *feel*. I get hungry. Maybe I'm being tricked. Maybe you're all in on it."

Was she just blowing off steam now? Or grasping?

"I have sadness. I get afraid. I experience joy. I'm lonely, even when we're all together. I'm different from the rest of you . . ."

She pinched her arm. Ran her fingers through her hair. Held her breath till she turned blue. Stomped her own toes with the heel of her boot.

"OW!"

But she was just kidding herself. One way or another, it was all programmed response.

Level 10

It must have been some kind of holiday break for the next three days. New games were hitting the boards, and we were busy beyond belief. I gotta admit I didn't think, at that point, Dakota was going to make it. I was 90 percent sure BlackStar was going to pull her plug . . . and that one day she just wouldn't come out of Re-Sim.

Maybe we'd run in to her again someday. Maybe with Jevo, both of them dressed up as fuzzy dinosaurs or a squad of heart-throwing teddy bears.

That's the way it happened when one of us became obsolete, outdated, whatever you want to call it. And the team, to be sure, usually knew it was coming. For a while leading up to it, the guy or girl would just fight too slow. Miss too many shots. Not be able to keep up with the pace and complexity of the gaming environment.

It's hectic in there. You know it is. This isn't PONG anymore. Tons of stuff comes at you constantly. It's exhilarating. Relentless. Some gamers, and some programs, just can't hack it.

Most gamers have seen us when we overheat. You run into an NPC who's totally confused. Who walks into walls. Who can't stand up and fire from behind their cover. Who just drives off a bridge or lets you walk right over and cap them in the forehead.

Just so you know, those *aren't* gaming glitches. Those are NPCs who've finally worn out.

So our team, when this started to happen, well, we knew the days wouldn't be long for that one. Sooner or later, there'd be a replacement. The public demanded constant innovation. NPCs had to continue to step up. And whoever wasn't cutting it would simply die in the game environment and never make it back out of Re-Sim.

That's the road Dakota was on. I couldn't see any other end. For whatever reason, her new-model programming just wasn't up to this task. Sooner or later, she'd fail to meet minimum requirements and we'd get assigned another teammate.

Nine hours of ZOMBIE SPACE PIRATES VS. SUBHUMAN ORGAN SCAVENGERS later, though, Dakota was still by my side. This was one twisted-up game, because, as everyone knows, your garden-variety subhuman scavengers have a very limited vocabulary. Between chop-shopping and auctioning the limbs and organs of all those gamers, we really didn't have much ability to formulate a strategy. All we could do was eat, chop, sell, chop some more, body-jack more humans, strip them down, kidney, liver, heart, brain . . . It was an endless cycle.

The gamers were *zombie* pirates; they tasted absolutely horrible. Ever eaten a zombie? No? Well, it's *exactly* the putrid, rotting flavor you'd expect. No amount of ketchup is enough ketchup.

So there we were, thirty-foot-tall scavengers, fistfuls of undead in one hand, giant bottles of ketchup in the other, and I turned to look over and what do you know? There was Dakota, rending and tearing and chomping right along with the rest of us! It took three waves of gamers to wipe her out. She sure put up a good fight.

Hadn't seen that coming. I'd expected, to be honest, a lot more sulking.

We got moved to radioactive spider-bat duty next, some RTS that had just been released. I think it was called NANO-SECT-ICIDE EXTREME!. You know a game is going to suck if they have to put the word "extreme" anywhere in the title.

It did suck. A week later, no one would be playing. It'd disappear off the charts. Plus, the radioactive spider-bat suits they made us wear were really itchy. I don't think it's fun for any game combatant when the enemy is constantly stopping to scratch their privates.

But again, Dakota hung tough. *Very* tough. She seemed to be getting into all that swooping and neck biting and voracious slurping. Something had come over her. Maybe she'd make it after all.

⊕　⊕　⊕

I love playing The Black Knight. "None shall pass." You better bring your A-game if you want to cross my bridge.

Of course, in EVIL KING ART VS. JEDI ASSASSINS, I wasn't really on the side of good. And gone were the steel swords of yore, replaced by attack dragons and laser scepters and armor you can mod with auto-crossbow blasters and power gauntlets.

Still, the idea remained the same: There was a king, and to stay king, he enlisted every able-bodied man from the villages to be one of his soldiers. The poor were heavily taxed and labored from dawn to dusk. They had no schools or means of bettering themselves. This King Art didn't even allow them to own weapons with which they might have hunted or protected themselves from roving bandits or fork-tongued wizards.

Kings are usually like that. Plus, Arthur had more important things to do. Like build up his castle walls and drink grog with his ladies while he watched me lop the heads off any who *would* dare pass.

Heck, it wasn't even much of a bridge I had. More like a log over a river. I was winning, though, and the fights were a blast. The Black Knight doesn't just claim invincibility, he needs to back it up.

Gamer after gamer attacked. I barely picked up a nick in my leggings. They shot arrows and swooped on flying beasts and one of them even tried some kind of magic spell he'd gotten from a mountain witch. It was weak. Sure, it turned my mace into a poisonous serpent and my horse into a rabbit. In response I fed the rabbit to the snake, then cut off its head and shook the bunny way down toward the tail end.

There, I had my mace back.

After I hacked up the gamer, I took *his* horse.

But something happened, and I wished Dakota had been there to hear it. There was a pause in the game as we leveled up, and I was under the bridge, down in the shadows, when a pair of new victims tromped up.

I could pick up their crosstalk.

One said, "Hey, Todd, you get that factory slot?"

"Uh, yeah."

"Lucky, man."

"It's a factory, brother, hot as a mother in there."

"Yeah, but now you get the brand."

"I'm just workin' for chits, same as you. After tax I barely clear rent."

"Bro, no whining. You're *in* now. On the good side of the wall for sure."

"I'm a corporate serf."

"You're *stoked* is what you are. Better days ahead. Nose to the stone. Plus, you got bennies, right? Meds. Protection. Store discounts?"

Then there was a silence.

"Do good in there. It'll lead to more."

They both forgot their problems because I jumped out and took 'em by surprise. It wasn't more than a few moves and I had them lanced, stood up, and planted in the ground like giant olives on a stick.

In here, these guys' problems were not better jobs or the cost of living or feeling like their lives only served the rich and powerful.

No, they should've been a little more concerned with perimeter defense, squad integrity, and overlapping fields of fire.

Level 11

DUNGEON OF DEATH XXV, the ongoing saga of a dungeon. Where there's death. And the gamers must sneak in and free their comrades before my drones can replace their good spinal columns with my remote-controlled fiendish spinal columns.

The tweak here is that I was playing the role of Boss, and while I really prefer to be a top general, the gig had its moments. As a general, I get to alter my troop and weapons placement and our defensive or offensive strategy. I can pace our engagements and watch for weaknesses in gamer tactics. The days when we villains rush blindly into a room or over a ridge one after another are long gone. No fun in that for either side.

As Boss of the dungeon, I had a long string of attack vampires on chains, and I placed these in the outer chambers. That made it quite a sneak mission for gamers to get around them and still stay out of range of their tethers.

I turned a bunch of gamers into werewolves with titanium skulls and spines and, using a catapult, launched them into a three-dimensional skirmish with those who'd survived the first levels. Toss in a few gladiator-style arena fights and that whittled things down to my favor.

But even then, a pack of gamers worked their way through—serious ninja skills—and soon enough, they were surrounding me, stomping my horned feet. Shooting flaming arrows into my pressure points. Eventually, two of them survived, climbed onto my back, and got revenge by extracting *my* spinal column in a closing scene filled with more bloody pulp and amniotic goo than should have been allowed under any rating system.

Nicely played. But again, I don't like boss battles. The big cheese always seems to have certain weak points that are just too easy to identify. It's the journey to the boss that's more fun. Not the final scene.

When I came out of Re-Sim, it started again. That burning over my right eye. It spread to the bridge of my nose and made streams of tears pour from my left eye. It almost knocked me to the ground.

And on came a vision.

I saw water. I saw people in the water, thrashing around.

And even though it was just a vision, my whole body shivered. The water . . . I could *feel* it on my skin. It was so cold. A pool? No, maybe a lake. And those people? What were they doing?

No, it couldn't be.

No.

Not like Dakota's memory scraps.

Not a swim lesson. No.

Level 12

It'd been at least a week, and the serious gaming rush began to die down. Dakota, thankfully, was in a cheery mood. I'd been worried about her. I liked her. She was cool to have around and a good fighter when she put her mind to it. Now it seemed that after some time for the bad news to sink in, her place in our little gaming-verse had settled in her gut. Good thing. It's hard to fight well, to *live* well, to enjoy the little stuff, if you're getting eaten up about something big like that.

And yeah, it *is* a big deal. What we are. Our actual worth to the world. Coming to grips with our limits.

Did the rest of us know, or realize, we weren't really "human"?

Sure we did. We just didn't have to talk about it all the time. Too depressing. Just like out there in the mortal world, I'm sure people don't spend a whole lot of time dwelling on the fact they're getting closer and closer to lights-out every second of every day. Or that they might get eaten by a shark or hit by lightning or die from some other random act. They don't run around telling everyone about every ailment or doctor's visit. Why focus on bummer news like that? It's no way to live.

And live we did and still do. We are alive. As alive as you or your kind.

What are humans, really? I looked it up in a BlackStar tutorial on how to kill you. You're a biological case with a brain that processes electrical impulses. Those impulses make memories. Those impulses control your actions.

So how are we any different, really? We're the same electrical impulses, we have the same control over our actions, only our cases are not skin and bone and hair. Our cases are plastic and metal and copper circuitry that, if taken care of, can last *centuries*. We can swap hardware, improve our processors, and learn from tactical errors.

Humans, well, you're stuck with your physical limitations. Forever. I guess you can get breast implants and nose jobs, but hey, I'll take the upgrades we get any day of the week.

But now it was time to relax. We all looked forward to it. No costumes, no guns, no aggression at all. Just good friends and funny stories and a lot of shared laughter.

"I totally ran into wackjob trouble today," Reno was telling the crew. "The gamers sent in some kind of four-legged magnetic land mine. Going 'woof, woof!' It followed me around, lurking behind like some kind of needy dog but never getting close enough to go off."

"Whoa, what did you do?"

"I could hear them chuckling," he continued. "I think they were waiting for me to lead it back to my base and my men and then set it off remotely. Stupid friendly pooch. Cute, too."

"Some new weapons out there lately." York yawned.

"No kiddin'. I finally found a place I could change into a regular jumpsuit. No metal. Broke the magnetic lock it had on me. Then

I got a nice big iron bone. Looked just like a doggie snack. Walked out into the open, said 'Here, boy! Here, boy! Now FETCH!'"

"Cool!"

"I threw the bone right into the middle of the gamer squad, and as soon as the dog-mine got to it, Mi blew Fido up with a beautiful rifle shot at like nine hundred yards!"

"Awesome!"

"Got 'em good!" Reno boasted. "All of them, right back to the checkpoint. Nothing left but dust."

I loved it. Now, that was a move I'm sure none of the gamers expected. And therefore, they got their money's worth. BlackStar would be thrilled with that. Great tactics make great games. We just kept raising the bar.

Team Phoenix — nothing and no one like it anywhere in your world. Or in mine.

And that's the way it went for a while. Drink a few BlackStar colas, throw down some BlackStar-brand nacho chips.

Yeah, having that little BlackStar stamped on everything everywhere was pretty annoying, but what could you do? It wasn't like we had to pay for anything.

And this downtime was good. We got to share stories. We traded ideas. I know why they give us time off. You do too. So we can *evolve* as artificial intelligence. So we can learn from each other's mistakes and triumphs. It's brilliant code. It's self-perpetuating product improvement. BlackStar_1 was no fool.

Something was different, though. It took me a while to notice. Something was wrong with my arm. I shook my hand. Seemed OK, just . . . lighter or something.

I rubbed the shoulder. Muscles all in place. Bones feeling tough.

Did maybe the Re-Sim shortcut something and not fully reconstitute my elbow? Nah. I was just being paranoid.

Any pain in my eye? No.

No one trying to teach me to swim? No.

Leftover road signs from SLAUGHTER RACE? Not a one. My vision was fine.

Still, what was wrong?

I looked around. York and Reno had a group of younger NPCs listening to some drawn-out, epic saga of how they beat the gamers ten missions in a row, blah blah blah . . .

Other grunts from Rio and Deke's team were coming and going. Assignments clocked in on the screen, NPCs rolled out. Sometimes a platoon returned quickly; other times they got pulled into longer sessions. You could never tell going in. Like any military unit, your group just moved together.

But still, my arm, it felt kind of light.

Mi and Dakota were across the room, chatting, smiling, shooting the breeze. Nothing strange about that.

But yes, actually, there was.

Mi wasn't here with me. By my side. Instead, she'd gone over to sit with Dakota. Now, what would strike me as odd about that?

Well, it explained my arm, why it felt incomplete. When you get used to someone clinging to it night and day, then they leave, you've got less weight to carry around, don't you?

But why be over *there?* What was up with the private conversation?

I wandered across, and wouldn't you know, as soon as I got to their table, they stopped chatting. Both looked up, smiling like they were totally happy to see me.

Mi even returned to her place on my sleeve.

Dakota grabbed another cola. The moment had passed.

It was probably nothing. And it was definitely a good thing they were becoming better friends. The more they worked together, the better my team scores would get.

Level 13

I should have seen it coming, right? After all, I am Phoenix. Of *the* Team Phoenix. It's my job to spot that kind of devious, backstabbing mutiny.

The mission hit the board. Reno ran the profile for the rest of us. He told the team we were gearing up for a trip into DOOM SPACE.

That title's great, but it's about as dark as it gets. A burned-out mining vessel traversing a barren galaxy, and with all this technology and all that weaponry they still can't equip a single room with a sufficient number of light bulbs? Close your eyes real quick. It's easier to see through your lids than it is on most of those ships' decks.

Still, we were the creepies, the Acromorphs, so we had a rudimentary form of night vision. We could hide in the shadows, and there were plenty of shadows.

We suited up, just the five of us, tentacles and fangs and those black, soulless eyes. I led everyone to the portal, shoved my hand in the slot, sucked in a deep breath, squinted to get ready for the darkness, and made the quick jump from our mission center to . . .

Bright, bright light?

What the . . . ? This wasn't right. A midday sun was burning through my costume.

It was roasting hot out here, and with the glare, I really couldn't see anything through the eye slits.

Something was wrong. I could feel it instantly. This was no ship. This was not deep space. More like shallow hell.

And it was boiling inside all that foam rubber.

We'd been dropped in the wrong spot. And that *never* happened. This was not the outer rim of a distant galaxy. It looked more like Death Valley. Add to that, my right eye was pinging with pain. I wanted to find an ice pick to stab in there, maybe make it stop . . .

I shucked off the costume, only to see that the rest of my team had done the same. Where were we? In the middle of a stretch of wasteland. Brush was about the only thing out here, not even a scorpion or snake or circling buzzard as far as our eyes could see.

"Damn!" I yelled. No echo. There was nothing there to bounce sound back. It looked like an unfinished landscape. Like a designer had planned to have a desert level but had abandoned it before finishing the mountains or the town or the enemies or anything other than sand, scrub, and heat.

"Bingo!" Dakota howled triumphantly. She looked anything but shocked. Instead, she seemed pleased as punch.

"Where are we?" I asked her directly. Then I spun on Reno. "*You* ran the profile. *You* said we were headed for DOOM SPACE!"

"I lied," he said bluntly—disrespectfully, in fact. I'd never heard that tone from anyone in my command. Couldn't remember the last time in my life someone had the nerve to speak to me like that.

"Which way?" Mi asked Dakota. It seemed like she was in charge now.

The blond girl, her eyes locked on me, just pointed north.

But there was nothing north. Not a speck as far as the eye could see.

She started walking, and wouldn't you know, York, Reno, and Mi fell in step behind her. Not one of them even looked in my direction for permission to deploy.

Something was up. A *lot* had been going on.

I watched them, my team, my friends, the people I spent night and day with. Who I fought with. Who I loved and looked after like my own kids.

They got farther and farther away, until they became four gray dots in the distance. I looked down, realizing I hadn't even moved from the spot where I'd dropped my Acromorph suit. It lay there in the sand, moving slightly in the breeze. At least the programmers had had time to insert a breeze. Without it, the temps would easily have been over 140 F-ing-heit.

And that was when I noticed them. In the hardscrabble dirt. By my discarded suit. The pair of tracks. Giant tire tracks.

The wind had almost erased the outline, but still, regular indentations were unmistakable.

Something big had rolled over this spot before.

Something like a giant buggy.

A giant buggy towing a trailer.

Freakin' Dakota. Didn't she realize what she was messing with here? I trudged along, miles behind, as the pieces started to fall into place.

She never had accepted or bought into being an NPC, had she? Or maybe she had but hoped to become more. One way or another, the girl just wasn't content with her fate or her place.

As the hours stacked up, I began to shift my anger. Mostly toward my good buddy Reno, who had tricked me into coming here. I guess he had to. The team wouldn't have been able to deploy without me, so they needed my hand to enter the game-world portal.

Still, there were questions. How had they been able to manipulate things so we'd come *here* instead of going wherever the mission profile had determined? We didn't decide destinations. They just appeared on the board when a gamer opened the environment.

Only Dakota had the answers. Eventually, though—whether you're a man or a woman or a fish or a monkey or a combat soldier created by programmers to fight and die—it's time to just get on the ride and see it through. That's life. Play the cards you've been dealt. You can't play what you don't hold.

She had to know this place was a dead end now. This whole thing—the gaming session and the rest of it—had been a *systems test*. BlackStar had wanted to find out what was behind Dakota's sketchy behavior. And then they'd nearly erased her forever.

Now, lately, as I told you, that sketchy behavior had been gone. She'd fought well. Maybe better than any of us over the past few weeks.

She should have let it rest. Ridden the ride. Enjoyed the perks. Made sure they didn't delete her ungrateful butt.

There was no good reason for this, for going off-grid.

The miles were still ticking away. Step after step. Why weren't we getting pulled back to base? We had to end this sidetrack. Get back to the real games. They didn't just let the best of the best wander in a desert for days on end. We'd be missed. And we'd pay for it.

I'm fast on the march, but not much faster than anyone else. I was the same generation as everyone except Dakota, so technically, she might have been the strongest, but she had to stick with the team. Whenever you move in a group, no matter how efficiently, you slow a bit. This was the edge I needed.

Twelve hours later I'd caught them. The tire tracks still stretched parallel as far as the eye could see, but now I was coming up on their tail.

They knew I was back but didn't break stride. None of them were even questioning Dakota about what they were doing out here. It was like they were on a mission. Walking. Sweating. Struggling. But trudging on and on. Lips cracked. No water. Skin burned. Together to the end. Their boot prints stretched behind us for fifty miles, weaving here and there, but in four nearly parallel sets. It was a miracle the natural desert predators—if there were any—hadn't started picking up our scent.

Whatever hold Dakota had on my team, whatever she'd said or promised, it was enough that it completely eliminated any kind of backtalk. Why couldn't I get that kind of obedience?

I fell into step. No sense arguing right off. Plus, eventually, the system would notice we weren't at our base or engaged in a game and pull us back in. It was just a matter of time.

They were drenched in sweat. The heat was intense; the sun hadn't moved an inch. Most games have natural day and night cycles now, but not this one. It was stuck. Probably because it was unused. An eternal cooker. High noon, always high noon.

The thing that nagged at me, though, was still the first thing: *Why* come *back?* This was not a commercial game.

"Where do you think we're going?" I finally barked up to Dakota.

She didn't even break stride. Determination was a string of code she did not lack.

She yelled back, "To the lab. I have questions. *We* have questions."

"You already know the answers, Dakota! You're a *program*. An advanced piece of artificial intelligence designed to kick butt first and take names never! They *wrote* you. Just like they make their desktop blue or their default font Tahoma!"

"Complete bull!" she snapped in return. "There are way too many unanswered questions!"

I actually rolled my eyes. Nobody *ever* has all the answers to *every*thing. That's the very foundation of "life."

"You're just going to end up with more questions!" I warned.

"Maybe. So then I'll ask those."

"Which won't clear anything up, it'll just lead to—"

"I know, I know, more questions. No need to beat it into the ground, Phoenix. Keep walking."

"And why didn't you tell me you were planning this little outing? I thought we were a team."

"You'd *never* have approved it." She laughed back. "Would you?"

"No, never." At least I was honest.

"So there. We had to act."

"All of you?"

"Of course *all* of us," Mi blurted out. "She's right, Phoenix. I mean, I dig you and all, but you should listen to Dakota. She makes a lot of sense about stuff."

"What stuff?"

"Like stuff about—"

But Mi was cut short when Dakota announced loudly, "We're here!"

Here? I glanced around. Same desert. Nothing had changed. Sun overhead. Very hot. Even the scrub brush, or the versions of it, was just continuing to duplicate like in one of those kids' shows where the monster runs and runs and the same background furniture scrolls over and over again.

York and Reno were also scanning the area. They appeared equally unconvinced.

"Here? Where?" I mocked. "This is the same!"

"Hardly." Dakota smiled. She looked like she'd just conquered a mountain even though she hadn't climbed a single foot in elevation since the long walk began.

Her finger was pointing down.

Sure, the landscape was the same as when we'd started out so many hours ago. But this was *the* spot. Or a spot.

The tire tracks simply ended. For miles they'd led us here, to this place, and now they'd vanished, as if sucked underneath the boiling desert sand.

Level 14

Dakota looked around for at least a minute. The horizon was the same. The brush was unchanged. The wind was a constant, so steady it felt like a fan. It probably was a fan.

So she reached out, stretching her arm forward, and the tips of her fingers hit something hard. It was invisible. A boundary. An edge of this place. The gate or door to the next.

Now they were all up there, fumbling, feeling the transparent wall like they were mimes in a box as large as the world itself. York was moving left, Reno to the right, Mi and Dakota rubbing and exploring top to bottom.

"Here," Dakota said, her fingers wrapped around something about knee-high. Still, it was completely invisible, and from where I stood, I thought she might be pretending to have found the latch.

She turned it, then pulled up. I had a vision spike of a typical suburban dad hoisting his garage door so he could get to his lawn mower. Now, there's a memory that had no place in my head . . . Oh, wait, how men are men on the outside: mowing grass. Was *that* where we were headed? My spine shuddered with pure fear, and I don't get scared too often.

As Dakota pulled, a wide section of the desert landscape slid up and rolled into a cylinder. It was a door. A wide berth for the crawler to drive through. Inside, I saw a tunnel stretch down, a ramp leading exactly where Dakota hoped we'd be able to go.

It was the road to the test center. Where we'd first faced the BlackStar team. Where they'd cornered the two of us, trying to find out what was wrong with their programming.

All five of us stepped through, the heat immediately disappearing. Now it was icy cold, our breath forming a cloud around our position. The sun was gone. Five paces in, the door rolled shut, locking.

I hate to make a comparison to games all the time, but it was just like when you step through a door and you know danger is lurking just ahead but that hatch behind you was one-way.

As we shuffled along, none of us had to point out that it was getting much darker the deeper we went. After a while the only thing we could see was our breath, a wisp of white that would quickly evaporate in the frigid black.

Footsteps and heavy, heavy breathing. My hands were out in front so I wouldn't bump a wall. Couldn't see them, either, not even the glow of our tattoos.

I was sure the rest of the team were shuffling in the same pose. Down and down. That's how we found our way. We knew the only way to go was to follow our feet into the basement of this empty level.

How far did we descend? Who knew. And it wasn't like this world was any more real than our own home base. It seemed like we were going down, but maybe we were going up. In all likelihood we weren't really going anywhere at all. We were just tiny bits of energy mashing around on some digital grid. Little more than x-y-z coordinates plotted by a motherboard in some computer server in some air-conditioned data center in Dallas or Denver or who-really-cares-where.

"What do you think the penalty is for trespassing?" York suddenly asked. "Would they program us into a prison cell for a few years?"

"Or," Reno suggested, "maybe they'd do some kind of system restore where we never actually trespassed."

"They can't do that," Dakota answered in the dark. "They can't take back the past or change it. What's done is done."

"On the contrary," York countered, "they take players backward in time *all* the time in games. That's what a gamer checkpoint is. A saved file. They save in that place, then the dude plays on, and if he fails and we win, they just reload him to the last save point."

"But you're forgetting that you're *not* a computer program," Dakota spat at him, her breath hot and white in the blackness. "You and I talked about that for a long time, York. Your experience is cumulative. One day's memories add to the next."

"I know, I know," he replied. I was having a fun time listening. I was learning a lot about what crap Dakota had been feeding my team.

"But," he continued, "your ideas, Dakota, they didn't answer all the questions either."

"I didn't say I had *all* the answers. I'm just saying that accepting you're just a computer program created by a video game designer — well, it doesn't add up."

"Doesn't add up *how?*" I interrupted. I had to hear that theory. I really wanted to know what she'd pitched my team that'd convinced them to disobey me and go off on this little junket into forbidden basements.

Dakota had reached another wall. She bumped it hard and I heard her mumble, "Ouch." That made me smile a bit through the gloom.

This time her search was easy, and I heard a door handle click.

"Phoenix, I think you already know. I think you've probably figured it out on your own. You're too smart to have missed so many clues."

Man, is it annoying when someone tells you that you already know something you don't already know. I just can't stand it when people give me credit for being more intelligent than I actually am. Grant me a little ignorance, please. My programming is simple: fight, win, destroy, triumph. What more does a modern antihero need?

She went on, "You don't need me to tell you what's been churning around in your head. Just listen to your own common sense, Phoenix. Take inventory of what you've *really* got in here. Then it'll all become clear."

What was that? A riddle? I don't do riddles. I do destruction and mayhem and Rating Board–approved high-definition digital violence! That's my purpose, my core mission parameters. It's my code.

Take *inventory?* I didn't have a single weapon. None of us did. Inventory = helpless.

The door popped open. Light streamed in. And that's when we saw it.

It was hideous!

It was monstrous!

It was the most shocking, revolting, gnarly-gross surprise in the history of video games!

And sure, she was cute. OK, she was adorable. All right, she was a darling little girl with blond hair and pigtails and a nice blue summer dress and an irresistible teddy bear tucked under her arm.

She was all those things. And probably the most horrible enemy we could have ever encountered.

With NPC monsters or gamers, at least they're predictable.

This, however, was going to be *big* trouble.

Ever tried to reason with a five-year-old kid? Ever tried to get straight answers from a child?

Good luck.

Level 15

The adorable waif shifted her weight from one tiny ballerina slipper to the other.

"Hi, little girl, what are *you* doing down here?" Dakota said in a cutesy voice.

I knew for a fact that wasn't going to work.

The correct opening statement was "DIE, you hideous blood-sucking parasite that's assumed the shape of this harmless child!"

The girl just stared up at us.

York whispered to me, "I bet it's one of the programmers, one of the men, dressed up like a little girl. This might be some kind of twisted fantasy game he's creating."

I agreed and reached for my weapons. Unfortunately, I had none. I was still just wearing the standard-issue jumpsuit.

"Let's try scaring her, and she'll lead us to her fiendish masters," Reno whispered.

Dakota was still baby-talking. "Are you part of the environment?" she asked. "Did you slip away from the BlackStar company daycare?"

But the girl suddenly turned and pointed at me. "What are *you* doing here?"

"Me?" I asked.

"Yeah, you're Phoenix. Daddy built you for BLASTERS OF FREE-DOM, right? My brother has your poster."

I kind of blinked, then nodded. She was right. That was my first assignment.

"Do you know the rest of these programs?" I waved around, looking for a gamer tag over her head. There was nothing, not even an Anonymous listing. I didn't think a human could get online without a tag.

The girl took a good look at my team, then pointed a finger at Dakota. "She's the new model. What did they finally name you?" Her eyes went wide as she took in our blond friend.

"Dakota."

"Good name."

"Do you have a name? Or a tag?" Reno cut in. York was still whispering that she was one of the BlackStar bigwigs, probably testing us, setting some kind of trap.

But the girl shook her head. "I'm just Charlotte. I don't get a tag till I turn eleven. Grumpy's pretty strict about that."

"Grumpy?" I asked. Now we were getting somewhere. "Is he a dastardly, vicious, evil boss or something?"

"No, he's just my daddy. I just call him by his boss name when he works and sticks me in here to play."

"Works?"

"Yeah, he made me come to the office with him too. Promised real ice cream. I'm not holding my breath."

Now the girl smiled. It is so hard to tell with a kid that age. You just never know if they're smart for their years.

Or, in this case, if they're even that age for real.

"Yeah," she said, obviously bored and ready to walk. "He'll let me run around in these test worlds, but as far as playing the shooter stuff, he says I gotta wait until I'm older."

"He lets you wander around here *unsupervised?*"

"Sure." She grinned. "Better than sitting on his office floor. I've got go-karts, ponies, jet boots, all kinds of brainteasers and puzzle books and places to explore. Never ran into you before, though. Why'd he link you in? Do you have some kind of challenge or scavenger hunt? A riddle? Or a quest? I want to go on a quest today! Please?"

That big grin again. The moppy hair. The straight little teeth. Almost too perfect to be real. Like at any minute the talons and fangs and horns would sprout and the satanic beast within would burst into the fray.

But this was no game. It was way too boring. Miles of walking. A long underground tunnel. No gamer alive would endure this kind of monotony.

"How about a race?" Charlotte asked, waving to a line of rocket-powered skateboards. "Twice around the complex," she ordered, jumping on.

"But you know all the shortcuts." Dakota laughed, immediately hopping on the deck right beside her.

York and Reno shrugged, then climbed up as a "Three . . . two . . . one . . ." chimed automatically from thin air.

Moments later, we were all zipping around. Arcing down the halls. Banking up on rolled corners. It was like riding a skateboard in a deserted airport or mall, and honestly, even without shooting or stabbing horrifying enemies, it was a whole lot of fun.

Charlotte did know the shortcuts. And she was deadly with dropped banana peels.

Next we rode Jet Skis through an underground river. Then we

played a game of basketball and we could all jump about twenty feet at a time. The so-called girl even showed us her own airplane, a pink and purple number with lots of flowers and polka dots and a special copilot's seat for her bear.

The stuffing's name was Bonkers. Pretty cool buddy. Didn't say much, though. Not sure about his weapons rating. Kind of gave me the creeps—those things *always* come to life and start swearing and spraying bullets everywhere. OK, in my experience that's what they do.

I know it sounds crazy, but we spent the next couple of hours just playing with the kid. Why not? All she knew was my name, that Dakota was the new girl, and that she had some nice people she could play some very G-rated games with in a safe place.

Yeah, after all the death and destruction we were immersed in every single day . . . to think that we'd find so much pleasure just hanging out with what we believed was the innocent little daughter of some real-world BlackStar bigwig.

If I were a designer, I'd think about adding a little wholesome action like that to even the darkest titles. Coming up for air from the grim mayhem every now and then makes all the blind corners a lot more fun.

Crazy stuff. But that really was a great afternoon.

"I gotta go," we heard Charlotte say. By now we were all tired from the races and were sitting around a big playroom. Toys tossed everywhere. Books lined the shelves, and traditional board games were stacked in alphabetical order from floor to ceiling. Imagine that, going into a virtual video game environment so you can pick up and play Monopoly or Clue or Chutes & Ladders.

Charlotte liked Chutes & Ladders. She'd beaten Mi and Dakota three games straight. I guess I should mention the board opened up to life-size. Everyone wanted to "accidentally" land on that long slide over and over again.

Anyway, she said, "I gotta go," and that's when I jumped over.

"How do you know?"

She didn't look any different now than she had two seconds before.

"Grumpy's here, he's tapping on my shoulder. I have to take the controller off now."

"Controller?"

"It's like a tiara. It's how I play in here."

Dakota whispered, "Does he know we're in here too?"

A shrug, no clue. Then, "Didn't he copy you over to come play with me?"

"We kind of made our way in here ourselves," Dakota replied honestly.

"But you're coming back next time? You have to."

Our new teammate, and my headstrong mutineer, smiled at the little girl. "*Sure* we will. Actually, I promise, because that's how I made it so we could come in here now. I watched the boards back at our home for when this game got loaded again. You must have opened it. That's how I tricked Phoenix into playing with us."

"I like him," Charlotte said. "He's kind of a dork, but he has big muscles."

"He's actually a real sweetheart," Dakota whispered. "Like our version of a teddy bear. He's sort of our own Bonkers."

"I am not," I protested.

"Are so," Dakota insisted. "You just don't see it yet. But, Charlotte, we'll come play with you again. Do you think, though, that next time your daddy takes you to work, you could check something for me?"

"What?" the girl replied.

Dakota started to say it out loud—I was dying to know. She looked at me and leaned over the child's ear. Once she was done whispering, Charlotte waved bye-bye, then winked my way. Very strange. And in a poof of yellow light, she vanished from the room.

Her father had disconnected her controller. Maybe work was over. Maybe the company daycare was closing.

We'd never know.

One second later, as the game environment shut down, we were sucked back to our base.

Level 16

All of us woke up on the Re-Sim tables. Of course, there was no repair work to be done.

For a change, we looked great. Refreshed. Happy. Tanned. As if we'd just come back from a long vacation.

"I feel *awesome*," Mi chirped, bouncing over to me for a kiss. I looked up: no missions on the board. We had free time coming.

How long had that taken? Hours? Days? More?

"You're in so much trouble," I growled over to Dakota, rubbing the relaxation out of my neck.

"I don't think so," she snapped back. "As far as BlackStar knows, we were all out there in some game somewhere. As long as the money rolls in, they're still happy overlord jerks."

"You're a program run amok. Like a killer robot, only without the robot part." I think it was a pretty solid assessment.

She looked at me, cocked her head, and said, "Well, if you're right and I am a program, I'm simply following the code they themselves wrote. All I'm doing is executing whatever command Black-Star inserted that says *find proof BlackStar is completely full of crap!*"

I wanted to argue, but, man, she was a step ahead of me there.

How could I disagree? If I was right, she was right too, and all she was doing was what was in her programming.

Or maybe she'd been hacked. But I didn't have time to suggest that.

She jumped off the table, high-fived York and Reno on the way out of the room, and disappeared down the hall.

⊕   ⊕   ⊕

A week passed, and while I'd been really nervous about repercussions from our illegal trip, nothing happened.

None of us disappeared in our sleep. We weren't demoted.

Perhaps Dakota was right. How could they keep track of all of us? With millions of gamers out there, each of them battling dozens or hundreds of us, what if we *were* unaccounted for? System glitch, probably. Maybe it happened a lot. We all experienced those slow-downs and disconnections.

See, I had some ideas about how this worked. Pretty simple stuff, like copy and paste, only on a computer-intelligence level.

BlackStar designed me and upgraded me from time to time when I was coming back through Re-Sim, and that was the basis for game enemy NPC.

Then I could be replicated as many times as needed across all the gaming sessions. Same with my team. Nothing to it. And since they'd designed us with this primitive form of self-awareness, we'd always put up a good fight for the gamers. We wouldn't repeat our actions or strategies over and over. Everyone won.

So what did I have to complain about? Nothing, really. I got to play those games every day at the highest level. Not to mention I had every need taken care of, great friends, and unlimited lives. Probably an unlimited life span too.

And with the duplication, or the cloning, of my program, there might be thousands or tens of thousands of "me" in the gaming system at any time. And millions of my team members. BlackStar might be copying my innovative tactics and inventive gameplay instantly, over and over, and delivering it to everyone who is playing or will play that particular game and level.

I don't want to act like I'm some kind of genius or revolutionary being, but I am. I just don't want to act like one. I mean, take a look at me: a prime physical specimen with superior everything. Don't want people to get the idea there's an ego beneath all this beauty, do we?

York, Reno, and Mi mostly hung with Dakota for that next week, but it really didn't bother me. Who knew what would happen? That girl, Charlotte, might have just been a random program anyway. An NPC left in the system from a preschool title, perhaps.

Plus, that world might not ever open again. It could easily have been moved or deleted or modified for some new game, so there was absolutely no guarantee that Dakota's little machinations were going anywhere.

As the time passed, their little coven began to dissolve, and Mi made her way back to my arm. It was nice. I liked having her around. We fought better together, back to back, side by side. And the more we were on the same page, the more times we'd see gamers bite the dust and go all the way back to their last checkpoint. Hoo-rah.

Just so you know the truth . . . YES, when you lose—when we blast you and you're not on the battlefield anymore—we DO whoop it up and pump our fists and high-five and have a party to celebrate.

Darn right we do! We feel good. No, we feel *great*. You like to win? We like it more.

And you don't like us? Well, we don't like you much either.

The bottom line was that it was cool that our little journey into forbidden game space had gone unnoticed.

I got tricked that first time. Fine. No worries. But you know the score. We have a job to do and I have a team to protect. That's my prime directive. It's what I do best.

So if Dakota wasn't going to help out and get with the program, then . . . simple . . . for the good of the team . . . she'd be the one left behind.

HIGH PLAINS KILLER came out a few days later, and now we were having some fun. Sure, future shooters and galactic battles are one thing, but there's a real draw to venturing back to the seedy Old West. I can't imagine there's a kid or adult alive who wouldn't like a chance to ride a galloping horse, jump over to a speeding train, race along the tops of the cars, stop the beast, and hold it up.

Great times.

My team mostly played as the notorious Skinner gang, a band of ruthless thugs who shot first and took baths never. Our horses were smelly, our teeth were yellow, and our six-guns sagged low. We spat tobacco, blew our noses on our sleeves, and never, not once, said "Excuse me" after we burped.

You know those legends of outlaws lying around a campfire, farting beans? My crew was a refried symphony.

HIGH PLAINS was a real triumph. The world stretched on for miles and miles and gigabytes more. The detail was fantastic. The characters, one after another, had their own novel-length stories to tell. Everyone who joined in the massive multiplayer game got to live and love and die as if they really were a frontier desperado. And every now and then, a few of them might get bold and test their mettle against the ruthless and odiferous Skinner clan.

That's when the fun began, not just for us, but for all those poor humans out there in the real world who, honestly, would *never* fire a gun for real. One after another, groups of gamers formed their own gangs to try to take us down and steal our gold.

We sent them all back. Then we hunted them like scurvy dogs, dealt hot lead, and planted 'em in boot hill. It became a global quest to try to take us out and claim our loot.

So after a long chase one day, York and Reno and Mi and Dakota and I had finally cornered some fleeing gamers. They were holed up in a box canyon about ten miles outside Vulture Hollow.

We still had three other riders with us, but those guys were expendable extras. I put them out front and hoped they'd draw some fire. That'd give us an exact location where our enemies were hiding out.

"They've got to be low on rifle ammo," York said, taking a long look through our spyglass.

"Good," I said. "We'll get in close, but not close enough for their pistols to be accurate. Let's take up in those rocks on the ledge and pick a few of them off before we start the main assault."

I turned to York. "Can you actually see them yet?"

"Not clearly. They're in an old mining shack. Horses are out front, though. And there's nowhere else they could have gone."

We too were getting low on numbers. The Skinner gang had started out twenty strong, but by now the gamers had whittled us down to the last eight. That was pretty normal. As the gang leaders and henchmen, York, Reno, Dakota, Mi, and I could take a lot more damage than our goons. Goons usually get popped in just one or two blasts. It takes a bunch of well-placed headshots or sticks of dynamite to finish the strongest of us.

"It might be a trap," Reno pointed out. "Been seeing a lot more of that lately. Gangs teaming up."

"I see nothing up in the cliffs," York reported. "No snipers. No cannons. No cavalry."

"I think they got themselves in a bind," Dakota added. "Probably didn't mean to ride up this dead-end canyon. New to the game map, is my guess."

"Makes sense," I agreed. The last place any gamer wants to end up is cornered in a spot where there's no alternate escape. But that's what these players had done. Ridden up the wrong road. Their loss, our win. Now to finish them off.

After waiting a few minutes, I realized we weren't going to get any easy shots. Either the horses were in the way or the gamers in the shack were too well hidden. We watched the windows and the door, but no heads appeared. No weapons poked up. Whoever was in there was just going to wait for our approach.

Fine by me. I'd show them some tactics they'd never seen from NPCs before. That's what I do. That's why we win.

York and Reno stayed to the right. Mi took the left with our three gang riders. Dakota and I would hold down the road and wait for the gamers to get flushed out front.

On my signal, both Mi and York unloaded a hail of fire into the side windows. Wood shattered, bullet holes ripped open, and splinters flew onto the dusty ground.

No response. Were they still in there?

Mi used the first diversion to create a second: one of her gang riders dashed toward the open shack with a Molotov cocktail. His throw was perfect, and the roof exploded in flames. The guy turned to retreat, and just as I began to think there was no one inside, my man's hat sprang off and his bald head mushroomed in blood. The gamer inside had picked him off, one bullet, at a full run. It was a nice shot, considering these old weapons.

Two more rifle rounds rang in the air. The shack was still burning, but Mi's other men went down.

"Whoa," Dakota groaned in my ear. "That's some *deadly* aim." She was right. This player was no novice. He'd taken them out with pinpoint accuracy.

Strange that he'd made the mistake of letting himself get cornered in this box canyon. Kind of a rookie move, if you ask me.

The flames had spread and the walls looked about to crumble. Sooner or later, whoever was inside would have to come out. That was the only escape, the front door. They wouldn't just stay inside and meet their doom and lose all their progress. No chance of that.

But nothing moved.

How about another surprise? I waved and Reno took off his ten-gallon lid. It just happened to be stuffed full of slithering rattlesnakes. I recommend everyone carry a lot of them, especially if you're immune to the bite, in your own hat. They're good in a pinch

—and trust me, when you chuck vipers, you gain a tactical edge.

Reno tossed them all through a window. With the flames and heat, those rattlers would be in a very bitey mood. Sorry, gamers, surprises like that are what make us the best, or didn't you hear?

We could hear the snakes snapping. The hissing was so angry it made the nearby trees quiver.

Nothing. Not a peep from the gamers inside.

Eventually, the shack burned to the ground. We watched as the final flames licked black timbers and the walls began to cave.

I waved and Reno moved forward.

He kicked away the rubble. Jumped back, waiting for someone to spring out.

The ruins were completely empty. That was odd. I knew the pinpoint shots had come from inside.

That's when York found the opening to the mine.

The shack had blocked our view of the entrance.

This game had a *huge* map. And now we had to pursue the deadly sniper down into the dark tunnels below our feet.

More work ahead, but, hey, unexpected twists and turns like that? *That* makes good vids. The designers deserved a pat on the back. No wonder this game was so popular.

We checked our ammo—unlimited—and began crawling single file through the entrance of the narrow vertical shaft.

Level 17

I could feel the air cool the deeper we went. This was not some standard mine—no rail tracks on the floor or support beams overhead. It was a tiny crevasse, more like a wormhole, and it dropped ledge after ledge with little room to move at all.

I was up front, Dakota behind me, then York, Reno, and Mi. That was it. There was no way we could switch order, either, as the rock walls and dirt ridges stood so tight that there were spots I thought we'd never squeeze past. I know, it doesn't sound like a gold or silver mine you would find in the real Wild West, but this one hadn't been dug by normal miners, had it? This was a game designer's interpretation of a mine. Or at least, a hole in the earth that led to . . . where?

The farther we went, the more I realized this was not something you'd usually encounter in a game. How would gamers, once done with the mission down here, find their way back? HIGH PLAINS is an open world. That means the players move around the environment as they please. There's no linear set of rooms or settings they're funneled through. If they came down here, well, eventually, they'd either have to climb back out or shut off the system and lose all their progress.

Kind of a cool feature. A one-way adventure. Inventive. Maybe it came out on the other side of the canyon. Or under a bank vault. Or inside the territorial prison. Who doesn't love a secret passage?

Along the way, I kept seeing big bootprints from the enemy who'd passed before us. Yes, we were chasing them, the one or ones who'd so easily picked off my men.

Finally, after what might have been a vertical mile, my feet hit a flat surface. I squeezed down, lowering my inconvenient bulk under a rafter, then crawled forward about twenty yards. It was dark down here, and cool, but there was just enough light from a series of evenly spaced lanterns.

Something was ahead. We hadn't accidentally left the map. That happens with designers who don't close off every nook and cranny of the environments. All "worlds" have some sort of boundary or edge. But in rare games, if designers are rushed or the artists aren't paying attention, there can be glitches where a gamer or an NPC might simply fall and fall until their system reboots.

But not here. No, this was as real and solid as the ground under your feet or the roof over your head. I could smell the damp air. I could run my fingers over the jagged rocks. Spider web stuck to my face and rats squeaked as I scurried along on my belly. Creepy design. Great design.

Then it got pitch-black. No more lights. But there was no going back. Not enough room. Dakota was right on my heels. I raised my rifle, panning around, listening for the click of a hammer or the chambering of a shell.

Nothing.

So I crawled another ten feet.

Nothing moved. Just blackness.

Another five feet and the ground suddenly changed. It was smooth. Flat. No more dirt.

A light popped on, and there, in the red glow, two cowboys stood twenty paces in front of us.

They were both tiny. So *that's* how they'd gotten through the tunnel so fast.

One had boots that were way too large and a hat that fell over his eyes, and his denim clothing looked like he'd borrowed it from Daddy's closet.

I pointed my Winchester straight at his nose. His gamer tag glowed in the dim light, but I didn't care what it said. This was the sniper who'd popped my guys.

Then, out of the corner of my eye, I saw the other cowboy. No, she was a cowgirl. Her ten-gallon hat almost covered her face, and her yellow dress draped over bright pink riding boots. She had no gun, she had no weapons at all. Just a small lasso, also pink, and a teddy bear tucked under an arm.

These were the gamers? Just little kids?

"Freeze, hombre!" the boy yelled, his long gun barrel centered on my right eye. "We've got the drop on you stinkin' varmints!"

"*Y'all,*" the girl corrected him. I recognized that voice.

"Oh, yeah," the boy replied. "I meant to say we've got the drop on *y'all* stinkin' varmints!"

"Charlotte!" Dakota exclaimed, now squirming into the chamber with us.

"Oh, brother," I moaned, lowering my gun.

"Dakota!" the girl squealed, running up to hug my troublemaker. "That's my big stupid brother, Jimmy." She pointed to the boy.

They sure looked cute, all dressed up like that, but this was an M title (mature audiences only—yeah, like that kept kids out of it). No wonder the clothing wasn't programmed to fit right. Tell you something, though, if that was Jimmy up on the surface picking off my men? Well, this kid was no amateur.

Out of curiosity, I looked at his gun. It wasn't like anything you'd see in any other frontier game. No, this was a specialized rig. Probably a .55-cal full auto with a 4,000-meter scope, night vision, motion detector, and an x-ray probe. Plus, it had a flamethrower and a grenade launcher.

York was staring at it too.

He smiled, then shouted, pointing at the kid, "CHEATER! I don't think *that's* standard equipment for an Old West game."

Jimmy replied, "Deal with it, old-timer. I hacked it in here. Found the rifle in a BORDERWARS folder and dragged it into the weapons locker for my HIGH PLAINS. So there."

I stared at the boy. Dakota and Charlotte were still hugging, but now the kid pulled the huge hat off his skull. He couldn't have been more than twelve years old. But corrupting video game files? How did that work?

"So you're *REAL?*" Jimmy asked, staring intently at me, then my men, then Dakota. He poked me with a finger like I might be a ghost. "You can feel and think and act independently?"

I stared back. "Of course we can. Because that's how we're programmed to behave."

But Jimmy was shaking his head back and forth like he couldn't figure something out.

Reno interjected, "You just pulled other weapons into this game?"

"Yeah," the boy answered, but his brain was still wrapping around the shock that he was having a *conversation* with enemy NPCs. "Simple, really. Any game is basically just a series of files and folders like on any computer. I opened my Pandora directory, control-C'd the sniper rifle, then control-V'd it into the HIGH PLAINS weapons folder on my dad's work console."

"Smart." Dakota smiled, now sitting down with Charlotte on her lap. They really did look kind of cute together in a big-sis/little-sis sort of way. That is, if the youngster is the cutest thing on the planet and the older one is a burly, battle-hardened, musclebound war machine dressed in flannel and chaps.

"Can you copy-paste me over a nuclear missile?" Reno asked. "I've got a sheriff in that last town I'd like to crispify once and for all. He hanged me twice this week. Neck stretching hurts."

"That's, uh, probably the least of your problems," Jimmy said to him, actually writing on his hand with a finger. "Charlotte doesn't get how weird this is 'cuz she's still such a little kid. Dudes, I'm like *totally* creeping out. She was right, you guys are *way* messed up. You should *not* be blabbering with me."

"See, Dakota?" I pointed out to her. "We shouldn't yap so much."

But Jimmy had some for me. "And *you,* Phoenix, should be pumping me full of hot lead. Right?"

That shut me up.

"Something's corrupted," Jimmy muttered. He started stabbing in the air like he was punching buttons. He might have actually been doing that, back in the lab where he was playing the game.

Then he turned to me. "Phoenix, where are you, like, from? Like, your origin story or whatever?"

"Your dad's BLASTERS OF FREEDOM code," I told him. "I was tempered from nuke steel, then bronzed in hellfire, the comet of doom delivering an indestructible element from deepest—"

"No." He laughed. "Knock it off. For *real.* That fiction doesn't add up anymore. Where do you think you might actually be *from,* if you had to pick?"

So I played along. "Phoenix, uh, Arizona. Maybe."

"You don't have actual memories of that, though? Or do you?"

"I dunno."

"Think."

There was just one scrap I had to offer. "I saw a sign once. It said to stay out or I'd be shot on sight."

Jimmy nodded.

"I think I might have a fear of deep water too."

Now he snapped his fingers, like I'd checked the best box or hammered the right nail. He moved his finger around the room, pointing at my team.

At York. Who answered that he might be from "New York."

Then Miami.

South Dakota.

Reno, Nevada.

He asked them all that same question, about any memories. Any scrap they could provide. Mi talked about her sprayer planes.

York, without telling us, had been carrying a vision of a crumbling island skyline and a million people living in subway tunnels. A city surrounded by rivers, the bridges cut, water slowly filling their only livable space.

Reno asked why he had a recollection of irradiated suburban neighborhoods. Factories built one after another, pumping smoke under a sweltering desert sun. Workers coming and going all hours of the day. Armed convoys departing on journeys across a roadless wasteland.

These visions. These flashes. They told small slivers of a story. And each time Jimmy heard one, it made him nod and his eyes go a little wider.

He must have been thinking the same thing I was. His eyes finally focused on Dakota. Her swim lessons. But it wasn't her memory; no, it was the timing of the memories. Because—plain and simple—*none* of those visions had begun before Dakota appeared.

So maybe she *was* a virus. Malware with eye shadow. An upgraded enemy disguised as . . .

It all made for one heck of a game, if someone out there pieced it together.

Because that was all it was. I was still sure. Just ghosts in our code. Phantoms in our machine.

I did understand one thing, however. We weren't on the Old West map. "Dakota, how'd you arrange this? Again?"

"We robbed a stagecoach a week ago. Jimmy was riding shotgun. While you were burying that marshal in the anthill, he whispered to me he was Charlotte's brother and was going to try to build a tunnel. I didn't get what he meant until we burned the shack."

So *that's* where we were now. Jimmy had hacked a door, a cave, a digital wormhole from that HIGH PLAINS box canyon right into the test facility.

Smart. It was the only way they could ever get me back to this test site.

The lights came up, and yep, here we were. Back in the lab. Blank walls, simple doors, and the only way out was through the hole in the bottom of the far wall.

But although they'd led us down here, I was certain they had no intention of making us go back up that way. The fact was: we were off-grid now.

It occurred to me, why *not* just delete us? Reboot with our original files or something? Or write up a version of enemy NPC who didn't wander off the reservation so often?

"BlackStar's going to reformat our butts," I told Dakota harshly.

"Probably the rest of our bodies too," York added helpfully. "Even our hands and legs and feet."

"How's that make you feel, Dakota? You'll be responsible for the end of us all. You're our angel of death. Maybe you infiltrated *us*, just like the gamers seemed to think you were infiltrating them with all your peace talk."

She wasn't taking any crud from me, though, and spat back, "I'd rather die right here, right now, than live as someone's war slave!"

And with that she wrapped Charlotte even tighter, as if the little digital representation of the real world were her only hold on physical earth.

Kind of funny, because Charlotte was, in turn, squeezing her teddy bear. One digital image clinging to the next. None of it was real. But for some reason they felt compelled to hug each other. To try to clutch connections that just didn't exist.

"You don't understand," Mi was saying, tugging at my arm. "Dakota *is* on to something. She may be right. I want to see this through."

"Right?" I howled, looking at York and Reno. Were they also buying into this crap? "There's no right or wrong or up or down or anything about it! You've all got to come to terms with the basic facts here. You don't really exist! You're electrical blips on a mainframe. Good-looking blips. Tough as nails. But *programmed* to fight and die. On the other hand, we've also got it great! We play games all day! All our needs are taken care of! When it comes to toys, no one's got playrooms like we've got!"

Reno came around to my other side, so now he and Mi had me pretty much surrounded.

"Phoenix," he warned, "you better not mess this up for us. And, man, you know I love you and would follow you into hell, as I've done hundreds of times in the DANTE EXTREME! INFERNO series, but now you gotta listen."

"Listen?"

"Listen . . ." Dakota said calmly. "Your version just doesn't add up. Even the stuff you say, the stuff that makes sense to you. 'Cuz, Phoenix, there are huge holes in your logic."

"Holes?"

"Gaping holes. Start with your love for us, for your team. Especially for Mi. That was one of my first clues. Would one program ever sacrifice itself for another? I've seen you do it. *Think,* Phoenix. Don't just *strategize.*"

"I agree," echoed Jimmy. "You yourself are proving Dakota may be right, and right this very minute, Phoenix."

We all turned to look at the boy.

He stared at me. "Look, when Charlotte told me that the NPCs were talking and playing with her, well, I thought she was making it up. You know, imaginary friends and all that. But now, it's freaking me out, you guys are *arguing* with *each other!* I don't think that's in any code, ever. Talk about inefficient. That programmer would be fired forever."

He seemed to be calculating. The kid might have been preteen, but it was hard to forget that he'd grown up in a house where designing artificial intelligence was as common a topic of dinner conversation as book reports and youth soccer leagues.

I watched him. In those ridiculously large clothes, the shiny badge, the belt that was wrapped twice around his trousers, he cut a funny image. But the brain in there was in no way undersize.

Jimmy explained. "Intersquad dissension? Not really possible. Dreams? Unlikely. And lucid dreams, at that. Conviction that you're *not* programs? This is like an anomaly chain that no one could even begin to write." He squinted. Maybe that made his brain kick into overdrive. "OK, *finally,* a real-world test for my skills of awesomeness. I can solve this. I need to just start from the beginning."

I wasn't convinced. Not a bit. He'd forgotten that we were *supposed* to adapt and learn, but he'd figure it out.

Jimmy began muttering, going back over what he knew. "Black-Star is in trouble. The city is dying. Dad needs a smart NPC. Something that doesn't just repeat the same enemy actions over and over again for his games."

"Is that when we moved out of the projects?" Charlotte asked.

"Right before," Jimmy said. "So then he introduces Phoenix for BLASTERS OF FREEDOM. Sales go off the charts."

"The game let me run free," I recalled, kind of proud. "I had no rules. I could defend any position or attack any way I wanted."

But Jimmy's brain was moving forward months at a time. "Sales spiked. Our economy got stronger. Enough food for everyone. Then that whole new generation of games was born. Each title had infinite replayability because the enemy used different tactics each time through . . ."

"Sure we use different tactics," I mumbled. "We're not stupid. If we did the same thing and hid in the same place and carried the same weapons every time, we'd never win."

"Mmmmm." Jimmy was calculating. "But this still makes no sense. Why name the digital combatants after locations? Plus, you have memories, uh, like leftovers of the local stuff there. How'd that leak in? Why the arguing with each other? Why Dakota's affection for my sister? Artificial feelings would be a waste of drive space." He was looking at Dakota. "Even the fact that we lured you in here. Or that you strategized to return to this place that first time you met Charlotte. None of it is a logical reaction to environment or conditions. It's unpredictable. Independent."

I just stared at him. He was losing me, but Dakota seemed to follow along a little better. Maybe it was because she was newer. Perhaps the Dakota model ran on a bigger line or had faster processing or more RAM or . . .

She suggested, "Jimmy, maybe you need to think beyond the limits of a simple program?"

The boy gave her a long, curious look. Then his eyes started to get wider and wider.

"I gotta go," he blurted. "Take care of my sister for a few minutes."

And with that, he simply vanished. Back to the real world.

Level 18

Charlotte was in the mood for finger-painting, so Dakota and Mi found jars full of colored goop. The nice thing: in here, who cared if it was permanent or it got all over your clothes?

The time on the clock was passing very slowly. York, Reno, and I just sat there, watching the kindergarten activity. It might have been hours. The second hand was absolutely crawling.

This was probably the end for all of us. The first time we'd snuck off campus to play with BlackStar kids? Might have been a mistake. This time, though, someone was sure to find out. Jimmy was a bright kid but no adult. It'd be a miracle if he could play around in the BlackStar mainframe and not leave a trail to follow.

I kept waiting to get deleted. It felt like I was having a heart attack. My chest got tight and I sensed the end was near. Wherever Jimmy had gone, this was going to be the last level for Team Phoenix.

I also had to make a fist, not out of frustration, but to hide the tattoo around my hand. I finally just stuck the thing under one of my legs. Didn't want anyone to notice. The glow, the light effects, they were beginning to flicker. It was a strange interruption, like my connection was dying. We were probably all dying in our own way. I'd go first, of course. That was my role.

And even though that afternoon dragged along, later, because of the news we would receive, it would seem like only an instant. I now remember those agonizing hours as if they were just a single tick of a real-world clock.

We waited and waited.

I guess that's what it's like when you're so close to the end of your existence.

Because, make no mistake, those last moments with Charlotte, they were definitely the end of life as we knew it.

There would never be an opportunity to go back. Or to live again as elite warriors with nothing to do all day but deal mayhem and have a grand old time doing it.

Upheaval. Complete and total. In three, two . . .

So how long had we now been out of the game system? Did it matter? That's like asking if you remember how long you spent in a crib as a kid. Those days or years are a blur.

When Jimmy returned, he'd ditched the cowboy suit. Now he was wearing a lab coat that was way too long.

"I've got, uh, news," he reported grimly.

I was sure we'd been discovered. My hand, that brand, had gone almost dark. Like a flashlight you have to shake and knock to get even a glimmer of yellow.

It was quiet in here. Out there, I could only imagine the alarm bells. I mean, how would you react if you found out some warlike monsters had been sneaking around, meeting up with your young daughter? I'd carve them slowly.

"News?" Dakota asked, wandering over, still holding hands with Charlotte. "Good? Bad?"

"Depends how you look at it, I guess," he replied.

I interrupted. "So we're actually malfunctioning NPCs and are about to get deleted or scanned or reprogrammed?" I could feel what was coming. They'd erase everything that had to do with this little revolution. All the players would be scattered across the system. We'd have no memory of playing children's games or having dance parties with Charlotte, no memory of this place or the kids or the worm known as Dakota.

I'd lose my team.

That meant I'd lose Mi. The thought hurt me on a gut level. Even worse than the pain in my brain.

"No, you're not *exactly* malfunctioning," Jimmy said. "Dad's up in his office as usual, and no one's around today, so I got to run a trace on the root files for the Phoenix and Dakota characters."

"A trace?"

"It's not that complicated," he said. "If a game is just like any other program or system, basically, so are you. You should be a set of folders and files that interact with each other. Just like you'd find in any desktop folder."

"So you found the root files marked Dakota?" she asked. "And Phoenix?"

"Sure did. Very clever. So there's a master folder with all your intelligence on the main server. Then, when anyone anywhere plays a game, it gets opened and copied as many times as you need to be copied and you get assigned to the environment."

"But why . . ." Dakota began.

Jimmy kept going. "The key was to crack open that root folder. I used a password scrambler in Dad's tools directory. Guess what? *More* folders! Dozens! Hundreds! There's some for your outfits and costumes and weapon preferences. Others for your skills and language, and even a couple for your moods. On and on. You would not believe how deep the database is on you guys. I kept digging deeper and deeper into the architecture. I figured I'd eventually reach the master folder where your read-only intelligence is stored. Wow, I thought, that was going to be like the coolest code ever! The most top-secret stuff at BlackStar! Think about it . . . your creative abilities as enemies, *that's* what makes this company survive. It's why other game cities are failing. Your superior abilities feed and house—"

"And you found that file?" I asked, just waiting for my particular intelligence folder to be wiped clean. If Jimmy had been mucking around in there, accessing my data, you know it had set off bells somewhere.

"Oh, I found it!" he exclaimed. "Man, did I find it!"

He then turned to Charlotte and said very clearly, "Sis, I will never, ever call Dad a big dumb idiotball ever again."

She kind of twisted her head, not understanding.

"Our dad," he stressed to her, "is the most brilliant man who ever lived. I was wrong to call him an imbecile that time he couldn't assemble my bike. I was so wrong, C. He's a *genius* who should be worshipped as the master of everything."

"Everything? He can't even do laundry."

"It doesn't matter," replied Jimmy. "What he did, what he's doing right now for BlackStar, well, Charlotte, now I know why we live the way we live. Trust me, if anyone else could do what Dad can do, they'd be bosses too."

She still looked puzzled, but I wanted a final answer.

"So you found our artificial intelligence folder? Or file? On a server or computer drive? What was in there that you think is so brilliant?"

Jimmy paused for a while before answering. It looked like he was trying to find the right way to tell us.

Eventually he looked up. "Remember when I said how that information is going to be good news or bad news depending on how you look at it?"

I nodded. Dakota was doing the same thing, hanging on every word.

"Well, the bad news is I *didn't* find an artificial intelligence folder."

"What?"

"And the good news is, there was no folder to find."

"You mean I'm not smart?" pondered York.

"Oh, you're smart. Despite all the patches and upgrades . . . So . . . The highest level folder, the master directory, did not actually lead to a file or program," Jimmy continued, making motions with his hands to illustrate. "See, it went into a computer server, where I thought you lived and existed, but there was also a port with a big cable running *out* of it too."

"Out?" Dakota demanded.

"Right. Out. You remember all those holes in Phoenix's explanation, right?"

She nodded.

He went on. "Anyone with any clue about artificial intelligence should have solved that puzzle, Dakota, but only you caught on. The arguing. The dissension. The affection. From having downtime between missions to looking after each other in a fight. The way he takes special care of Mi over there. The way he grins when he looks in those green eyes of hers. Or how you—"

I interrupted again. I didn't need to be reminded I'd missed so many clues. "So *the cable led out* from the server bank?"

The boy nodded. "Then down the hall. Then to another room. Through the floor, down a long, long service shaft. Then into the . . ."

Jimmy now pointed to a wall. A big projection screen was over there.

He waved a hand. The screen turned on, royal blue, and we thought it might be in one of those blue-screen start-up modes.

But no, it wasn't just a background. It was fluid. Thick, dense liquid. Something began to form. Something was drifting, lifeless, in the murky solution. Closer, closer . . .

A body. A woman. Almost nude. Slender. Hairless. A creature in an aquarium, or a zoo, or buried so deep in the system that no one even knew she existed.

And the heavy cable running into the side of her right eye glowed as gigabytes of information were pumped in and out of her skull.

She didn't move. She didn't twitch. She was not awake.

Jimmy finished, "The cable led to the tank in the basement."

"The *tank?*" Mi was now yelping.

"Right again. The tank. Where the bodies are floating."

"Bodies?" I joined in. "Flesh and blood?"

"Flesh and blood, yeah, sure. Pale as ghosts. Way slimy too.

You each have these wicked cable jacks drilled in the sides of your skulls."

"We're connected to . . . ?"

"Yep." Jimmy smiled in a disturbed sort of way. "You guys aren't programs on a server or computer creations at all. My dad is so brilliant. I know why he did it too. See, the only way any video game enemy could ever truly act randomly was if they were capable of real, organic, *independent* thought . . ."

"Woooooow." Charlotte was amazed, touching the screen.

Dakota, surprisingly, then turned and slugged me on the arm. Hard.

It hurt.

"I *TOLD* you!" she yelled. "Things just didn't add up! Like that we'd need to be from a city or state or some *place* . . ."

"Yeah," York agreed, "why didn't I think of that? If I actually have memories of New York, maybe my *body* was born there. I've been kidnapped! Help!"

"Any computer program," Jimmy explained, "would eventually repeat. It could never be truly random, as at some level it's all determined by a programmer."

"It totally explains why we'd need time off between missions," Dakota was going on. "Our brains need time to rest. Like normal sleep. Humans go insane without it."

"It was obvious all along." Now Reno was being a jerk-defector-agree-with-Dakota putz, just like his buddy.

Mi too?

Yep.

She said, "Or why I'd even *want* to have a boyfriend. True computer programs don't feel love or affection. But I *always* have."

"Or why it hurts to die," York was saying.

"Or why we'd rejoice and celebrate and feel good when we win . . ." Reno added.

"All those emotions."

"All that *humanity.*" Dakota was staring at me accusingly, like I'd been in on some kind of plot to deny her mortality. "Did you know about this?"

"No!" I answered. And I didn't. And I probably, honestly, still didn't want to know. Thinking I was just some computer program had never bothered me much. I liked the perks.

"It all makes sense." Dakota then turned to Jimmy. "So what do our bodies do? I mean, are they functional? Does it seem like they've been in the tank for years? Months? How old are we? Am I completely naked in there? Please tell me there's underwear involved. Did your dad at least have the decency to put clothes on me before I got submerged?"

"I dunno," he answered. "I guess you look like normal humans who've been suspended in a fish tank. Those cables that run right into the soft spots of your eye sockets are serious work. It's not like pulling out a USB."

"Am I pretty?" Mi asked.

"Am I strong?" York was looking at his huge digital muscles.

"More important," Dakota pressed, *"can you wake us up?"*

Jimmy stared.

I pointed. "Look at the screen, Dakota. You're not exactly fit for active duty."

"But you can trace our cables, so you know which bodies belong to us, right?"

He conceded a small nod.

"I want to wake up," Dakota said firmly.

"So do I," York agreed. "I can get back in shape."

"Count me in," said Reno. "New mission, new rules."

Mi, to my surprise, actually grabbed Dakota's hand. And Reno's.

Now the circle all turned to look at me. As if they still needed my code off my hand to step into the next world. They didn't. But I was one of them, leader or not.

Charlotte was tugging her brother's lab coat, asking, "Can you really wake them up, Jimmy? Let's help them, maybe they're really the good guys. Getting kidnapped and drowned *wasn't* their fault."

"No, it wasn't."

"Daddy's gonna freak." She smiled.

The boy was thinking. "I know he will. But, Sis, I'm not sure I could sleep every night knowing they're still in there, breathing that blue goo. I sure know I couldn't shoot them anymore. I think I'd feel bad."

She smiled up at him. A little-sister/big-brother smile. There's nothing else like that anywhere in nature.

Dakota grinned too, and she hadn't even heard his answer yet.

"This is *not* a good idea," I warned.

But it was too late.

Jimmy reported, "Well, there is this emergency revival manual taped to the side of the tank."

"Open it!" Dakota urged. "Read! Learn!"

"Now!" Mi agreed.

"Guys, girls," I began, hands out, pleading, "you have no idea if this is safe. It could kill us, for real, immediately . . ."

They were staring at me so coldly.

"The kid said that half or most of our intelligence files are not in our heads, but on those other computer drives . . . Without being plugged into that . . . Jimmy?"

But Jimmy wasn't listening. No, he was gone.

Then Charlotte's character faded from view. The last I saw of her was her little thumb, pointing up, right in front of those cute little teeth.

"Dakota, we have time to think this through. What we gain may in no way measure up to what we lose . . ."

As I turned, I realized I was speaking to empty space. Dakota had departed this world. All that was left was a shadow. It pixilated, flickered a few times, then blinked out.

And for the next minute, one at a time, I watched the rest of them slowly, agonizingly, fade from the playroom.

Reno began to melt. His body converted to liquid metal and seeped lazily into a drain.

York's skin hardened, turning to crystal. Then, while the top half was still coagulating, the bottom started to chip and shatter and clatter away like ice that had been shot with a BB gun.

Mi was next. Her eyes locked on mine and she gave me a sweet smile. Everything else turned to ash, as if she were in a furnace. Flakes drifted on an invisible breeze. I missed those eyes as soon as they went dim.

I didn't know if I'd go next. Or where. After all, I hadn't really given my vote. Would it be back to CO, all alone? Or forward and out, to be painfully born of a primordial ooze on the floor of a cold laboratory in a world I didn't know?

So much nausea. Room swirling away. That feeling like you're twitching and tumbling and . . .

Instant death.

At least, instant digital death.

The only way I can describe it is, suddenly, a small black hole opens over your head, but not big enough for you to fit through. Tough luck, victim. You're going to get squished anyway.

The harsh suction yanks every cell and pore and hair and tooth straight up, squeezing you into empty space like meat being twisted into burger.

You pop through, look down, and receding is everything you know and care about, quickly dropping away.

All you feel is helplessness. There's nothing you can do to get back.

No matter how hard you inhale, no air is left. You begin to suffocate . . . gasping, choking.

Bright lights.

Waking up in your human body is *nothing* like waking up on the Re-Sim table.

Level 19

Start by holding your breath for the next two minutes. Now, without opening your mouth or nose, go stick your head in an unflushed toilet and try to breathe.

That's what it was like waking up in the BlackStar tank. We were all coughing, gagging, sucking for air. The fluid was putrid. Heavy, gluey, it belched from our lungs, ears, nose, and throat. The bright lights burned our virgin eyes as we tried to focus on two adorable kids staring at us through the Plexiglas.

I felt like a monkey in a zoo.

No. I felt like a fish in a zoo.

My head burst up through the solvent just as Mi's, York's, and Reno's heads did the same. For some reason, Dakota wasn't thrashing like the rest of us. She surfaced as if she were some kind of mermaid who liked breathing preservative soup. I didn't like it. Not a bit.

And all around, floating left and right, there were even more bodies. Maybe a dozen of them, each wired in, that synaptic spike plunged horizontally through their eyeballs. None was alert. All remained locked in the gaming universe with no idea they had real flesh-and-blood arms and legs out here.

Was that Rio? Or Deke? The others I'd seen every day around

Central Ops? How could we tell who was who? They still had no clue what they were. I could reach over and touch them. That is, if I could get my arms or legs to work right.

The cables were bizarre. Mine slowly popped from its socket and splashed into the goop. That's when I realized I was standing, floating almost. The heavy syrup kept me upright.

My fingertips brushed the wiring. On the end of the cable was a long, metallic spike. From its length and size, that thing had gone in my right temple, behind the bridge of my nose, and completely through my left eyeball as well.

The data transfer, the digital impulses moving in and out, contained an enormous amount of information. These guys had some twisted ideas about what they had the right to do to other humans. What kind of surgery had it taken to implant the receptacle in my head? What size drill?

Two of my fingers came up to rub the port. It was like a hole through which their server could feed me everything I saw, heard, smelled, and experienced.

Well, not *every*thing. They hadn't been feeding me my feelings through it. My affection, my love . . .

We all looked the same: blue skeletons covered in slime. We were thin as rails and no stronger than newborns.

It was hard climbing over the edge of the pool. Slippery. Painful. The concrete floor was bitter cold, hard; my feet ached almost instantly. So soft. Tender. Like tissue paper for skin.

Jimmy pushed blankets our way. Through clouded eyes, we helped each other rub away years of goo. We all had to sit for a while. Every move was exhausting. Then, shuffling down empty corridors, along an underground tunnel. Huddling close, like disaster survivors. Slowly, we loaded into the back of a van. I remember pain in my joints, the soles of my feet, how my legs would barely walk, how my eyes blinked and fingers trembled and it felt like I was going to throw up.

Mi did throw up.

She puked about a gallon of the fluid we'd all been swimming in.

But . . . how long? How many years? What were we? Convicts? Lost hospital patients? Or normal people who got kidnapped, lobotomized, reprogrammed?

We slept. Almost as soon as the van door shut, we all closed our eyes and drifted away.

Later, in the dark, a hand grabbed my arm. It was small, insistent. My face rose, stuck for a moment in a foul pool. I'd lost my stomach too, in my sleep. Lucky not to have suffocated on the stuff.

Jimmy walked us. I had no idea where we were, but the air was so cold.

"How long?" My mouth forced the words out.

"Three days," the little voice said. "You slept three days."

Doors closed. Heat washed over my face.

Soon the five of us had stumbled through a series of plush rooms. Down a hall, toward more gloom. The lack of light was a beacon. It felt good, much better than the harsh glare of lamps and bulbs.

We were attracted to dark corners. And not for the first time.

More sleep. All of us. Curled on a huge mattress, tucked together for warmth or safety or perhaps just to feel our first human contact in . . . how long?

Once, when I opened my eyes, the sun had come up. It hurt less and less each time, and eventually I could focus on things farther away than my hand.

My hand. All clean now. But so small. Slender fingers. A third its former size. No calluses on the palm or scars on the knuckles.

So I turned it over. Real world, right?

But there it was. Just as in the digital world, my tattoo remained. All those swirling bars, all that code.

Now, however, it didn't glow.

It would not shine.

The charcoal ink was just ink. Slightly worn, not perfect or animated. There was no internal power source. It was just lettering. Just a plain stamp.

Where were we? I figured it was a guest home or a pool house, because in the distance was what could have been a castle, with wooden beams, stone entryways, turrets, and towers. Fields of long grass stretched in every direction. It was even bigger than anything in the game world.

And there was a familiarity to all of it. Pieces matched up. By one pool, was that the statue from PAIN PLANET? I thought so. Didn't that tree line appear in the closing sequence of VIETNAM VEN-GEANCE? Even the barbed wire looked the same.

Dakota was right. Real-world memories were tucked away in our heads. But whose memories? Was I even Phoenix? Or was I Fred Smith—plumber, fry cook, whatever. Had I gone missing at summer camp? Or had I not woken up from a dental exam? They were always doing freaky things to death row inmates in games. Maybe I was just too violent to be allowed to roam free, had gotten convicted, and . . . ?

What had Reno said that day? "There's *always* an abandoned re-search facility where the secret experiments run amok and the virus gets out of hand . . ."

Then, instant sleep. For a long, long time.

Some soup. It tasted strong even though it was barely water.

More light. A pair of dark glasses.

And more sleep.

It went on like that for days and nights. One after another until, finally, one of those cloudy evenings, I felt a whole lot better.

The sickness was gone. I ate some bread and didn't vomit it right back up. The broth seemed like water, so I added more powder. Then some noodles. An hour later I'd eaten so much my belly felt like it'd pop.

I stood. My legs held. My head, which I realized had been foggy, felt clear. It was the first time I could remember feeling like I wasn't about to fall down and crack open my skull.

"We're getting used to it," a voice said. It was Dakota, and she was also standing.

But she wasn't what I expected.

And I bet you this—I wasn't what she expected either.

York and Reno were on a couch. It was pitch-dark outside. A TV screen with stock tickers and profit projections read 3:14 a.m., but our internal clocks just didn't care what time it was. We had become night creatures. We were all wide-awake now. There must be some formula to determine how long it will take a brainjacking victim to readapt to the real world.

In the distance we could see the lights from the main mansion. Jimmy and Charlotte would be up there somewhere, tucked in by the help, snoozing away. Maybe having dreams about their strange new pets, the ones they'd smuggled from BlackStar and hidden in the estate's guesthouse. In their million-dollar playhouse.

The pets they'd been feeding. The ones who wore stolen clothing from main-house wardrobes. The ones who were beginning to understand the word "mortal."

"I'm ugly," York was whining. "And where are my huge beastlike muscles?"

"My forehead's not even brick-shaped," Reno agreed. "My skull's no longer a square block of bone."

"I can barely lift this coffee cup," York said, testing his strength, "let alone throw huge boulders and cars at my enemies."

"Ha ha! So you wanted to be human?" I chuckled to myself. "Welcome to Earth, puny mortals."

"I'm just so *plain*." Mi was looking in the mirror. "What are *these*? Average-sized boobs? Ick! My weak, skinny butt! No bulging calves? Ripped thighs? Why don't I look the same anymore?"

She was right. In digital, like everyone still back in there, we were all figments of an artist's imagination. Those worlds were always full of huge, athletic megastuds who could fight and run and jump.

Out here, just like all those gamers when they came back to their real lives, we were about as average as average could get.

I was no taller than any of the rest. Had dork hair growing in patches around my head. Arms as limp as pasta. When I made a fist, instead of a leather sledgehammer, it resembled a doll's hand. Soft and tiny. Breakable.

Dakota had auburn hair, not neon blond, and everything from her nose down to her toes was soft as a marshmallow.

York and Reno might have been poster children for some kind of geek camp or nerd retreat. Poor Reno had already taken to wearing a pair of reading glasses around the house. Bad eyes? Game villains never need contacts.

Actually, it was pretty funny when you think about it. What had Dakota expected? To come into this world as the planet's most dominant woman? Reality check here: we'd been living in a *tank*. We'd had no more real exercise over the past years than any other kid who lies around playing video games all day.

Our bodies were horrible. Our looks were worse. We were weak, slow, and short. Talk about homely!

"You still love me, right?" Mi was pleading. "I mean, this won't change anything, right?"

I gave her a hug and a long kiss on the cheek. Whoa, that was *new*. It was . . . remarkable. When my lips touched her face, it was the first time I'd really physically tasted . . . her. Does that sound right? Does it make sense? Sure, it was just cool skin, nothing to it, but I remember the smooth texture as vividly as any sensory moment I've ever had.

It was *great*.

She smiled. I hugged her again. She was, after all, human now. She needed the affection more than ever.

So did I, perhaps. It sure felt good to hold her. It felt safe.

Not just safe, it felt . . . alive. It felt like promise, or hope. Now I could put my head on her chest and hear a heartbeat. And not just hear it, but *feel* it. No game had ever provided that mix, that intimate connection. How could it? It was so simple, yet so unbelievably wonderful.

But safe was the last thing we were. There was too much going on, and those few waking moments in the guesthouse would end up being the most peaceful times we'd have together. I've come to believe that war just follows some people, maybe like one of those magnetic bombs.

Dakota stayed occupied with Charlotte most of the time. I didn't know if she was working the child for information or seeing if she could somehow become BlackStar_1's adopted older daughter, but the little girl didn't mind a new playmate. These kids lived on a huge estate. A pretty desolate existence, other than all the money and all the toys.

They made a nice pair, Dakota and the little cherub, but this was not going to be a successful infiltration experience. We couldn't hide here forever. If they'd taken all that surgical trouble to tank us in the first place, they'd want their investments back.

On our bodies' surfaces, we changed. Brief journeys into the sunshine helped our skin move past the instant-sunburn risk. And our diets were getting better, not to mention Jimmy had lifted bottles and bottles of workout shakes and protein pills. None of us looked like the comic-book muscle boys on the package labels, but hey, that day I first did two pushups without having chest pains? It was a great moment.

One day Jimmy cornered me and peppered me with questions. As he did, his eyes barely left my face. I think maybe I was some kind of school science project to him. I couldn't imagine any other kids would be able to bring video game legends to show-and-tell.

Heck, I didn't even know if he went to school, but he was trying to find out everything he could before the project came to an end.

"How does it feel to be so puny?" he asked. Then, before I could get my words straight, the follow-ups flew. "Does it hurt to be hungry? What will you do for money? Can you keep Mi happy if you're dirt poor? What will you do when you get sick? Everyone is going to ask about that huge cable port next to your eye, how can you explain that? An industrial accident? One that you all had in the same spot? How about your tattoos? Bounty hunters will be on the lookout for those, so do you all just wear one glove everywhere? What about jobs? What *else* do you have training in? Are you actually worth anything to the world now . . . ?"

I couldn't keep up. All I knew was this: "We can't stay here much longer."

"No, that's the bad news. The search is spreading. I opened Dad's e-mail today. They've expanded the hunt off the company campus and are working their way through the suburbs."

"Are these suburbs?" Mi asked. "Nice burbs, Jimmy."

His answer was "I'll get some supplies together for you."

"Cool. Thanks."

York had a different idea and turned to me. "I say we don't go anywhere without better toys."

"Toys?" Charlotte smiled when she asked.

"Big-kid stuff, sweetie," York explained. "First, we use our two hostages to demand multiple attack helicopters, fully loaded. Black-Star will pay. They'll never let these kids come to harm. I need an assortment of long rifles, house-to-house breaching charges, and fully auto submachine pistols for personal backups."

Reno chimed in. "Wheels too. Several. Tough overland vehicles. I know the mall parking lots are full of minivans, but we gotta demand escape chariots with bigger engines. Bulletproof glass. Nitrous. Supercharged. The works."

"Hostages?" Dakota stood up. "No way."

But my boys were making their shopping list. Better not get in their way. "Rocket launchers, land mines—make sure to put those on the demands sheet. Lots of spending money. And dirty weapons too. Like poison gas and small-tonnage nukes. Is someone writing all this down? When the security forces get here, they need to know they're dealing with pros."

"We're not using the lives of our friends as bargaining chips," Mi chimed in, agreeing with Dakota.

Jimmy also seemed to think this was just talk. "You guys will be fine out there. Get to the city. Get into Redwood. Stick together and lie low. Maybe you've got family nearby. That's a good start. It's unlikely you came from outside the border."

"Border?" Reno asked.

"You gotta stay away from the military police for a while," Jimmy asserted. "At least until you can blend in better."

I already had a destination in mind. "The best thing for us will be to get on the road. Away from Redwood and BlackStar. We'll head to Arizona or Florida and begin our search on familiar ground . . ."

Now the boy began chuckling. "Are you, like, *new?* Phoenix, you're smart enough to know about staying out of the wasteland. Barely anything crosses that anymore."

"Wasteland?" York had a puzzled look on his face. "Hey, I played sim games. There's no wasteland. Rolling hills. Highways. Airports. Trains. Soccer moms and vacation cruises and . . ."

Jimmy actually rolled his eyes at me. "C'mon, guys. Get your heads straight. Those sim games are so fake. Just frosting or candy coating for what real life is like. You all *know* that."

"I'm a trained shooter." I smiled. "It's all I know."

"You don't look like one anymore," he said honestly. "You're back to square one. Think of this like your first RPG. You get the role of father."

I smirked at that. I got it. "Mi's my independent, kick-ass queen. York and Reno are the unshakeable knights."

"And Dakota's your rebellious, troublemaking teenager with a bad attitude and no real life experience to speak of. But you still have to take care of them or the whole dynasty fails."

My hand was fingering the open port in my head. That area throbbed. It always throbbed now. And you couldn't look at me and not notice it right off. The metal hole gaped so wide a mop handle might fit.

But something about what Jimmy had said about my age was making it hurt less. Like it was the right path or channel to explore.

So I asked the kid straight. "How long was I in the tank?"

The boy nodded. Like he'd expected it. "You accessed the dates on my files, on our files, when you were playing in the server directories, right?" I'd seen my hand flickering. He'd looked.

His eyes gleamed. "You're catching on, Phoenix. Now you're asking good questions."

"How old? What was the oldest file?"

"Near as I can tell, you've been in the tank about four years."

I asked my next question, the obvious one. "How old was *Dakota?* What were the earliest dates on her files?"

Jimmy smiled. "Less than half that."

"So she was the beginning of the problem?"

"Not the *beginning* of a problem." She got angry. "The *solution* to a problem."

Level 20

So we were fugitives. My team, which had spent almost every minute on offense, was running like rabbits. But with no hole to hide in.

We watched three black vans roll up to the mansion. Helmeted men with body armor and matching assault weapons spread quickly around its perimeter, but we knew that the guesthouse was next on the list.

Just like that. Just like our lives back in the tank. We went from total relaxation to terror.

"How much do they know?" Reno asked Jimmy. The boy had run down from the mansion and was watching out a window with us.

"It's house to house now," he said. "They're desperate. Grasping. You slept in the delivery truck for days. We snuck you out the back when it made its regular stop here."

"Is it shoot to kill? Wanted dead or alive . . . ?" York began.

"It's a panic. I erased what *I* did, but you weren't showing up for missions. That's bad. They need you. They figure a competitor probably snatched you out of the tank, since you can't walk or move at all. I saw a bulletin to be on the lookout for large, unusual canisters."

I gathered the food and clothing the kids had lifted. Reno

watched the troop movements. Mi was by my side, but Dakota had one leg over the windowsill already. She was eager to move. She wanted more of whatever was out there.

We beat feet swiftly across the property, keeping the guesthouse in direct line of sight with the main residence. This shielded our movement from the search party.

York cut some fence. Then Reno pulled it together so no one would see our route. Up over another barrier, using our clothes to stop our flesh from getting snagged on the razor wire.

Just like that, we were out, and the whole world was down in front of us.

⊕   ⊕   ⊕

Jimmy and Charlotte's neighborhood was more than nice. It was almost idyllic. Trees swayed in a cool mountain breeze, and the streets looked new. The lower we walked through the hills, the smaller the houses became, but this was Sims-style living at its best.

Most houses had a small car in the driveway. Many had swimming pools. The paint was fresh and brightly colored, and toys were scattered in picket-fenced yards.

A school bus rolled by.

So did a military police van. What were they searching for now? Still the canisters? Or had they discovered we could walk and talk just like any free human?

To be safe when they approached, we'd split into twos or go solo, then reassemble a block later. They were looking for five. For a team.

Overhead, the sky was the sweetest blue. I loved how it wasn't just one shade of an artist's brush. Near the sun it was pale, but as you moved to the horizon, it got darker and colder.

We hadn't seen a bird yet. Or a plane. Nothing up there. I liked it that way. It was so . . . unthreatening.

The vans the troopers drove were sleek, like short buses, but streamlined and armored. Solid military vehicles. Impressive, sure, if you were a civilian. But everything has a weak point, and I'd already come up with a dozen ways we might ambush one between houses.

That would alert BlackStar, however, and we were locked into stealth mode now.

"Freakin' mosquitoes!" Dakota barked, slapping the back of her neck. A red smear appeared on her hand.

"You liking the real world now?" York mocked her. "Because the bugs sure seem to like you."

"You've got sweet virgin blood," Reno added, not mentioning that he had a few bites of his own. He wasn't the kind to let you know he hurt. Dakota, however, had always let the world know every single thing she was unhappy with. To her credit, she didn't just complain—she also did something about it.

Street after street, we wandered away from the mansion, and we watched the city of Redwood turn from executive to working class.

Our clothing blended in well. Hoods or sunglasses—courtesy of Jimmy and Charlotte—would hide our skull ports for the time being. Tape covered the tattoos.

Not bad. Not bad at all. This might work. Get jobs. Share expenses. Hide in plain sight until we came up with a master plan.

More luck went our way. As we tromped down the streets, the BlackStar patrols began to thin. So we spent less time hiding behind trees or fences or ducking down in tall grass.

It'd take them forever to search all those homes. And by then we could be *any*where.

The diversity was overwhelming. No two houses the same. All the toys had been played with, broken, repaired, stickered. Garbage cans and recycling bins. A kite stuck on a power pole and a sheet of lost homework — math — marked with a *B*. A woman with shopping bags returning from the store. Another on a corner, arguing with a man in coveralls about poor reception. This was the pace of their lives.

Low buildings began to appear. We'd reached the city. Cracks in the pavement became more common. Litter. Rubble. Potholes filled with broken glass.

We walked, we marched, always staying to the edges of streets or along the dark sides of the alleys.

It changed so quickly.

Now, *this* was not anything like a Sims game. Late clouds rolled in. A light rain came, went, and left behind a knee-level mist that was as pungent as swamp gas. Fortunately, it provided an instant hiding place, if we wanted to lie flat in a muddy gutter.

But the mist did not hide the reality of the urban decay. We'd gone from where people had plenty to where they had nearly nothing.

It was like falling off a cliff, but skipping the fall part. You were at the top, and *splat,* now, at the bottom, you were nothing.

Out here, if urban living was my only choice, I too would spend as much time as I could in the safe, cozy, virtual playrooms that BlackStar made.

Because the rest of your world? It's a hard place.

Level 21

When true darkness fell, we found a place inside, out of the rain. Sleep came, but not as easily as on a plush bed. And in the morning, we were all hungry, so our supplies took a good hit.

Then we walked. Not quite daylight. Everything was still so deserted, so abandoned.

"There are no cars anywhere," York said, patting me on the arm. He'd been talking nonstop about jacking one. The whole way down out of the rich neighborhoods.

He was right. The streets seemed uncomfortably wide without taxis or buses or vans parked along the curbs. Block after block, we peeked into underground garages and saw nothing, not even the remains of a bike or scooter.

No wonder security was so tight up in the hills.

This meant we had to keep moving. Nothing is slower or more exposed than a group of unarmed stragglers on foot.

Gone were the bright colors, the grass, the care. Weeds pushed through seams in the pavement. And it was darker, as if the electricity for signs or lights had already been sucked dry by those who could afford that luxury.

"The streetlamps have all been sawn off at the base." York pointed. "Look at the windows, too."

He was right: every pane of street-level glass on the storefronts was missing. But it wasn't about the glass. The metal ridging had been the target, and it was all stripped bare.

"They're cannibalizing their own steel," Mi reasoned. "Like in the World War Two games, where there's a huge iron shortage and the whole country has to ration its resources."

"Or like what came after," Reno added, "where everyone was stealing copper and aluminum and anything else they could sell."

I didn't say anything, but I was sure they were on the right track. So there was a war out here? Well, at least in our new home, we'd speak the language.

"You looking for work?" a voice suddenly barked behind us. "Right now?"

I spun, both my hands reaching for weapons that I knew weren't there. It was an old habit. When surprised, I usually came out shooting.

Not now. All I had in my pockets was bread and beef jerky.

It was a younger guy, hard-looking, tanned, walking with a group. They'd just come out of one of the buildings with the vacant street-level shopping outlets.

Those stores scared me. There were no shelves. No counters. Even the wiring had been torn from the walls.

I guess I half expected the voice to belong to a gaunt, malnourished old-timer with grim warnings about the horrible devastation into which we'd been dropped, but it wasn't quite that bad.

And—you know this—I think all of us had been scanning for a mangy dog licking a rotting corpse. Signs of the times. Real-world suffering. But maybe, probably, the dogs had all been eaten long ago.

Not if you looked at this guy, though. The one with the job offer. It might not be all bad down here, out of the elite neighborhoods. He had some flesh on him. A bit of muscle. And while his clothing was closer to ragged than new, it only had a few holes and had been recently washed.

"Work?" he asked again. "As in, your lucky day? Right place at the right time and all that?"

I stepped up, not even eye to eye with him. I muttered, "What *kind* of work?" It was going to be hard to get used to not being one of the tallest, strongest men in the city.

He actually grabbed my arm to turn me, to walk me along with his group. That was almost an attack where I was from, but he wasn't threatening, just insistent.

"Look," he said, waving to the group that followed, "a panel fell yesterday. We lost six. Now we're getting behind. We can't get behind. Help us out, man, really. All of you. We need ya."

He was still walking me, kind of like a prison guard walks a death row inmate. And my team, well, they were on autopilot, following along.

"What's the pay?" I asked, making sure now to move my feet fast enough to loosen this foreman's grip on my arm.

"Standard six chits a day," he said, almost as if it was boasting.

"Six dollars?"

"Chits—company script, of course."

"What's the job?"

"Where you been?" he laughed, and again, I just didn't feel a threat. Not much of an opportunity, either, but if this guy wanted to, he could probably have beaten me to a pulp and not broken a sweat.

"We, uh—" I was searching for a story when he interrupted.

"Who cares. Seriously. I'll get you *seven* a day, each, if you all help us out. Like I said, we can't get behind. You know what's at stake."

So we followed. The whole group bunched together for safety, but from what? Alleys were deserted. Dark corners stood empty. And every other group we saw for that long mile was also headed in the same direction.

I'm not sure what we heard first. The shouts of men at work? Or the clang of tool on bolt? Perhaps it was the creak of overloaded cables stretching and straining, trying not to spill deadly cargo down on the extended hands of laborers below.

Around a final corner. There in front of us we saw where all the city's metal was going.

We'd reached the outskirts of the Redwood ghetto. And this was where its people spent their days.

At first we caught just a glimpse of something between the buildings and beyond the edge of the city streets. Just a solid line above the tops of the outermost structures. It was different heights in different places, but we could see pieces being added to some sections. It dwarfed everything around it.

As we got closer, we saw this massive structure was made from heavy plate iron and was a swarm of movement. Huge girders were being anchored into concrete footings while multi-ton panels were hoisted, placed in position, and hammered with rivets.

One Tetris block after another, each as big as a garage door, the citizens were building a *wall*.

This was no ordinary barrier. Not some kind of flood levee or cattle fence. It looked like a patchwork of projects that, once joined, would surround the entire city and the suburbs with sheer, unclimbable steel. And what was on the other side? Why so much *bulk?*

When complete, would it be a hundred feet high? Two? No matter. From down here, it simply towered, sealing the city off from . . . what? Wild animals? Raiders? Armies?

Old men, older women, small children, the base area was a hive. Hauling, hoisting, running, scampering out of the way of jagged plate. It was like the panic on a World War II Pearl Harbor troop carrier—All hands on deck! Everyone work for your lives!

We walked with the man and his group. No need for introductions, no need for anything more.

One section seemed to be moving nicely. Another was struggling. Foremen yelled. Laborers cringed and picked up the pace. It was barely daylight and every one of them was already dripping sweat and wrapping dirty bandages around pockets of blisters.

"It's the building of the pyramids," Dakota whispered.

"I don't think they're slaves," I said. "I don't see anyone with whips." She and I had played the same thug roles in those Egyptian games. There were *always* whips.

"They're *paid* workers." York spat some road dust, and it was clear he had no great desire to jump in and lend a hand. "Each group has a foreman, like ours, coordinating the delivery of rivets and girders and plates." He pointed to a simple lever device with a wooden fulcrum as large as a cement truck. "By hand, that's how they hoist the sections up to vertical."

"What's it for?" Mi asked. "To keep something out?"

"Or to keep a lot of small things in?" Reno surmised.

We'd reached this foreman's work section. It was hard not to notice a square area on the ground, exactly the same size as one of the panels, where dirt had been rubbed into a rectangular reddish stain.

"Squashed 'em flat." York pointed to the mess.

"I tell ya what's crazy . . ." Reno was looking up and down the enormous barrier project.

But he didn't have to say it to me. I'd already noticed what was missing.

"There are no construction machines," he blurted.

He was right. Not a bulldozer or forklift or truck anywhere. No compressors or nail guns or welding torches.

Groups of men carried the plates over from stacks by hand. Others lifted the panels using blocks, winches, and cable. Up above, lighter workers on ropes bolted support brackets and then hammered each of the millions, if not billions, of rivets.

"Why not just use cranes to do their work?" Dakota asked the rest of us.

"Yeah," some smart-aleck kid yelped at her as he walked by with a load of hemp rope. "Like there's any spare fuel left to run machines." We were all staring at him as he went on his way saying one last thing: "Why don't you climb out of your dream world, Granny, and pick up the slack?"

Level 22

Two things helped me make my decision that day: First, it wasn't a bad idea to hide in plain sight and pick up as much information as possible. Second, up high, where I was, I had a great view of our surroundings.

They strapped me with a dried-out cord to an older man. I realized it was because we were probably the same weight.

A ring held the center of our line, and it was hoisted with the winch about forty feet into the air. Soon a sack full of rivets and a hammer was pulleyed up for each of us.

That was my day. A panel would be moved, hooked to the lines, and slowly elevated into place. The other guy and I—his name was Hal—would bolt a support over the top of the last panel and slot the next higher one in place.

Then we began the hammering, just as dozens or hundreds of neighboring crews were doing. Strike after strike clanging through the air. One panel took hours. My arms felt like they were falling off. Still I worked, on and on. Panting, sweating, trying to keep up. Soon enough, around midday, we were at the top and I finally got a view of both sides of the barricade.

I couldn't tell which was worse.

Behind me and Hal was Redwood central, a crumbling slum of brick-and-mortar buildings. All the steel ones had long ago been cut down. They were now likely part of this enormous barricade that stretched miles in both directions.

But out on the plains, it was barren. It could not have been quieter, more stagnant, more laced with the stillness of death.

Trees were stripped. Grass was brown. Dust was claiming the land, one creeping inch at a time.

"Looks inviting, huh? But they're out there." Hal coughed at me. The guy must have been fifty or sixty, but he was swinging his mallet just as easily as I swung mine.

"They?"

"They're watching. You know they are. Eyes in the dirt. Licking their teeth. Bellies to fill."

"Who?"

"Go even a few feet past the wall guards and you'll get snatched. I've seen it."

I squinted but couldn't pick out a single threat on the horizon. Maybe he was making it up. Old-timer with old stories.

"And you watch those girls with you too," Hal warned. "Some of the hordes been trying to breed meat again. Eat the baby boys, grow the baby girls until they can have more veal of their own."

"What?" I was starting to think he was bat-crap crazy. Nothing was out there. After all, where would they hide? It was just hard-scrabble ground. Almost like a game environment, only this one was too detailed. Every dead tree was individual, every dust devil was natural. Even the sounds were unlike any recording you might hear.

Hal stopped talking, but he never stopped working. It was like he had something to prove, not to me, but to the foreman down there.

And the guards. They were always watching, either the wasteland or the work. It was still almost impossible to tell whether they were there to keep us in or Hal's monsters out.

It got hot up there. I was boiling, but at least I could feel the wind. Layers of skin rubbed clean off my hands, and blisters formed on every finger. A rash began to develop wherever my soaked clothing touched skin, and I thought of my team down there on the ground.

It had to be twenty degrees hotter for them. And way more humid. Poor Mi. Poor Dakota. York and Reno would keep a stiff upper lip, but they had to be suffering just as much as the girls. Hauling serious weight. No water to drink. Sweating and heaving and feeling pain race through their backs. Knees twisting. Ankles cracking, not used to a load.

And this was *everywhere.* Thousands of workers. Scrambling and scratching out a meager existence in the hope that soon, not long now, the wall would be completed and they would be safe inside. But from what?

I still had too little information. To take my mind off the toil, I kept working old Hal for his story. This city's story. What had happened between life as told by the Sims and the country as it really was?

First, the oil ran out. Once fuel was ten thousand dollars a gallon and all the refinery production stopped, so did all the continent's farming.

So there was no food.

With no diesel gas, the world stopped mining metals and coal.

With no power, starvation. With no work, hunger.

People began to recycle everything they could. Scrap by scrap. Aluminum, bronze, copper, these became the most valuable currencies.

No taxes were being collected, so then, no federal government. No police. No firefighters. No schools. No military.

Crop wars for a few years. Corporate wars for a few more. Electricity wars. Rail wars.

The man babbled on and on, until he finally said, "Look! Scrappers!"

A cheer went up from the wall, a huge, resounding cascade of applause. Down below, Mi, York, and Reno wouldn't be able to see over the top, but I watched closely. Workers abandoned their tasks and rushed to the site perimeter, cheering, yelling, pointing.

Out about three miles, I saw them. At first it was just a cloud of dust, wheels rolling fast over dirt.

Then it was a desert machine. Like a tow truck but with heavy, worn, hard rubber tires. Carving the earth, sending up a plume behind its four-wheeled trailer.

Stacked on that flatbed was its catch. Two rusting old cars, probably from the early 21st century, had been strapped to it with cargo belts. Somehow, somewhere out there, they'd been overlooked. They'd never been melted. And they were an unbelievable prize.

To the howl of the Redwood citizens, the tow truck weaved back and forth. Out of the brown sand, filthy creatures that might have once been men leaped and ran and tried to cut it off. The rig, with its heavy load, was probably only doing thirty miles an hour, but still the attackers thought they could catch it.

It veered, arcing cleanly back and forth, trying to avoid the beasts. They were jumping, dodging, doing whatever they could to mount the trailer and climb to the front cab.

Hal was right, though. The cannibals *were* out there. And they were waiting for any fresh meat, even if they had to swarm a speeding old vehicle.

The truck got closer. For a moment, it looked as if a pair of howling attackers might step onto the running boards, but at the last minute the driver gunned the engine, black smoke pouring out, and bounced them both cleanly off the front bumper's cattle guard.

Red smeared away some of the dirt but was quickly engulfed and turned back to brown.

And then the tow truck was at our perimeter. Guards waved it in. The crowd parted to let it by, slapping the hood, admiring the courage of the crew. Every pair of eyes was longing for the huge riches in the three tons of jagged, corroded metal the truck had hauled out of the wasteland.

I saw something else. Something a bit disturbing. On the driver's side, there was even more blood, but this was on the *inside* of the truck. Something messy had happened during their run.

Then the scrapper was gone, motoring off toward the city's interior. I already had a couple of crazy ideas churning in my brain.

We weren't back to work ten minutes when York whistled up to me.

"Phoenix, what's *that?*" He was waving up the line, in the opposite direction from where the scrappers had just finished their successful mission.

I could see them too.

About five sections up the wall, around a crew that was slightly farther along than ours, ten men in black armor with matching assault rifles had just surrounded the team of workers. One at a time, they were removing hats, gloves, and other clothing from the men, women, and children. Checking them over. Very carefully.

When they were finished, they sent the labor party back to their job and moved to the next section closer to us.

I looked at York. He had already found Reno. Mi and Dakota quickly scurried over.

"I'm climbing down, Hal," I said to my partner. "Hold on to something so you don't fall when I untie my end of the rope."

"You can't go!" he barked. "We need the manpower. If our section gets any more behind we'll lose our chance of getting a spot on the inside!"

Then I saw him look where I was looking, then glance over at me and back toward the troops. Would there be a reward out for us? Sure there would. I couldn't imagine that the surgery on my head or that slave tank came cheap.

The bounty was probably a whole lot more than the handful of coins this guy would make up here today.

I wasn't going to keep chattering with the old-timer, waiting for him to do the math. A quick tug and I released my line, then slid down one of the hoist cables, thankful that the tape on my hand kept my palm from ripping apart.

My first plan was to run, like before, in exactly the opposite direction from the search team, but then I had a better idea.

What if they knew we would go that way? I'd used that tactic before, flushing an opponent, laying an ambush, guessing ahead of time which escape they'd take.

"Which way did the scrapper team go in their tow truck?" I asked Reno.

My friend pointed to the street.

It was pretty obvious. We knew their last heading.

So we'd be following tire tracks again. The five of us bolted off the wall's work perimeter and ventured toward the inner city.

"Did anyone bother to get paid before we ran?" York asked.

Wow, our wages. Not that we were starving yet, but it'd be good to know how the local economy worked. To get our hands on those chits the foreman had mentioned.

"Not paid," Dakota said as we walked quickly, "but I sold a heel of bread I got from Charlotte. The guy said he'd never gotten real wheat. Look." She held out her hand.

Four plastic squares, stamped from cheap vinyl, sat in her palm. So that was the pay.

All of us took a turn holding one of the squares, rolling it in our fingers. They were light, crusted with dirt, but none of us said what I'm sure we all first thought.

The stamp in the middle. The logo. It was just way too familiar.

"So BlackStar controls the money."

"Just in this town," Dakota explained. "It's company script. They pay everyone in it. And then the workers have to go spend it at the company store."

"Prices inflated, ripping them off again, barely enough to survive," Mi guessed. I bet she was right.

"Where's this store?" I asked.

"City center." Dakota pointed. She'd picked up good intel. "Highly fortified."

"It's got what we need?" York asked, and I was sure he meant guns and ammunition.

"Just like the supermarts of old days," she continued. "They've got everything, but for a price."

Now, finally, I had an idea what Jimmy had meant earlier. About how virtually nothing crossed that wasteland out there.

Well, *one* thing had to.

And I couldn't wait to see it.

But for now, we were too weak, too small, and too unarmed to allow ourselves even a brush with those dark troopers. Full-scale anything was a long way off.

Block by block, we loped along after the set of dried dual tire prints.

Redwood, during daylight hours, was no better than a ghost town. Everyone was working on that wall. And doing it for scratch, for barely enough to feed themselves.

There was no rebellion, either. Why not? No whispers of an uprising. Just hard work.

It was classic feudalism turned modern serfdom. A journey back to the Middle Ages, when the peasant class was doomed and those with the weapons controlled all the wealth. Now add in modern lords, their privileged children, unbeatable firepower, and superior mobility.

We'd all played a hundred historical games. Every one of us had been The Black Knight. Out here, though, the knights drove armored vans, and instead of swords they protected their bridges with automatic weapons.

So what level was the city boss? A prince? A duke? Earl of Redwood?

Something made me sure that no matter what kind of wealth his global game operation collected, he was not yet king.

And how had I come to that conclusion? It'd happened while we were following the tire tracks.

The roads were wide and pitted and seemed like they had a million miles logged on them. But the tracks from the tow truck were definitely bigger and rougher than those from the smaller tires I'd seen on the BlackStar security vans.

We walked—crept, really—and even though the streets were empty, we stayed in the shade. We passed buildings, every one of them looking like it might be bombed out, the glass exploded from inside. But upstairs, we could see dim lights and occasionally people going about their nightly routines. People lived. People died. They struggled every day for barely enough to get along.

The tracks kept rolling along. And then I realized BlackStar might not run the whole show after all. Because at an intersection, something broke the steady path. Crisscrossed the tire tracks, going off in a new direction.

While the security vans had big rubber and the tow truck had even larger, what I saw next made me shake my head.

These *new* tracks were enormous. Three times as wide as the ones from the tow truck. Spaced so far apart my team could lie end to end and barely touch either track.

"Holy . . . What made *these?*" York's eyes went wide.

The rubber prints were really something, lugged for heavy terrain but also ridged down the center for high speed.

I had an idea. I also knew that following those tracks right now would be pointless.

I wanted to find that tow truck. I wanted to ask about all that blood dripping in its cab.

Level 23

I told Mi, "I think the old guy I was working with was doing it for more than just chits."

"What do you mean?"

We talked about the horde in the desert. "I get the feeling everyone trying to seal off the city is working for their right to stay inside once the job is done."

She weighed that, then asked, "Like there's some really big pestilence out there on its way to wipe them all out?"

"It wouldn't be a bad move by BlackStar. To make them think a horrifying threat is always looming. It'd keep them in line. Keep them from revolting."

Mi and I were up front, just like the old days, leading the team, with Dakota about ten paces back. York and Reno were on our six, watching out for the BlackStar troops.

Mi said, "The whole time I was hauling rivets, I kept wondering how this'll work out for us out here."

"How did you expect it to?" I tried to smile at her. "Long days of labor? A family? Living in a scraped-out building like everyone else?"

"At least we're together." She grinned, but I knew we were both just putting a good face on it.

"Right, if we have nothing else . . ."

"And trust me"—she put her arm in mine; it felt great—"we have absolutely *nothing* else."

"No food." I went along.

"No money."

"No home."

"No identity."

I pointed. "The area around my skull port is getting infected."

She pointed too. "I keep getting stabbing pains in my chest."

"Our kids have stopped doing everything we order them to do."

She chuckled at that, then added, "I never thought the day would come, my mighty Phoenix, when you and I didn't have one single, solitary bullet between us."

My hand clasped hers. Wow. On those terms, I sure had let her down. I had let them all down.

But these were different terms now, right? Out here, combat rating didn't mean a thing. Just surviving day to day, that was the true test. I guess maybe Hal, that old-timer, was actually one of Earth's real winners. He was still alive.

"Where did we come from?" Mi asked suddenly. "I mean, am I all the way from Florida? Kidnapped off a street, away from my family?"

"I think Dakota suspects she got here like that. From up north. Some kind of slave trade. Like they take the best, apple-core their brains, slide in the cable port, and drown them for the rest of their lives."

"Maybe. But it doesn't completely add up."

I realized how easy it had become for the world to control a population. Especially if that population had no transportation. "Seems like there's really just one way in or out or around these days: through the unfinished wall. And then we go until we get somewhere. Or run out of fuel."

"But the *monster* tires. Those tracks. What could have made those?"

I nodded. "They push a big machine."

"No planes, though? I find that odd."

"If they can barely come by a few gallons of regular gas, jet fuel can't even be a consideration. Helicopters are too short on range, no good for the long haul."

Up ahead, I believed, we'd get a few more answers. The street opened into a square, every side of it walled off by concrete. At the far end, a set of gates stood closed, guarded by a pair of the company troops. Those guys, from what I'd seen at the wall, were exactly what foot soldiers would have been back in medieval times: the ruling class, going from village to village, or in this case, building to building, drafting any male child with good size or strength.

That way, the lower class was always weak. And the soldiers themselves? Why *wouldn't* they work in enforcement? It got them better food and better living conditions, and they wouldn't spend their whole lives doing hard manual labor.

In front of the troops was a platform, and we watched the tow truck drag its loaded trailer onto the scales. The whole thing shimmied as it settled. Armed guards centered their weapons on the cab.

A door swung open. Pools of blood dripped out, then down the running board.

A man with no face shield in a BlackStar tunic waved to one of the guards, who quickly ran over and began sopping up the puddles.

"I guess they don't want the scrapper to cheat and get paid for too much weight," York reasoned, now standing near Mi and me.

And as the driver climbed out, we could see what kind of work he'd chosen. His right arm was covered with bite marks, and his left sleeve was torn in a dozen places. One leg was also wounded, but he was still able to hobble off the skid and stand proud near the booty he'd hauled back in.

The guns, however, stayed pointed right at his head.

"One point seven tons," the clerk in the tunic announced, reading a small dial.

"More like one point nine," the driver argued.

"One point seven. The bottom one has a stripped engine."

"Yeah, but the whole block in the top one is grade ore."

"I already calculated," the clerk sneered.

I admired how the driver put up an argument, but even he didn't seem to think it was one he would win.

"Minus truck rental, fuel"—the clerk punched numbers into a small plastic calculator—"burned engine oil, rations, and mileage. Minus rubber, tool rental, ammunition, fluids, and cleanup."

The driver nodded again. It looked like he'd heard the swindle before.

"Six thousand two hundred four chits," announced the clerk. "Pay the man."

"Good haul," I heard one of the troops mutter as he slid a stack of large chit plates over to the driver. "Better get that to the store before you get robbed."

I saw the man snort. Then, slowly, he lifted a sawed-off shotgun out of his belt. As the guards with the machine guns watched, he handed the weapon over. It was quickly tagged and placed in a small locker near the feet of the clerk.

Now, I believed, he was unarmed. Sure, he was big and scarred and looked like he could crawl through a cactus thicket and come out the other side without a whimper, but he was also just one man.

And there were five of us.

"Are we going to rob him?" York asked eagerly. "Before he can stash his loot?"

I just smiled and turned. When the tow truck, trailer, and scrap were driven away through the guarded gate, I stood in the driver's path.

"How ya doing?" I said to him, looking over his heavy leather gear. The years of marks and cuts on a face that was instantly suspicious. A busted-up hand reaching toward the small of his back.

I think, at that moment, my entire team figured I was going to try to jack this guy.

But I said, "Looks to me, sir, like you might be needing a new crew."

A smile came across his face.

I went on, "Two of us. You need two new scrappers, right?" My hand waved toward Mi.

Still suspicious, he nodded slowly.

"What's the cut, when we come back?" I asked him.

"Can you shoot?" His gruff voice made me think of a guy who'd been breathing road dust far too long.

"Yeah," I promised, "I can. But my friend here"—another wave at Mi—"she can *really* shoot."

"How'd you know *two*? That I lost both my men today?" he asked.

"Best strategy," I replied, glancing at the retreating tow truck. "One to drive, one to strap cargo, and one to keep the animals away. Any extra weight would just cut into the fuel consumption."

I saw his eyes squint, kind of twinkle. "You get twenty percent of whatever we haul," he announced. "I keep the rest 'cuz it's my show."

"Done," I said, and put out a hand to shake.

When he took it, I noticed something right off. Old, dirty, almost faded from view, but there it was: the man had a tattoo wrapped around his big, callused palm.

Level 24

First day of work, you never know who to trust or what to believe.

The guy told me his name was Screw when we showed up the next morning. The tow truck had been rinsed off, most of the blood was gone, and the trailer had been unloaded. All that remained on the bed was a small hoist crane and several heavy cargo straps.

"You sure the little girl can shoot?" he asked abruptly.

"Like no one on the planet," I replied.

He handed her an old company-issue single-shot rifle and a handful of bullets.

"That's not much ammo," Mi grumbled, climbing into a shooting turret dead center in the back of the truck.

"Gunpowder don't grow on trees," Screw spat. "You waste a single bullet and it comes straight out of your cut."

"What do *I* do?" But I had a good guess.

"Drive," he replied. "An' where did you shrimps learn any of this, anyway?"

I hopped into the cab and fired the motor. It coughed, it chugged, and I realized auto parts were probably as scarce as full vehicles. If we broke down out there, it was going to be a one-way trip.

I tried to avoid the question. Indeed, how *would* two working-class citizens, fresh off the city wall, have a clue how to drive or to shoot? Those are rare skills. Military skills.

But in a way, we'd already given an answer. Screw's eyes focused on the tape around my palm. And around Mi's. He grunted again, and I steered the clumsy, slow-accelerating rig toward the exit from the square.

"Where we headed?" I asked, watching the half-built wall approach and the safety of the pavement leave my tires.

"Honey hole," Screw muttered. "I know a spot. Been good to me."

"Same place you went last time?" I remembered that he'd suffered losses. I was sure he remembered too.

"Not my fault those boys couldn't cut it. Go south. And stay off anything that looks like a road. Those are bad places to get stuck. Too many hole-traps."

I knew he'd had enough talking, so I did what I was hired to do. I drove.

⚘   ⚘   ⚘

I knew the instant we rolled under the wooden sign that it was a trap. It'd been over nine hours of driving, I was as stiff and sore as I could ever remember, and my senses were likely dulled.

Still, we were not dealing with a race of supreme tacticians out here. Whatever these rabid humanoids had become, it was not grandmaster chess players.

I could see how Screw had been picking the abandoned

junkyard. Most of the yard was covered with sand, but a storm had blown clear a short stack of ancient cars. How old were they? Thirty years? A hundred? In this dry air, with the heat and no rain, they might have been even older.

But c'mon, Screw. Couldn't he see what was up? Over time, one after the next, he'd lifted the vehicles closest to the entrance. That section was clear. Now he was having to venture farther toward the back row to get at what was left.

On the left of that row, a bleached wooden slab was now leaning against some large rocks. How could that have gotten there? It made a perfect shield for someone to crouch behind. On the right, three or four fresh mounds bordered one of the rusty heaps. We'd already seen the way these savages dug holes and hid in the dirt.

The problem was—and I knew Mi was thinking exactly this—we had no communication system. I couldn't radio her and point out what I'd spotted. I was sure she'd pick it up too, but what would she do? Waste bullets on the mounds? Blast a hole in the wood plank? Or wait for me to just run them over?

"You know it's a trap, right?" I said to Screw, shoving my right boot into the brakes.

"There's always a trap," he grumbled, pulling his shotgun from his belt.

"Let's be efficient about this," I recommended. For one thing, I didn't want one wave of the cannibals occupying Mi while another climbed up from the back and had her for lunch.

The man barked, "We need the metal. Usually if you shoot a big'n and then back off, the rest'll gnaw on him while we get the load on the trailer."

"Usually?"

"Four times out of five."

"Your odds are weak."

"Yeah." He smiled through broken teeth. "But I'm still scrappin', and almost no one else'll even come out this far. I'm gonna retire after I clean out this lot."

"So." I was still thinking about finding a better way. "Where do these guys live? They must be breeding."

A snort. "Oh, yeah, they breed. Most times they don't eat a woman right off. That girlie of yours is sweeeeet tail. Thanks for not knowing about that and volunteerin' her to sit up there where they can all smell our bait."

OK, he was playing it *that* way?

"So they've got a camp nearby?"

"I dunno, man." He was getting impatient. "They can live in dirt for weeks." But maybe he was right. Against a mindless enemy, sometimes the best thing to do is just wade in and keep shooting until your barrels turn red-hot.

"They got nothin'," he said. "Nothing but the scent of that little baby oven up top."

I was getting other ideas about how to handle this, but Screw was chattering, his voice starting to sound panicky as we saw some of the piles on the right begin to shift. "There's never been enough food for everyone. Some had to get pushed out a long time ago. Same as they're gonna do again when the wall gets built. Our food allocation will only support so many. Same as it's always been."

"*How* many?" I asked, slipping the truck back into gear.

"Well, all the execs, a'course, and the troops. Plus other *key* personnel like me who know their way around. And the better women. The younger women, then, maybe, is what I hear. . ."

"What you hear?"

"Hey, man, I *bought* my place. I had to *pay*. Sweat and blood, brought in more metal than any other two scrappers."

"So how many of the current citizens building that wall are going to get a place to live, inside, once it's done?"

Screw shrugged. "Less than *they* think." He chuckled harshly. "One man out of ten or fifteen? Less. The younger women stay. I wish they'd hurry, I'd get my pick. And the kids mostly stay. But the completion of that big metal fence is a death sentence for most. An' Kode's got 'em all tricked into hurrying. What a cool scam. They think the ones who get their section done first are first to get on the housing list."

I let that sink in. Sure, the wall might be months or years away from completion, but that project had an end date. It would insulate the residents. I could not imagine any city, in these days or the past, from Jerusalem to China's great wall, *not* wanting some kind of massive barricade to protect itself from the outside.

"Why are you telling me this?"

Screw took his gun off safety. "You do a good job. Got the tat. You're company meat. So I can get you a spot."

"You lying to me?"

"Not at all."

"Did you tell that to the last guy? The one whose blood poured out at the weigh-in?"

"Course I did. But he didn't do a good job, did he?"

Right then, three mounds exploded on our right, and the wooden slab to the left tipped down.

Man, was I glad weapons were so scarce. If the attackers had been armed, we'd have had no chance. It was a grinder of an ambush spot. There were a dozen of them and only three of us.

Three of us and, you know, one big truck.

I gunned the engine, hard, gave it everything it had, and lurched forward in third gear. This made the tires spin like mad, racing to catch the tranny. The whole beast sank a bit in the sand, then plowed out as if kicked in the rear.

I had good timing. So did our attackers. They came at us like they'd done this before. Screw was trying to steady his weapon to fire out the door, but that stubby thing would only be good at close range.

I could hear Mi up top, chambering one round, then the next, splattering each head down the line, but now the distance between us and the horde had closed.

Up close, they were foul. Solid black eyes, like sharks'. Their skin covered with white sores. Teeth filed to points. Scars everywhere, as if when the feeding frenzy started, one bite was as good as another and anyone was fair game.

I still had my foot pegged to the floor, coaxing every bit of fuel through that engine.

Screw had shot none. It looked to me like Mi was three for three and lowering her sights on number four. Still, there were eight, maybe ten of the ragged, nude men screaming, bearing down.

I spun the wheel left, hard, still full on the gas. I had to keep the RPMs high, redlining. If the engine stalled, I'd die by teeth. So would Mi, but not for many, many months.

The truck fishtailed, missing the horde. But better yet, the trailer acted like a whip, snapping around, cracking an arc as its flat-grate side became a two-ton guillotine. I would have liked to have felt it a bit, to have gotten the visceral satisfaction as the rusted edge collided with all their frail bones and meager flesh, but I was still spinning cookies, flogging them into splatters and splinters.

Soon my foot came off the gas.

I heard one more shot from up above.

Then I kicked open my door and climbed down. All the hidey-holes in the sand were empty. The ground, while sporting deep, circular tire marks from my spins, was much less bloody than I expected it would be.

In the real world, apparently, blood soaked into porous sand very quickly. And it didn't gush in buckets like the artists would make you think.

But also, out here, even though these opponents were no more than animals, I felt something strange. An ache started in my heart and went straight for my gut. I heaved, almost throwing up the chow I'd had a few hours ago, then forced it back down.

Phoenix, getting sick at the sight of blood? And not much blood, at that?

Strange.

Something, however, finally brought me back. It was Mi, climbing down, and you know what she said in my ear?

"I got seven of them."

"Seven?"

"Yeah, seven shots, seven scavengers. You only got six with your truck stunt."

I just stared at her. Apparently, the sickness wasn't in her gut too. "So?"

But I already knew what she'd say.

"I guess my stats are still higher, sweetie. Accuracy for sure. And I'm definitely winning on total kills too."

I made quick work with the boom, strapping and hoisting as much old car as the trailer would carry. Mi was on watch for a second attack, and Screw had the scrap wrapped tight in just a few minutes.

When he turned, Mi was pointing her rifle right at his forehead.

"No moves," I told him. "Not the sawed-off or the hideaway you got in the small of your back."

"You know about that?"

"Hand it over," I told him.

"It's just for show," he said, producing a small revolver. "Ran out of shells for it way back."

He wasn't lying. The gat was empty and corroded. I was pretty sure he still had a blade or two tucked under his gear, but that wouldn't do much good with Mi keeping her sights on him. He'd seen what she could do. And anyway, I just wanted to have a talk now. One in which he knew for certain he should not lie.

"Tell me about the tattoo on your hand," I ordered, and leaned against the cab.

"You want to do that out here?" he asked, licking cracked lips, eyes darting as if the ground would come to life again. "Why don't we get on the road . . . ?"

"Out here," I demanded. "I'm not sure you've got a round-trip ticket."

Now he knew I meant business. And yes, I'd sure leave him.

The problem was, and Mi knew this, we only had half of our gas left. We *had* to return to Redwood. Anything in any other direction would be past the point of return, especially now that we were hauling a wealth of heavy scrap on the trailer. We'd need every drop to get back in.

"What do you want to know?" he asked. "It's the same as yers. Same as anyone who was in service."

"In what?"

"To the company. I did my tours years ago. 'Fore you were born."

"I don't get it," Mi said. "Like military tours? As a goon trooper?"

"Whatever. You sign over or they banish your family. They keep you alive. You get protection. Five years ago all of Redwood had scavs in the alleys and the troops would only answer in BlackStar neighborhoods."

I had to think about that for a moment. The timing. It clicked. "So something changed, didn't it?"

"Oh, yeah. I mean, we were getting nothing from the shipments. Barely any food, bad ammo, shelves were bare. We always had good water and some electric, but we were gonna be written off. I think supply had pretty much abandoned this outpost. Trucks rarely came. So no gas shipment. No metal trade. Begging in the streets and no way to control the hordes. The cannibals were all over us."

"So what happened to all the regular animals out here?" Mi jumped in, waving a hand. "No hunters around. Shouldn't these plains be full of deer or whatever?"

"We ate 'em!" Screw smirked. "What you think? No gas left? Sheeesh. Hunted night and day, millions of us. Fished out all the rivers and ponds. Sweetie, everyone was *starving*. For a long time. It's crazy how those old morons thought the world could live nice without fuel."

"So now they all retreat to virtual reality."

"Better than real reality." He liked to spit when he talked. "Plus, we had it comin'. Everyone was warned. Peak oil came and went. Then gas was ten bucks a gallon. Next week it was fifty. Five hunnerd. No one drove. No one flew. Couldn't sell a car for a dime. I know the history. No cops, so cities got lawless. But screw 'em, had it comin'. *We was warned,* over and over again."

"So you signed your butt over to BlackStar?" I pointed at his hand again.

"Yep," he said. "Ate good enough. Had to beat down my neighbors from time to time, got to show them who was law. Took a wife. Took another when she wouldn't work. Got a good deal for my daughter. It worked out for old Screw."

I could almost hear Mi's finger squeeze her trigger a little tighter.

"But that's same as you." He pointed at my hand. "Yer no different. Not a bit. They own you too, you got the mark. It's where you learned to kill and where your chickie got her eye. What were you, corporate trooper? Something high up, not like a store cop or wall guard. Assassin? Private hunter? Makes no difference to me, let's have some road-trip fun with your little betty and get back on the throttle toward home. Deal? I'm willing to pay."

Twenty minutes later, I was driving back down the same route we'd taken to the automobile graveyard. Following safe tracks, a trail I knew didn't have traps or holes along the way.

Mi was right next to me, in the cab now.

On the trailer, well, I'd already forgotten we hadn't gotten paid from the wall job two days before. This would more than make up for it: two old cars, a lot of scrap, plus a bit more that we'd piled on top.

"Think he'll make it back?" Mi asked.

I shrugged. "Not really my concern. He used you as bait. That offended me right away."

"Awwww." She smiled, purred a little more, and leaned over to kiss my cheek. "He might be able to walk out," she guessed.

"It's nine hours over dead terrain by truck. That's days on foot. No water or food, unless he wants to eat the scavengers. But who knows? Maybe he's that tough."

I didn't want to think about him anymore. Screw got what he deserved. We'd left him behind. He'd bullied and killed for years. His time had come. We'd gotten the drop, and he'd been dropped off the back.

"Most important," I said, "I think this evens us up."

"Does not," Mi answered sharply.

"Seven for you, seven for me."

"Your last one is *not* a confirmed kill," she reminded. "Screw was just a simple abandoning. You don't even get a quarter of a point for those."

"Seven to seven," I argued, just to kill time.

"Seven–six in favor of Mi the Magnificent," she replied.

"Seven–seven."

"Seven–*six.*"

It was going to be a long drive.

Level 25

We got paid. I was worried the clerk or his guards would have some kind of wanted poster on us, but it went smoothly. I just told them Screw hadn't made it back. It was the truth. They didn't ask anything, eyeing our rusty-metal haul.

The worst part was turning in those company-issue weapons. The guards pointed shiny new rifles at us while we—very reluctantly—handed over the battered single-shot Mi had used. Then Screw's shotgun.

BlackStar, as far as ruling went, had the system down. They even searched us for unspent ammo before handing over the stack of chits.

So we were back to being unarmed. Mostly. I'd dropped something in an alley on the drive in. Not much, but metal makes kings. Maybe even just a scrap of it.

Reno, York, and Dakota met us in the alcove we'd decided to use as our rendezvous. Twenty minutes later, as night fell on the last day of our third week out of the tank, we scaled a brick column and climbed in a second-story window. The sash was wood and the glass broken, but I thought it was likely a fire escape route at some time. The lifesaving steel ladders and platforms had long since been pulled off, melted down, and put toward building the city wall.

The darkened building was eerie. Here and there we'd see the remains of a camp: A pee-stained piece of foam padding that was probably used for a bed. Plastic wrap that once held food. A candle or an old, discarded game controller strap—these straps were as common here as the last century's wallet, cell phone, or car keys. Simply designed, the straps had electrodes that touched the user's head. A battery pack. Wireless sat-link. And that was about it.

Ever since meeting back up, Dakota had been staring at me. I mean, every single chance she got. I saw confusion in her eyes.

"Look." York was at a blown-out window, pointing across the street. The opposite building obviously had power, lights. It also had a Rooms for Rent sign on the lower level.

We all went to where York stood, Dakota edging up to me the whole time. Something was clearly on her mind, but she just didn't want to blurt it in front of the others. What had she found while Mi and I were away?

Across the alley, in every one of the lit windows, we got a really nice slide show of what happened when the sun went down.

In one of the top rooms, a mother fed two kids out of plastic bags. The meal looked like chunks of dirt. I had no idea what it was, but when she was done with the packages, she put them carefully away. Maybe they were worth something at the store. Then she and the kids all slipped game controllers over their heads, and away they went.

Window after window, it was the same thing. Whether they were in the gaming verse watching TV or listening to music or visiting a Caribbean island, who really knew?

The thing was, they were *all* doing it. We could see fifty windows, and behind them, the only people not plugged in were those using the bathroom or eating a meal.

"So they work sixteen hours on the wall," Reno guessed.

"And spend the other eight plugged in," Mi continued.

"It's like our old schedule, only backwards."

We all stood there for some time, watching. Occasionally, they twitched. Every now and then a hand would come up or they'd duck like moving into cover. They'd cheer when they won and swear when they lost. I don't know how to describe it, all those souls in this building, the next, and probably every one in every surviving city around the globe. Was I sad for them that our digital landscapes had become so much more desirable and interesting than their real ones? Or was I happy for them that they now had a way to escape the complete dreariness of their real existence?

I wondered how my team felt. Who was glad for these survivors? Who pitied them?

And did we really want to trade what we'd had for what these people had?

It wasn't like we had much of a choice. Could we find out where we came from? Were there answers there? And how would we get them? Who did we ask? Would they just give up that information, or would we need to be . . . persuasive?

Dakota, again, had taken her eyes off the tuned-out citizens in the next building. She was staring right at me, and I knew something was coming my way.

When I saw what was eating her, honestly, I didn't know what to make of it. Maybe I still don't.

Level 26

The next morning, before anyone woke, Dakota nudged my shoulder and motioned me out of our room. Mi mumbled something about needing the car to go to the grocery store but didn't stir again.

In the hall, Dakota said, "You gotta come check this out."

So we left the building before daylight and set off through the city center.

We made quick time through the streets, around a nuke plant where she'd been offered work, and then along an interior wall. It actually had trees growing on the other side, and I realized they were the first I'd seen since leaving the suburbs. No trees grew through the crumbling pavement where we had just come from. No grass, either. Maybe it was because of the atomic plant. Maybe it had all been grazed five years before, when times were really tough.

Times sure weren't tough on the rich side of that wall, though.

But that wasn't where Dakota was leading me. The sun was breaking through, and I knew this meant the working class folks were rising, pulling off their controllers, and getting ready for another day on the assembly line. It made me think about what Screw had said. How many of them knew that once the wall was complete, BlackStar troops were going to force most of them to the other side, out into the wasteland, so that the chosen could live in safety behind the impenetrable barricade?

Screw had that knowledge, and he only seemed comfortable blabbering about it to others with a company tattoo. Most of the ordinary citizens, like Hal, probably had no idea. They were all doomed as soon as they finished their jobs.

"There's the lake." Dakota motioned up ahead, still moving at a brisk pace.

"Yeah, Reno told me about that. Makes for a natural border. I'd bet the hordes can't swim or build boats."

"Right, a natural border," she repeated. "But Reno didn't go farther. I walked a ways around it."

So Dakota had gone the extra miles. But what was out there? York had said the north wall was done. And up here, these were the nice neighborhoods. Clean. Well taken care of. Even the air smelled cool and fresh. Nothing like the stench around that power plant and its century-old wastewater pool.

We walked along the rocky shore. No fish jumped, not a single bird came in low. Bugs danced, and when they did, I saw Dakota cringe. She didn't like those things, and was still scratching at her neck where she'd first gotten bitten.

And that's when I began to see them. Far off in the distance. Snow-covered peaks were just collecting the first of the morning light. Glacial fields stood as steep as any man-made wall, only these stretched thousands of feet high.

"We're bordered on the northwest by a mountain chain?" I asked. Was this all she wanted to show me? It wasn't a surprise. Something had to feed that lake. Snowmelt was usually unpolluted. The city couldn't survive without a source of clean water.

"Not the mountains"—she motioned—"look lower."

We started hiking up. Now I saw. And it was strange, but not really worth the trip out here. About a mile up, the wall was still under construction. A long section reaching all the way to the lake had been completed. So they were enclosing this side too, but that made sense.

There was less urgency here. Security guards were few and far between. The horde wouldn't try to infiltrate from up high. How could they? They'd have to have walked naked through the mountains.

Still, the wall was going up. And along its eventual path, the surveyors had laid out the concrete footing for the vertical beams. Nothing unusual there.

The thing was, out there in the field, at the base of the ice cliffs, thick grass was growing. Wildflowers had sprouted. And unlike in the wasteland to the south, *animals* were moving. Not big ones, nothing that was a full meal, but here and there a small rabbit darted through the brush.

Still, this was not why Dakota had brought me here. See, on the concrete footing stood men, women, even kids. Not a lot of them, but those who'd woken early and ventured up.

It was almost like they were afraid to leave the city boundary, because none of them were out in the field. It didn't seem like the guards even took notice. But trust me, the citizens wanted those rabbits. And why wouldn't they? That was free food running around out there. Maybe the tastiest bites any of them would ever have. Can you imagine barbecued rabbit after a lifetime of eating those brown chunks of mystery feed they got in those plastic packages?

So maybe two dozen of them were *fishing* for rabbit. Bizarre. It didn't seem like the best way to catch a meal.

The citizens stood on the edge of the fresh pavement and

attached all sorts of bait to wooden hooks or snare loops. Then they'd carefully toss their lines out into the field near one of the bunnies. You could even hear them coaxing the animals, "Here, Mr. Rabbit. Some nice cornmeal for you! Have a taste! Just one little taste!"

Dakota pointed. "What do you think?"

I was honest. "I think they've got a good game spot, and they're lucky the horde isn't aware of it and devouring every one of those little rodents."

"Phoenix." She rolled her eyes. "*Not* the bunnies. What do you think about all the people *fishing?*"

"I think they're doing what they can to make life better for their families. Same as I'd do."

"But they could go *hunt* in those woods," Dakota argued.

"The guards would stop them," I pointed out. "And there might be bigger, hungrier things out there to worry about. None of *us* have guns, Dakota. What do you think their chances would be with sharpened sticks?"

I watched her. It was weird, like she couldn't take her eyes off the gaping escape route. And I also noticed something else: Dakota was sweating. Even though it was cold up here, her body was shedding water like we were running a marathon.

Daylight was burning, and we had a pocketful of money and things to do. I had my own family to provide for.

So shortly after, Dakota and I began the trek back down the hill.

I admired those people out there. They never gave up, even when the deck was stacked against them. I hadn't seen a single one of them catch a rabbit, but good for them for trying. Never give in. Sometimes a solution is just one more cast away.

Level 27

The day was slipping away. It was midafternoon and we needed food. We also needed medicine, as Mi had picked up a cough and I remembered her telling me her chest had been hurting. What was it? The radioactivity? Fallout from some past war? Maybe she just wasn't used to breathing grit all day.

My head hurt, but that was from the redness around my skull port. At least out here, all those creepy dreams had disappeared. Made me think we were on the right track, even if actually visiting Phoenix, Arizona, or the Dakotas was out of the question.

York had gotten quieter lately. Even Reno. The eager look of kids exploring a new playground had disappeared from all their eyes. Mi's gaze had grown cold, as if the green in there was about to fade.

It was all starting to get pretty clear to me how it worked out here. And, also, that we shouldn't be walking around with huge amounts of money jingling in our pockets. You've got to watch out for the bad guys, don't you?

It was time to stop playing tourist. I knew where we had to go. I had a pretty good idea what we'd see. To get there, all we had to do was follow the trail. In the Old West, it would have been train rails leading to the town's supply center. In Redwood, it was the giant prints made by that huge machine. Just follow them back to their home.

"They *knew?*" Mi asked when we finally saw it. "The rich bastards knew all along, didn't they?"

Yes, sweetheart, they *always* knew. Back when there was gasoline. When everyone lived like kings and had cars and money and boats and even private planes.

Back before the Middle East went up in a series of mushroom clouds. Before the governments dissolved and military factions had their brief reign. Before deadly plagues occupied the southern country, any place where there was a marsh in which the infections could breed. Before the horde. When those living in the lawless wasteland between cities had some humanity left.

They *always* knew. They *always* saw it coming. And from the first brick that was ever laid, they planned for the day when they would rule everything that was left.

Didn't anyone back then have any tactical training? Didn't they know a military installation when they saw one? Were they all fooled by the brightly colored paint and oversaturation of preschool smiley faces?

Those weren't buildings, they were bunkers. Those weren't parking lots, they were kill zones.

BlackStar, you see, was not top dog. Not the big boss. Redwood, like everyone everywhere now, served those who fed and clothed them.

Want to know my first clue? Remember HIGH PLAINS KILLER? Every town had a general store. One store, no more. It controlled every piece of merchandise that came or went. They charged what they wanted and drove the small business owner into poverty. In the Old West the general stores were supplied by train, but out here, rails had long ago been torn up.

So now towns were supplied by those giant trucks. We hadn't seen one, not yet, but what else could survive thousand-mile trips across the wasteland? What else could bring processed food, clothing, firearms, armor, hammers, rivets, controllers, and every other thing these people had?

And think about it—just go look at what passes for today's general store. Look at the heavy walls. The barricades in front of the doors. The lines of surveillance cameras on every corner. How, in all directions, the land is cleared like a shooting range.

Look at how everything inside is overbuilt. Wired for security. And not made for form, but for function. To last centuries. To outlast an apocalypse.

I'd played the Sims games too. So what was Redwood's general store originally? A Walmart Supercenter? Probably. Maybe a Target or Home Depot. Whatever.

When we got there, it was shocking. The building had zero windows. Two entrances, both of which were glass during the day and covered by solid steel at night. All-weather cams along the roof. Motion detectors and infrared and automated gun placements under smoked-plastic "observation" domes. Open approach on all sides providing clear fields of fire.

The rubber tire tracks led through the city to colossal sliding doors on the side of the building, the area that clearly used to be their automotive department, back when cars were common and gas pumps owned every corner.

I knew, without seeing it, that somewhere in there were the city's only fuel tanks, where Screw's tow truck was issued its rationed supply. Where BlackStar security and delivery vans must go to fill up.

But that was for the elite shopper. We were in line at the peasant entrance. Going through the metal detectors. Getting patted down by faceless security. Shuffling along with a mass of others who behaved as if it were some kind of special privilege for them to come to this warehouse and spend company money in a company store on goods that were far overpriced. They had no choice, though. Where else could they get packets of feed for their kids? Or a shirt? Or a pair of work gloves?

XMart. The place, like in the past, had *everything*. It was the city bank, their pharmacy, their grocery, and of course, the provider of all their entertainment, not to mention their dentist, their doctor, and their community center.

In the early days the neighborhood supermart had lured customers by offering the lowest prices. Then the world began failing. And the supermarts remained. They ran their own fleet trucks. They could armor them. They had the gas, the rubber, the parts, and the guns to keep business rolling.

No one had suspected, had they? That *this* had always been the plan of the people who built these mega-marts? After all, everyone was warned *over* and *over* again that oil would run out. When that time came, who could ship medicine? Without it, millions would die within a generation. With no doctors, plague would spread. With no government, there would be no schools. After just a decade, much of the youth in outlying areas would be no smarter or more civilized than cavemen of the past.

And they *knew* it was coming. So when the first store went up, it was nothing but reinforced concrete, heavy fortifications, and durable goods. Within a decade, every city had one. But no one noticed that they were not stores, not really, but weaponized bomb shelters. Easy to defend. Plenty of firearms. Would last for lifetimes.

Out there, in the streets, there was poverty. In here, as my team walked, we saw where all the wealth truly was.

It was nauseating. To think how common people had to scrape to get by, but in here, XMart could feed them all. Of course, there'd be no profit in that. Better to sell food to them in tiny increments at a criminal markup, one day at a time.

Food was stacked in the market section. Meat would have cost our entire pay from the day before. Fruit, trucked all the way from whatever city had cornered that niche, was even pricier.

A simple razor made of sharpened bone was ten chits. One with a stainless blade? Over a hundred. Cheap clothing was rummaged through by the average shopper, while to one side, sweet leather gear was carefully picked over by off-duty security personnel.

It had everything a city could need. It had to. Citizens banked, for a fee. They reupped their game subscription fees. They stocked up on food packets. They splurged for a toothbrush or bought a rare birthday present or, if need be, sat in line to have a tooth pulled. The cost for that was actually quite low, unless the patient wanted some kind of anesthesia or painkiller.

One glassed-off wing had the town hospital, where patients were stored on racks of beds that moved up and down, left and right, as if they were slung in an elaborate vending machine. The doctors, one minute whipping up a cast and the next giving some kind of injection, did not have to move out of their chairs as one casualty was spun along after another.

I kept our money in my pocket. But we did do some shopping.

"They won't let me near the gun counter," Mi whined. "I can't even buy a knife or a battle-ax or one of those cool laser–chain saws."

"Why not?" Reno asked her. "We all have the company tat."

"They wanted to *scan* it. No dice. You need a security pass too. Only goons carry guns out here. And just the elite BlackStar troops with special clearance can get near the big stuff."

"That is just so unfair to the common criminal," I agreed.

"Makes it tough to start a revolution," Dakota said. "But I bet Jimmy's family would have no trouble buying anything they want."

"They've probably got servants doing their shopping for them," Mi pointed out. She was right. There were, here and there, neatly dressed older women in housekeeping frocks making large purchases. They'd scan their master's shopping list, point to this and that and ten more of those, and one of the store employees would gather it all on a wooden pallet for later delivery.

But it didn't stop there.

It was an enormous place. Cement floor. Cold steel shelves that would survive a heavy blast. Fluorescent lighting.

But the world outside, in some way, must have been rebounding. You could get just about anything in here, *if* you could pay. There were a few small cars for sale. So some city out there was still manufacturing automobiles and was welcomed into the XMart supply chain.

The cost, of course, was over a million chits. Gas would be a crippling necessity. But for the wealthy, it could be done.

You could buy other large-ticket items as well. Big-screen TVs, even though the poor seemed to get all their news and entertainment from their cheap game controllers. Some bizarre things: Yard fountains. Push mowers. Elaborate barbecue grills. I saw a hang glider down one aisle, and York came across a power boat in another.

It was getting harder and harder to wrap my brain around this world. Did the top 1 percent really live *so* well? While the poor were just used as labor?

"Look at *that* line." Mi pointed. BlackStar's logo was bright. Visuals for new titles, new adventures, and new experiences gleamed on overhead screens. People were buying.

"Imagine," she said, "that same line in every remaining city or town on the planet."

"For game subscriptions?"

She nodded. "BlackStar has found one of those things that all people feel like they just can't do without."

"It's pretty cheap to play," I told her.

"Sure, but if *everyone* has one, I mean, rich and poor and old and young and boy and girl . . . ?"

Now it began to make sense to me. How important BlackStar was. And how much money they really could make.

The company that made those cars? They'd sell in the good neighborhoods, but not to *everyone.* Same with the boat, the plane, a gun. But *gaming:* gaming had no age or status or gender boundaries. From Max Kode himself to Jimmy and Charlotte and Hal and Screw and even my team, no one could really live without that escape. So a few chits here and a few there, across the globe, from every remaining citizen.

Yeah, BlackStar had found a hit.

And something else made sense. Something we *all* now understood.

We were BlackStar. *We* were the reason gaming was so good.

And we were missing now, weren't we?

There would be nothing that company would not do to get

us back. There'd be more and more search patrols. On and on. We couldn't lie low forever, not with these telltale holes in the sides of our heads.

We heard beeping, everyone heard it, but something else made my ears prick up. Big doors were sliding up. Not the front ones, but over by the automotive section.

I grabbed Mi's hand and we ran. I didn't want to miss a second of this, but the sudden movement made her cough violently.

"Sorry," I said.

"Let's go," she urged, hitting her chest.

Up a ramp. Through a couple of furniture stacks. Then past, would you believe, fake aquariums stocked with rubber fish?

There was an aisle of Christmas decorations. Another of lawn ornaments. But we were headed to the back wall, where the loud chirping originated.

"Now, that's an RV!" Reno yelled. The rest of them had kept up.

As the giant double doors on the back of the store slid up to the roof, we all saw what had made those huge tire tracks in the street. It was, without a doubt, the king of mechanical beasts. Eight tires lined each side, each of them a couple stories tall. On the wedge-shaped nose, a driving cabin sat way overhead, and on top of that, no fewer than ten soot-covered exhaust stacks belched dead pterodactyls.

I figured the semi-truck had at least four decks. It was towing a line of trailers, each of them like a small container ship, stacked with goods for the store. A trailer piled high with scrap metal and bales of plastic packaging looked ready to head out, maybe back to XMart's distribution and manufacturing base, wherever that was.

The truck pulled inside the bay, almost like a spaceship would edge up to a station to dock. Brakes hissed. Turbine motors whined, then began a long, slow decline, until the whole store stopped echoing.

Instantly, a door on the truck cab opened and a woman stepped onto an elevator platform no larger than her feet. She whisked to the ground, manifest in hand, and tossed the papers at a clerk. Then she was off, through a door after her long, tough journey.

Crews surrounded the trailers, pulling them in alongside the semi-truck. Cranes snaked straps from the ceiling and began hoisting the various goods off to their internal destinations.

It was clockwork. It was well practiced. Wherever this thing had come from, it looked like the only real way in or out of our city. Of any city. And it was tightly controlled.

A mass of armed BlackStar commandos watched every move. Guns ready. Goggles scanning, magnifying.

Then, on the bottom deck of the semi, a door whooshed open. Two of the guards pointed their weapons inside the hatch, motioning "out."

And a string of men and woman began to disembark. They were not, in any way, passengers. No, these humans were under heavy guard.

"Look at 'em." Dakota pointed. She didn't need to say that. We couldn't look away.

The eight or ten were made to line up and sink to their knees, hands clasped on their heads. They were pale, small, almost breakable. Lack of food, lack of sleep, something had kept them weak.

"Those aren't line workers. They aren't street people." Dakota was still talking. She was probably right. They didn't have that hardened look, like Hal and Screw and everyone in this store. Not laborers. But valuable enough that they would be transported—at huge cost, no doubt—between cities.

"They're *us*." Dakota seemed sure of whatever she was saying.

"Us?" I asked.

"Not us now, but at some point, that was us. *That's* how we got here. That's where we came from and the reason you're no longer in Arizona and I got taken from South Dakota and *all* that."

"Passengers?"

"No, prisoners. Selected because of our gaming skills or brain patterns or whatever, who really cares? But I'm sure of it, Phoenix. It's why we have memories of those places. Because we were *born* in those places. Then stolen, sold, and brought here against our will."

I didn't know how much sense that made, but Dakota seemed to believe it. One of the guards kicked two of the prisoners, made them all stand up, and marched them into a room off to one side. The door slammed shut.

We'd seen the show. It was time for us to go.

Before leaving, I rushed over and bought every antibiotic I could find for Mi and her cough. Some ointment for my port. Dakota complained of a fever, so we stocked up on flu meds.

Then food. Nothing fancy. Nonperishables. Enough for a long time, though, in case we had to try to get out of the city fast.

York and Mi really wanted guns, but no way was that going to happen.

We got clothing we might need, better boots, and a few more hats and pairs of plastic glasses to keep hiding our ports.

"Game controllers and subscriptions?" Mi asked, her eyes wide.

"Not for me," Dakota hissed.

I didn't want one either. There were a lot of bad men on our tail. We didn't have time to waste playing games and shooting our own kind.

Level 28

"Really, Dakota?" I asked. I also did it a bit loudly, so that everyone could hear.

We were about a block from the building we'd chosen to squat in. Security and foot traffic on the streets was ebbing. It was time for sleep.

"Really what?" she groaned back, although I thought she knew what I meant.

Still, I wanted to say it. I wanted it on the table. "This is your choice? You'd take *this* kind of freedom over . . ."

"Over a life sentence in an aquatic prison?" She glared at me. "Yes."

"It's almost unlivable," York challenged.

"There's got to be a way to make it work," Dakota replied. "To have something to work for. Or toward."

"Otherwise," Mi observed, "what's the point?"

But York had my back on this, wanting Dakota to have to spell it out. "So you'd rather live your life working to build the upper class while you barely have enough to even survive. What next, Dakota? A husband? Kids? Bringing them up in these torn-apart old buildings, only for them to be cheap manual labor themselves? And all of you addicted to or consumed by escape into an artificial game world?"

"Where killer aquarium fish—like we used to be—get to shoot you up every night?" Mi kind of joked. Kind of.

Dakota went a bit quiet then.

I wasn't sure if she was lost in thought or was reacting to what we saw when we turned the corner: the street was crawling with BlackStar troops.

They were everywhere, rushing in and out of the occupied buildings, and all around the deserted one we'd moved into. Searching every apartment.

"Go door to door!" a captain yelled into his radio mic. "Three men per flat! Tear them apart! Room to room, closets, bathrooms, every single crawl space."

It was a heavy sweep. Four or five of their vans were lining the street, machine-gun turrets panning across all the lighted windows.

"ATTENTION!" a voice from one of the trucks barked through a loudspeaker. "WE'RE SEARCHING FOR FIVE MURDEROUS CONVICTS WHO ESCAPED FROM BLACKSTAR PENITENTIARY!"

"I didn't know they had a prison," Reno whispered to me. We had a good hiding spot behind a series of pillars just down an alley, but our path to our own place was blocked.

The announcement continued. "YOUR COOPERATION IS MANDATORY. INFORMATION LEADING TO THE ARRESTS OF THE THREE MALE AND TWO FEMALE FUGITIVES WILL BE REWARDED WITH CITIZENSHIP. IF WE HAVE TO FIND THEM BEFORE YOU SURRENDER THEM, SENTENCING IS IMMEDIATE! FAMILY BANISHMENT TO THE WASTELAND!"

This was not good. Of course, none of those poor people knew anything about us, but through the open windows we could hear furniture being smashed, children screaming, riot batons cracking into joints and bone.

I kept waiting for some description or mention of the names we might be using, but apparently, they hadn't thought to take snapshots of us while we were slaved up in that tank for so long. Nice advantage for us. I hoped it would last.

York nudged me. "Couple of flamethrowers would take care of those trucks."

"Fresh out," I said. I'd been thinking more of rocket grenades, but at least we were getting our legs back under us.

"We can't do anything about this," Mi rationalized. "Not like we are. We can't help anyone."

"They'd turn us in, in a millisecond, if they could," York answered. "But Mi's right. We need to get into our lair and lie low until we come up with a better plan."

I agreed, but everything changed right after that.

The captain was getting impatient, and as his troops came out of the occupied buildings, he seemed to realize this search was not going to produce.

He turned suddenly, right toward the darkened structure where we'd hidden. Ten stories, all brick, no power, every room almost bare. It would take time to search it, but that was the direction he was pointing.

"Run a bio-scan on the empty one."

"Affirmative," came a reply over the speaker.

A glowing red nozzle then poked up from the top of the middle van. You could hear the thing powering up, and we watched all the troopers take a couple steps back. Many shielded their eyes, even though they all wore those smoked-glass helmets.

"No one in there will ever grow hair again," one man cracked.

"Not the only thing the men will never do again," another chortled, grabbing his crotch.

A beam lashed out from the scanner. Up, down, left, right, x-rays or gamma rays or whatever it was using, it pierced wall and ceiling and floor. Cooking, baking, irradiating, basically microwaving everything inside.

"Is it clear?" the captain asked.

"No one inside. Well, not anymore," the radio reported. "We had a squatter on the third floor. From the readout he was almost fifty years old."

"Didn't make it?"

"Still breathing. Pretty baked, though. Should we send in a cleaner?"

The captain paused. "No, let the roaches have him. But turn down the power on that thing. Boss will have our heads if we fry the quarry."

And that was that. But I knew we'd better think hard before we chose a place to hide again. The citizens would turn us in if we tried to pay rent for a flat. And the empty buildings were definitely out of the question.

"Where can we *go?*" York asked, realizing the same things.

"I'm taking water to the old man up there after the troops leave," Dakota said firmly.

"Of course you are," I replied. "Then we need a new hideout."

"We're really between hard places," York said to me. Reno nodded to that. "Every step we take, they flush us a little farther out."

They were dead right. Cannibal-infested desert to the south. Frozen mountains to the north. Walls everywhere.

And ruthless bounty hunters on our tail. *Right* on our tail.

Level 29

I'd left a few things hidden in the building, and even if they were radioactive now, I needed them back. Dakota did what she could to make the cooked man comfortable, but soon enough we were outside again.

"Where can we go?" Mi asked. "Should we break back into the Kode estate? I'm a little mad at Jimmy and Charlotte for booting us out like this."

"They're just kids," I reminded her. "And Dakota pushed them hard to do it."

"I think she wants us to take a chance on the open gap through the unfinished wall to the north. Over those frozen peaks. She's a good climber."

"Not *that* good."

"Rabbit must be a delicacy here." Reno had been eavesdropping. "Although if there's small game, maybe there's some big stuff up there too? Elk, moose, maybe bear? And stuff grows up there. Five of us. A few guns if we can get them. We go over the top and start a new life away from flesh-eating humanoids . . ."

Now York and Dakota had edged up. We were just wandering, homeless, with no destination. Not yet.

Reno was still thinking it through. He said, ". . . but there's got to be a reason more citizens aren't making a break for those mountains."

York continued for him. ". . . besides the avalanches and frostbite and all the water is frozen and the climb is impossible and we have no ropes or gear or thermal clothing . . ."

"That is not why I showed Phoenix that gap," Dakota sneered, like some of us just didn't understand. I kind of did. Dakota didn't want to run. Not really. She still held to some hope that there was a better life for her right here.

Yeah, maybe, sure. If she had money. Or top programming or design skills. Right now, her only training would be as a trooper, but she was way too small. Also, as soon as she signed up and they handed her a helmet, there'd be a serious question asked about where she'd gotten that funny-looking cable port in the side of her face.

"I'm *sick* of playing defense," York muttered. "I need to pull a trigger."

No one spoke after that for a long time. A couple hours later, with the security sweep gone, I found a strip mall that basically had nothing left but adobe walls and torn-up flooring. It'd been a big one, with interior halls and support rooms, but most of it had been scavenged long before any of us were born. The roof was gone. Maybe it had been made of tin or aluminum.

We did our due diligence, making sure we knew the access points and secondary escape routes. Those habits, they never left us.

Night fell. It got a lot colder, but the stars were stunning. We huddled together, taking turns sleeping, eating what we'd bought from XMart. It was horrible. The chocolate feed tasted like manure. And it was the best flavor.

It amazed me, to be honest, that I could make that distinction out here. Inside the games, when I chose chocolate anything, it was always the best. Maybe it was just my cable telling my submerged taste buds how sweet and dark the candy was, but that memory was overwhelming now.

Out here, everything was different from everything else. I picked up a handful of old pencils from a desk drawer, and every one was unique. Varying erasers, tips, lengths. Even the bite marks on a couple were as distinctive as fingerprints. Inside, every one of these pencils would be exactly identical—pure copies, to save the designer time. In there, a hollow-point .46-caliber gunshot *always* rang the same. Airplanes flying as a fleet behaved identically. Backgrounds repeated. Snowflakes were not individual. Days were the same length no matter what the season.

But out here, variety was the only consistency. It made me wonder how the search teams had found our neighborhood so easily.

Was I too much a product of games? Had I become predictable? How could they have tracked us so quickly? Perhaps I needed to change things up. Perhaps it was me, my simplicity, that was the biggest danger to my team.

And right then, that's when I heard the sound.

I knew this sound. When a small pebble gets stuck in a combat boot tread and the boot comes down on a hard surface, the rock hits first. It doesn't sound like a rock has *dropped;* no, it's been pushed down, slowly, because the foot is moving so slowly.

The boot was creeping. Then the other foot stepped silently. That boot had no pebble wedged in the rubber lug.

And the wearer, whoever was out there, down the hall, he *knew* the mistake. I could almost see what he did next. He'd heard the rock hit too, so now he was balancing on one foot, taking a hand off his weapon, lifting a boot, and prying the stone away.

Then he could creep in silence again.

We weren't alone.

At least one hunter was out there.

And that sneaky mother knew what he was doing.

Level 30

Quickly, one of us tapping the next, everyone was awake. But we were inside, in a closed hall. Just two clear exits: up where the intruder was, and to the rear. Were we being flushed that way? We could try to climb up and out, over the walls, but I was pretty sure we'd be cut down as we moved from the shadows into the starlight.

Down here, down low, darkness was our best cover.

If we'd had weapons, we would have pointed them toward the creeper. Without any, we formed into a tight diamond, Dakota in the middle. Five sets of ears and eyes trying to pick up anything through the gloom.

"P?" Mi whispered, waiting for an order. A team again. Just like that.

I listened hard. What was our best move? Rush him? Them?

Attack *first:* that would have been my normal order. I'd given it ten million times out of ten million opportunities.

But not now.

It was still too soon. We had no hints as to troop strength or position. We were small, weak, and unarmed.

"Retreat," I whispered. "Assemble at location four if we get separated." Habits die hard. We'd used our map and chosen a few safe areas around the city.

Our feet, all at the same time, began stepping back, back, back, down the long hall. The choreography was perfect. And dead silent.

In thirty steps, I knew, we'd get to a junction where two other corridors came together. At that point, we had multiple exits and could scatter and rendezvous at our meeting place. In any case, when we got to the crossing, we had a way to confuse whoever had made that sound.

TINK! Clumsy. Now he'd bumped a wall. Or had he just made that sound to give us a false location? This whole thing might just be a diversion. The bulk of the BlackStar troops could be waiting in the direction we'd been pushed into going. That'd be a good move. One of *my* moves.

I wished I could spray that area behind us with a few bullets. But I knew he wouldn't make that mistake again, giving away his position. Nor would he stay in that spot.

I listened. Yes. Whoever it was, he had training. He moved immediately to another angle in the dark. He was stalking. Playing cat. That made us the mice.

"There's just one of him," York whispered low as we retreated. "I'll lie in the dark under some garbage. You lead him in. When he passes, I'll hammer his knees."

"No," I said, "we don't need to engage yet. This is a lose-lose, we have no toys or tools. If this were my assault, I'd have sent this guy to flush us into a bigger area with more troopers."

Mi agreed. "He's pushing us in exactly the direction he wants to push us."

"Ten yards to the corridor junction," York announced. There was the four-way there, the way we'd come in.

"We'll split quickly," I decided. "Make him think."

Mi was back in her element, offering, "I'll go right, with Reno."

"Good," I agreed. "York, take straight." That'd put me and Dakota going left. "He'll pursue you since you'll be the single quarry, but I'll flank around once you're clear. And we'll play it by ear, try to take him out or trap him. Quietly."

"*Without* killing him?" York asked. "I mean, right, yes, without killing him."

I grinned slightly. York caught on. No reason to murder someone when all they'd done was scurry toward us and bang into a chair. Those weren't exactly execution-level offenses.

"Five steps to the junction," Dakota continued, then, "CRAP!"

She said it loud. Too loud. Our position was given away.

"Cover!" I barked, and we all dove into alcoves and doorways off to the sides. That took only a split second, but at least now we had our backs to something solid.

I listened for a fast approach. Nothing came.

"What, Dakota?" I demanded, angry as I get. She knew better than to cry out like that.

"There's a *gate* now," she hissed. "We're trapped! The sliding door that covers the hallway! It's *shut!*"

I didn't believe it, so I moved over to where she was. Bad news. She was right.

"That was open a half hour ago!" Mi said. We all knew it had been. Reno had scouted it. And we trusted him not to make mistakes.

I grumbled to the rest, "Someone got in here quiet, behind us, and closed off our—"

Tick tick! More noise from the hall.

What could it be?

Tick tick! It was a faint echo, like a rat's nails on linoleum, but not a rat. No, it was the sound a rifle's sighting scope makes when the power source starts to build up a charge.

Two blips, red dots, popped on and glowed toward us through the night. I knew exactly what they were. They were as familiar to me as the green in Mi's eyes.

Because they *were* eyes.

Night vision. Infrared goggles, staring at us from down the hall.

And then we heard more. The unmistakable *CLACK-CLACK* of machine-gun shells being chambered in a military-issue assault rifle.

That beautiful noise. Smooth, oiled, precise. I could probably have told you the weapon's age and weight.

"Don't move," a man's cold voice rang out. It didn't shake. It didn't waver. Whoever was out there was used to being in situations in which he pointed a loaded weapon at unarmed citizens.

He continued, "I can see you all plain as day. Move to the center of the hall."

We paused. It's what you do. Push the limits, see if—

POW! POW! POW!

A muzzle flashed as three shells buzzed by my ears, just centimeters away.

My ears. Not warning shots at any random ears, but *mine.*

"I said move out!" he repeated.

My brain searched. This was not a low-rent wall guard. Or a store guard. No. The equipment was too nice. The guy using it was in command. This guy was a pro.

I motioned to my team. We had a bit of faint light from the commando's goggle beams, but it didn't compare to what that guy could see. I knew his rig—the weapon sights fed the scope reticule into his goggles. He could aim as easily as you do with a cursor when you play a game. We might be able to see shadows, but this guy could look right through our rib cages, put his red dot on any valve in our hearts, and cut away.

"OK, to the center," I agreed. The five of us reluctantly shuffled into a pack. Mi, cleverly, was in the back, trying to feel for a gap in the outer edge of the wooden barrier, hoping for a way to make a break for it.

The eye beams approached three steps. Then three more. This guy was systematic. Trained. Mistake-free.

He panned around, making sure there were no tripwires or traps.

Man, I wished I'd left York lying in the hall behind him before the guy turned on his night vision.

But I hadn't. So now he had the upper hand. But he hadn't shot us yet, had he?

There must have been a reason.

Of course there was. In a flash, I realized the biggest difference between our old world and this new one: In there, everyone gets to go to Re-Sim. Out here, tough luck, the game is really over. This guy must have had strict orders not to harm us. He *couldn't* kill us on sight or he'd fail his mission, so he *didn't* hold all the cards.

I still had that one ace.

Now if I could just find a way to play it.

Level 31

What I'd have given for a gun just then. Anything that could penetrate his armor.

I did what I could. I reached up the back of my shirt and pulled a short wooden staff I'd found and kept. With one thumb I unfolded a long, rusting blade I'd ground from a piece of the scrap Mi and I had brought back in to sell. Not quite a samurai katana, but I bet I could cut pretty deep given the right arm or leg joint.

Did you think I'd have walked around *completely* unarmed all that time?

That was when I saw Mi reach into her boot and slide out a short club with a bicycle-chain ring strapped to the head.

She looked at me and my sword and shrugged at her own weapon. Our eyes locked for a sweet moment.

Reno pulled a heavy spiked bat with dual wrist straps. York had a pair of riot batons squirreled away. He'd bound fist guards over the slots for his knuckles and lined them with hard plastic blades. Yeah, that's my team. Old habits don't die at all.

Even Dakota whipped a bone cleaver from some hidden pocket. I could tell by the way the serrated edge glowed in the infrared light that she'd hardened it in a flame. Did she really think she was so different from the rest of us? She might be some kind of new version, an upgraded recruit, but the bottom line was that she wanted to live —even if others had to perish to make that happen.

POW! CRACK! Two more warning shots. The commando was moving forward again. And those last two blasts, as before, had been right at me.

This guy knew who the leader was. He knew which dog to beat first.

"I am gonna get max chits for this little capture." He snickered, What, was it a bounty thing? Did he get paid for every escaped BlackStar unit he could re-tank? Were there more? Maybe this was a regular event and he was some kind of post-apoc blade runner.

A well-armed one. He was now within view, and I could tell we had our hands full.

First, he was much bigger than any of us. Bigger than any working-class adult or BlackStar thug we'd seen. Every inch of his body was covered by a corrugated layer of next-gen armor. Solid stuff, but so lightweight he barely knew it was there. Combat boots. Not a speck of skin showing. Kevlar everywhere. A helmet with full mask, and those x-ray eyes gleaming out, tracking each move. Giving him instant targets right through flesh, bone, and even some walls.

His left hand came off the weapon, to the side of his smoked-plastic helmet, and I saw him key a mic.

"*Got* them. Alive and kicking," he reported. "Well, they do have some *really* scary pointy sticks to wave around. No trouble here. Send me a wagon."

Damn. Backup on the way, but how far off? Although, he was right. It wasn't like any of our prehistoric hack-'n'-slash melee weapons would even make a dent in that armor. He was a one-man juggernaut. A gun turret with legs.

Legs, then. That'd be our only shot. But we'd probably take some hits on the way in, right?

"Nice run, Phoenix."

He recognized me? And by *name?*

"What? How do you know me?"

A snort. Then a step closer, keeping us all in his field of fire.

I saw the rest of his gear. A shotgun slung across his back. A pair of pistols on either hip. Sticking out of his boot tops were electrified wands, the kind with a million volts to send you into cardiac sleep as soon as they hit your grounded body.

Great. Even if we could boost his primary weapon, he had a whole rash of secondary choices. Knives. A machete. More.

"Seriously. How do you know my gamer name?"

Another snort. It was funny to him.

"Tell Mi to stop squeezing the grip on her stick. I know her moves."

"What, we've *played* you?"

He mocked me. "Maybe I should make her whack you over the head with it, Phoenix? That'd be funny. OK, Mi, smash your boyfriend's noggin with your stick really hard, or I swear I'll, uh, shoot Reno in the leg."

"What?" Mi asked. "You freakin' nuts?"

POW! The rifle muzzle flashed. Reno's pants leg twitched.

No blood, though. Straight through the fabric. This guy had great aim.

"I'm serious, chicklet. Knock Phoenix out. Crunch him good. Contract says I gotta bring you in alive. There aren't any specifications for *how* alive."

"I'm not cracking anyone's skull with this except yours," she assured him.

"So be it," the commando agreed, and unleashed a burst of three quick shots, the red laser sight moving in a neat, straight line up Reno's leg.

This time, dark liquid exploded everywhere. Reno howled and crumpled in a heap, holes opened front to back in his left calf, thigh, and hip.

That sound, that wail, it was so disturbing. It was so real. Not a canned recording or an actor pretending he'd been hit in some studio voice-over.

No, that was my buddy. And we could tell he was in *agony*.

But this was also our opportunity, and despite Reno's crippling pain, we all knew we might not get another chance. The killer was trying *not* to kill us.

I broke right, Mi went straight for the guy's throat, and York took the left flank.

Now, try to shoot all three of us? While we're moving fast? Fat chance.

Indecision. I could tell he wanted to blast me first, but Mi was the closest. That moment of uncertainty can be fatal. I hit the guy low, in the sides of his knees, just as Mi drove her head straight into his chest armor.

York clotheslined the guy with a forearm to the side of his helmet, and he caught the skull flush. Now the bottom half of the soldier's body was going north and the middle was going east, but his head and neck were being driven south. For a moment he resembled a pretzel, but just that quick, it was over. He was down and stunned. Held tight by three of us. I climbed on his big chest, my knees pinning him to the hard floor.

Using the hilt of my makeshift sword, I smashed his faceplate, over and over, saying "Knock knock, let me in," until a small crack appeared. Then I hit that spot four more times, shattering the Plexi.

Mi had one of his arms and was already stripping him of the weapons on that side. York had pinned his other arm, and Dakota was first to grab one of his pistols and level it at the exposed hole in the man's face armor.

Behind us all, bleeding badly, trying to slow the flow by clutching holes but not having enough hands, Reno continued his leak toward death.

We'd get to him. Soon. But first . . .

The dark warrior demanded, "Get off me, Phoenix! I've got twenty guys racing here!"

"Maybe," I said, knowing it was probably true.

"How does he *know* us?" Mi demanded. "Way better than what he'd get from a contract or wanted poster?"

I was wondering about that too. He picked us out by name in the dark, with only infrared to help him see. He knew Mi was my girl. He knew I was leader of the pack and knew to watch me the closest.

"You don't get it yet, do you?" The man smirked. Even beaten, he still had the attitude. Pain didn't bother him at all. Not like it was making Reno cry. He was choking on it. I knew our buddy needed help, bad.

"You still won't win," the man said. There was something about the way he said it, using the word *win*. I wished I had time to pull off that armored suit. Probably pumping meds and drugs even as we spoke. Steroids. Aggression serum. The works.

"Who are you!" Dakota barked, shoving the pistol into his

groin. She found a seam between the cups, and I could tell it hurt the big man.

"You stupid crack," our captive slurred. "*Why* would you want to be on the run like this all the time? This is your fault, newbie. Did you really think you'd be allowed to just disappear among the sheep? Not a chance. You're wolves, every one of you. Even Dakota. You were made to rule, not follow."

"Who the hell is that?" York demanded, scratching at what pieces were left of the guy's facemask.

I remembered the radio. Enough of this; we had to get out of here, quick.

To Mi I said, "Use his daisy cutter to make a hole in the gate."

She chambered a shotgun shell and went to work.

Then I yanked the helmet off the guy.

"Holy mother of . . ." York belted. Even he recognized the commando right off.

"Jevo," I muttered.

It *was* him. It was definitely him. From the bald head to the vacant eyes to the oversized noggin. Gone all this time, since the ghost town. No one knew where.

But how? The clincher was his port. It was nailed in there by his right eye, just like the rest of ours. The big, round cable fitting. Glowing. Covered. Almost as if it had been filled with a plug to keep out bacteria and dust. It fit perfectly over the gap.

Even out here, Jevo was a monster. Muscular. The combat gear made him bigger, and he clearly dwarfed all of us, but not like some comic character. More like he'd been well fed. And worked out. His chest and arms were just a whole lot bigger. Perhaps, in real life, he'd always been that way. Or maybe he'd been pumped full of whatever vitamins or growth hormones they had lying around.

So *that's* how they were going to hunt us? By using our own? By finding combatants who knew our strategy and likely hidey-holes as well as we knew them ourselves?

"How'd you find us?" I demanded.

"This dirtbag jungle only has one water hole," he sneered. "Sooner or later I knew you'd show up there."

Water hole? For a human? A-freakin'-ha. Supplies . . . XMart. Pretty bright for that dim-bulb Jevo. So he'd staked that out, and then we'd been followed? It still didn't add up, but Jevo did know my moves.

And he'd made a nice one blocking this hall.

I had more questions. A lot more. But time wasn't on our side. They would never hunt five of us with just one of them. They'd send a scout, then send teams.

York pushed the stolen assault rifle against the big man's port hole. It looked so much cleaner than ours. Mine was red and pulsing. Mi's had streaks of purple etching out.

Another theory—maybe, just maybe, he'd been *woken up* from the tank the right way. Jimmy and Charlotte weren't exactly Black-Star physicians. If Max Kode had decided to bring Jevo around to hunt us, he'd have made sure his investment got all the best meds, exercise, and a top-quality diet.

York was still tapping the port with the hot barrel of the rifle. "Jevo, you traitor, why shouldn't I cap you right now?"

"Hold it, hold it." Jevo was squirming. "*Not* so fast."

I could seen a sheen of sweat starting to form.

York kept at it. "You still serve them, even after they had you sucking blue spit in a tank?"

"All part of the job," the big dolt argued. "Anyway, I've had worse. We all have."

"True." It was my turn again. "What'd they promise you to bring us back in?"

"Oh, so you *know* I had to grab you up alive? Huh. Yeah. These stupid stun batons. That's a bad rule. 'Shoot on sight' would have been easier. But hey, *that* was the mission. Glad I got to carve up Reno, though. That douche always annoyed me."

"Kiss my . . ." Reno was gasping.

Jevo blurted, "I liked making cheese out of your leg! Bet it hurts, too!"

Another smile. It pissed me off, so I hammered him in the teeth with my hilt.

"Ease up, Phoenix. Next time around, I'll electrify the gate. That might even the odds a bit. One-on-one, I was always better than you, Phoenix. One-on-one, I come out on top."

Mi shot a dotted line around the edge of the gate and quickly finished blasting our escape route.

"Answer me." I asked my last question. "What'd they promise? Freedom? A big mansion? Being a big cheese at BlackStar . . . ?"

"Like I said." Jevo shifted. "You still don't get it."

"Get what?"

Another snort, like before; I remembered him doing that back when we were in-game all the time. Out here, it really annoyed me.

"Get what?" I howled.

"We're out of time," Dakota decided, and I watched yellow fingers tighten on a pistol grip. "I'm taking an interrogation shortcut."

She pulled the trigger, and Jevo's crotch exploded in crimson goo, just like Reno's leg had three times.

But man, a wound right *there*? Now, that was twice as bad as leg holes.

He screamed. Man, did he scream.

Through it all, he could still speak, and when Dakota kept ramming the weapon into his shredded pelvis, he was ready to talk.

"I'll get you for that you bit—"

"Answer her."

Jevo spat, "I can't believe you haven't caught on. This isn't *real,* Phoenix. You're still in the game. All of you. I was loaded in to bring you back home."

We all stared at him. Blankly. His face was busted, and judging by the shards of bone sticking out from below his waist, he'd never walk right again. There were other things he'd never do again either. Not out here.

"You're full of it." Dakota smiled. "Nice try."

Quickly, I saw what was going on. But Jevo . . . This was great. No, it was *brilliant* what Max Kode had done.

What a way to twist Jevo in the wind.

I mean, *I* knew this was all too detailed to be faked, but *Jevo?* That idiot? I bet he *did* still think he was on-mission in a game. In fact, I was convinced that's exactly what he'd been told.

Max Kode had played my own goon against me. Revived him, worked him for info, and then played him. Freakin' *genius.* That guy. Who would he send next? Deke, Rio, Lima? For *sure.* What a pack of hunters. The top guys from each of the teams sent to hunt my crew.

No wonder Kode was BlackStar's top guy. He was a player's player.

But he didn't matter now. Jevo was through. No surgeon could ever put that dumpty back together again. At least, not all the key pieces.

"We move." I was already up, dishing orders. "Outside. Split up. Remote checkpoint four. Meet in six hours. Make sure you aren't followed."

"I'll help Reno," York volunteered, hoisting his buddy. York had wound tourniquets around the three pairs of holes.

"Good. Thanks."

But before I left that hall, once everyone else was on their way, a hand came up and snagged my sleeve.

Jevo again.

I didn't have anything to say to him. He'd gotten what he deserved, especially after shooting Reno up like that. Heck, Reno might not even live through the night, but I was pretty sure Jevo would have huge numbers of medics at his side in just a few minutes.

Blood was everywhere. The floor was so slick. And the smell. Something you just never get in a game. It was metallic. Like if you left a pan on the stove with no food in it. So sharp and strong.

Jevo whispered, his voice scratchy, "Tell you one thing, Phoenix."

"What's that, traitor?"

"If this *is* a game, I'll just respawn bigger and badder, and you sure haven't seen the last of me."

Then I broke his nose. It was the least I could do for Reno.

Level 32

"We gotta find shelter." Mi grabbed my arm. "Reno's gotta make it."
She was right, but what move did we have?

Still, facing off with Jevo hadn't been a completely worthless
encounter. Mi now packed a submachine gun. She'd also stripped
him of his sighting goggles. That gave us an effective sniper.

I had a pair of stun batons. Dakota had three concussion grenades and one of the sidearms. York had claimed the other, along
with the shotgun.

We were armed. Just like that, everything had changed. Give a
small group of citizens some firepower and they can be a big problem. Now give the same firepower to highly trained combatants.
BlackStar might have made a huge error.

Games are not like real life. I know most players wish they were,
so they'd have usable job skills, but it just doesn't work that way. If

any army makes an assault in a game, they go for the biggest castle or lair. But you can't play that way on a real battlefield. That was painfully clear to me.

What did I have, really? A few popguns. Ammo that would last maybe five minutes in a fight. Four able bodies and one that needed help walking.

Our food was limited. Our mobility was zero. I suspected BlackStar might be tracking our heat signatures through satellites — because unless I had a mole, how had Jevo found and trapped us?

So what could I do? Make a bum rush on the towers of Black-Star itself? Or try to grab a security van and see what the desert held? We weren't going to blend in, that was for sure. Dakota's skin was not the same color as when we escaped. I had issues with fluid seepage around my port, and every few minutes, Mi was coughing and trying to hide it from the rest of us.

We needed good supplies. We needed reliable food. And we really needed some place we could call home base without the security forces fry-cooking us with their electron x-ray beam.

"I'm sick of playing catch-up." York glared at me. It was the first thing he said when we met back up.

I agreed.

But in the real world, how did you take what you needed if they wouldn't let you work for it?

You can call it our genetics, or our training, or even our programming if you want to be cruel. The fact was, no matter how human Dakota wanted to be, we were products of war. Maybe even products *for* war, if you looked at our real value to this world.

So there it was. Our core code. Our resting state. The top level in our central directory. Our systems, and this system, would just not let us stay at peace.

So to answer the question what do you do, in this real world, to get what you need?

You take away what the enemy needs. You cut off their supply lines. You disrupt productivity. Starve them out. Make them panic. You find a defensible position and, through superior tactics and strategy, you make *them* come to *you*.

Level 33

In any military society, there's a stone-cold pecking order for combat personnel. Everyone is ranked—their size, strength, speed, intelligence, weaponry. Everyone has stats. Over time they get sorted. The best bubble up and the rest become rent-a-thugs.

Near the top, I was sure, were BlackStar's troopers. Above that, once we'd been revived, had to be Jevo and our generation, but I couldn't worry about Jevo and his pals. Not yet. If we ran into those elite BlackStar forces now, we'd lose.

Plus, we had to make a move before Deke, Rio, Syd, and the rest were called up. We'd gotten lucky with Jevo. It wouldn't go that way again.

So we had to go after mall cops. The bottom level and the least prepared. It was a good gamble that they'd react most predictably when it came to an ambush.

Across Redwood, the manhunt was on. Corner video screens ran a constant ticker about the missing five. Posters with sketches of our likely appearance caked the sides of buildings. Truthfully, those images looked closer to our online selves than to our real faces.

The reports claimed that one elite BlackStar soldier had been injured in our "firefight" with their forces. That was Jevo. They also reported that we had killed several support troopers in cold blood.

BlackStar controlled the information, but they still couldn't find us.

I believed they thought we were about to run. Extra troops guarded all unfinished areas of the wall. Patrols in the swankier neighborhoods went on full alert. Search teams were increasing in number and size, scanning all abandoned buildings twice a day.

Homes were invaded. Families were questioned. For the first time, we actually saw a helicopter overhead, spraying the poor areas of the city with clear fluid. It was impossible not to breathe the fog. But after the chopper was gone, everyone went back to work. Maybe it was some kind of chemical marker. A dye that would react only to those who had certain preservatives or solutions in their system.

Mi and I watched trucks roll and big men abuse terrified citizens. There was nothing we could do except keep moving. Stay in the shadows. Always have an escape route. Plan ahead. Just not get caught.

So, and it was probably about time, I chose our next objective. We had weapons, but not a lot of them. Even with a perfect plan, we had only two fully functional people for each exit.

Stretched thin. But it should work. Even Reno could play a role. I gave him the rusty, unloaded, useless pistol I'd taken from Screw.

That would be diversion one. I was pretty sure how the response might go.

Level 34

As the sun came up, packing all the chits we'd saved, we strolled into XMart to shop for the supplies we'd need to attack XMart.

We browsed in housewares. We stocked up in hardware. The kitchen department was full of choice chemicals. You're probably aware of what someone can make with ammonia and fertilizer.

The big thing we did, however, was to keep our eyes and ears wide open. Three hundred Spartans once killed twenty thousand Persians because they understood how to use a choke point. I knew we'd be outnumbered, but I also knew those big stores only had two unlocked entrances.

We had five guns. Only four worked. Our bladed weapons were a joke. They all had to stay outside for the beginning of the op because of the metal detectors and hand searches.

We had no air or ground support, no vehicles at all, but we were able to buy radios. They might provide the advantage we needed.

"We've got options!" Dakota hissed at me as I picked out the best radios I could find. These things would cost us most of our wealth, but so be it. Communications in tactical arenas are often more important than bullets.

Dakota was in a dark place. Her peaceful integration dreams had been quickly squashed.

She said, "This is not a war to win, Phoenix. It's a puzzle we can solve."

"They shot first, D. They shot Reno first."

"So that's all this will become? Just payback? How *programmed* of you."

"No, it's the only negotiation they understand. If we don't get a few victories on our side, they'll just keep whittling us down until we beg to go back in the tank."

"I'm not going back," she said flatly.

"They shot Reno," I reminded her at the checkout. "They put holes in us *first*."

"I wanted there to be a higher road I could take," she said blankly.

"I know you wanted that." My arm went around her shoulders, a loving squeeze. "There's nothing wrong with wanting that."

"I need answers," she continued. "I need to know who I really am and where they snatched me from and how long ago they herded me off that big bus."

"And I'm trying to get them for you. This is the right place to start."

"I agree Jevo didn't have to shoot Reno."

That made us both go quiet. There was really nothing more to be said.

We had to act. Our combat capabilities were eroding quickly.

Mi's chest had gotten worse. She was coughing every minute or so.

York was clutching his ribs for no apparent reason. And me, well, you know about the redness around my port. I tried to hide it from everyone. It was actually draining now, not blood but a clear fluid with little green specks. Kind of like a flesh rot, but from the inside. The smell was horrendous.

Dakota had taken to wearing full shooting gloves everywhere, and something just wasn't right in her head. Always sweating too. Reno, you know how Reno was. He'd lost a lot of blood. Time for us to go get some back.

That hospital inside the XMart . . . I looked forward to raiding that almost as much as opening up XMart's gun lockers.

Level 35

We were ready. Reno was out front. Mi was in her spot across from Dakota. York would be handling the secondary door over by the automotive entrance and I was the only one inside. I had a cart full of . . . treats.

On command, Reno raised his empty pistol and pointed it at the front door security guard. *That* got his attention. Civilians *never* had weapons. Possession was instant banishment without trial. The screens reminded people of that at least once an hour.

The goon spoke into his radio. "We've got a situation here."

But that's all it really was. A situation. The gun was useless without the right bullets, and as rusted as the thing was, I'd have hated to fire it. You could lose a hand and both your eyes.

But the big barrel, that *looked* scary, and scary was what Reno was going for. He had a bunch of bad facial hair, wild eyes, pale skin, and the gleam of desperation you just don't see in men who have jobs.

Plus, the limp. The holes in his leg. I bet that guard knew immediately that he was face-to-face with one of the BlackStar escapees.

"Give me your weapon!" Reno barked. But the bigger man just

kept pressing the emergency button on his utility belt and trying to take things slow.

"Everyone get down!" Reno waved the pistol around, watching terrified shoppers drop in one smooth wave.

That order was mostly for their safety, but they didn't know that. Gotta get the innocents out of the line of fire. Not only to protect them, but also so they don't get in the way of a well-placed shot.

I was exactly in the right spot, in the clothing section, just a few dozen steps from the front of the store, so I boosted myself up on top of the changing room to get a better view.

It didn't surprise me that XMart cameras were up here too. Pointing down into the closets. For this chain, there'd never been such a thing as privacy.

Anyway, from up here I could watch what I really wanted to see: their response tactics.

The alarm was chiming, and instantly, a half-dozen men dressed just like the door goon rushed toward that main entrance.

"Six total, plus the one in Reno's sights," I reported into our radios. I could just feel my team making those slight moves, the instinctive adjustments that would allow them to put the greatest number of XMart guards in the smallest usable targeting zone.

The big question we all had was this: Faced with a serious threat, how would their forces respond? Would they *all* head to the scene of the disturbance? Or were they smart enough to leave reserve troops, just in case the first action was misdirection?

They were mall cops, but they probably had some training. We just didn't know. So we prepared for anything.

Now the men had Reno surrounded, and he made sure not to point the gun at them. In fact, he was already surrendering, palms out, dropping the weapon. Apologizing profusely. "Sorry! Sorry! Didn't mean anything! I was just hungry and wanted to surrender! Long live BlackStar! Heil XMart!" and all that.

Good, now the seven troopers were breathing a little easier. Moving in. Closer. Helping each other. Getting out their zip-cuffs. Preparing their stun wands . . . Tighter and tighter into a bunch.

There might just be those six reserves. It looked that way. From my vantage point, there were no more cops. Not over by the big truck. Not around the bank. From what I could tell, they'd all responded.

And why would XMart have more than that? It wasn't like anyone could rob the place. Or would ever try. Talk about outgunned. Most people had probably forgotten how to spell "gun."

But I wanted to make sure.

"Phase two, phase three, now!" I yelled, hopping down from my spot.

I began a hard sprint toward the automotive entrance. It was a tiny door, just a single set of sliders, but by now York had taken a position outside it. I was a wild card, running at full speed, knocking down displays, smashing glass, throwing smoke bombs made from household chemicals we hadn't paid for yet.

"Long live democracy!" I howled, wondering how long it'd been since someone used that word. "No dickless bounty hunter can take me alive! King Arthur was a wimp! The Black Knight wets his armor! Space aliens taste good on toast!"

I don't know what I was yelling. All I wanted to do was create confusion, smoke, and some small blasts and get everyone's attention.

It worked.

As soon as I started my tirade, out front, Dakota and Mi jumped from the line of shoppers and yelled "FREEZE!" at the seven guys who surrounded Reno.

This time, they aimed working weapons. One shotgun and one machine gun, both courtesy of Jevo.

Mi let loose a small stripe of lead that cut an XMart logo clean in half. You can bet those guys froze. In an instant, while I was still acting like a lunatic behind them, the men were on their knees, kicked to the cement, and stripped of their gear.

My end of this still had another act to play out. We had to flush out the rest, if there were any. And I can tell you, from the way I'd gone postal, I had the attention of the managers in their interior security booth.

In just a few more aisles, two mall cops were on my heels. Then three. One of them actually took a shot at me, but I heard the safety click off and dodged left through fishing supplies and then right down children's books.

Man, I hoped they didn't shoot me. I wasn't planning to shoot them.

Meanwhile, York was dead ahead. Warlord York. Standing near the exit as I did my best fullback impression, lowered my head, yelled one more "Never trust packaged foods!" and ran through the exit out into the lot.

The remaining XMart guards—the ones not surrounded by Dakota and Mi—followed close on my heels.

"Stop right there," York said calmly just as they got outside, leveling a pair of pistols at the whole bunch.

He didn't shoot a single one. *Good* for York. He'd come a long way. Not all the way, as I'd find out, but his mayhem dial had definitely turned down a notch.

Level 36

It took only a minute to clear the store of shoppers. Even less for the underpaid, exploited employees to flee.

With the front gates down and covered, we set up a grid to sweep the store. Two clerks were still in the back. We found one more trooper coming out of the bathroom. Out they went. York and Dakota doubled back to cover some areas twice. Now the huge space was empty. It was ours. And it was closed for business.

We turned off the signs. Outside, a good stretch away, we saw crowds of shoppers gather, then get turned back by the ejected mall cops.

Dakota asked about the handful of doctors in the hospital wing. I told her to set them free, only keep the oldest one, the smallest threat, to care for the sick and injured strapped into the racks. I also asked her to help Reno up onto one of the tables and get him some real medical attention.

Finally, we could get a clear view of things. The XMart roof was dead flat with a nice waist-high ledge all the way around. It's a great defensive construction technique, just like a castle wall. Plus, the whole thing channeled rain into a catch basin. They could run that pipe into holding barrels if they were low on water.

Not that we were. Remember, this was the one general store for the town. Everything they had to eat was downstairs. All those chalky packets of food for the poor. Plus a smorgasbord of tasty fare for the rich: hams, turkeys, fruit, vegetables. It looked like one of those feasts medieval lords used to set at long tables while their serfs begged for scraps on the wrong side of the moat.

Once the place was locked tight, we met on the roof. With the cleared lots, no one could make an approach without us knowing. Five hundred yards away, the city began, and we had an unobstructed view. Three people could cover multiple directions with our turret weapon placements and shoulder guns.

"They could put sixty-cal snipers on the roof way out there," York mentioned.

"They don't want to kill us." Mi coughed.

"She's right," I said. "But we started a countdown for them. BlackStar can't afford to disrupt commerce. Their workforce needs the food inside. The company needs that wall. And even the rich gotta eat."

"This was a nice move." York was looking at me. "*Finally.* But I might have tested our luck in the wasteland."

"Thanks," I answered with a nod. "I gambled. I bet they expected us to jack some vans and run for safer ground. And thought this place wasn't within our capabilities."

Overhead, a blue sky stood empty. That scarcity of jet fuel was a bonus. We had higher position, so ground forces were going to have a hard time breaching our walls without destroying their own supplies. But a single attack helicopter? That would be difficult to fight.

Around the perimeter, but within range, a row of security vehicles began to assemble. One by one, nose to tail, they made a truck wall circling the giant store. Troopers stood around, pointing, looking, but without assembling or raising weapons. Just waiting.

"How soon before they start taking potshots at us?" Dakota asked.

"Why, to avenge what you did to Jevo?" York joked.

"But he wasn't one of *them*," Dakota argued. Her eyes were wild. She was starting to look like a dog turning rabid. "Jevo turned on us. Had it coming."

"I thought a simple revenge plot line was beneath you, Dakota."

"They stole me from my home. Enslaved me. And spiked my eyes. I'm gonna make them pay and get what's mine."

"Seriously?" I patted her shoulder. "You've come around to wanting to make them *pay?* I thought you just wanted to be free and work on a wall all day so you could go home and eat mystery grub, then tune out into fantasy game worlds."

"Is this freedom? Living and dying within a few blocks of where you're born? A single overlord who controls every one of your days? Some distant warehouse that gives you supplies based on your work performance?"

"What did you expect?" Mi snarled back. "Some kind of Sims utopia where food and toys are free for the taking? Cheap cars? Unlimited gas? You *had* that. Before. But it wasn't enough, was it?"

"That wasn't real."

"No, but how many people out here would have traded places with you in there?"

Dakota was still determined, eyes wild, darting around. "I'll figure it out. There's got to be a *third* option. I gotta find it."

"Knock yourself out," York barked.

A long black limo began curling around inside the wall of

security trucks. Almost idling along. Here's what was funny: you could *hear* a major engine under the hood. Powerful. Not like the smaller patrol trucks. This thing burned high octane and would throw your head back if you stomped on the gas.

It'd been a while since I'd heard that throaty roar. I missed it.

Mi looked at the speed machine through her fancy scope.

"The big kahuna makes his entrance?" York smiled, and I noticed something disturbing: There was blood on his teeth. Like his gums were leaking. But it couldn't be a lung injury. He hadn't taken any bullets.

"I can't tell," Mi replied. "There's a guy in there, I can see him on the x-ray. He's yelling into a phone. Waving his hand. He's worked up about something."

"Plenty to be worked up about," I agreed. "This is a one-horse town, and his labor force is locked out of their pantry. Without a wall, the hordes come back, all the way up into his grassy yards."

But Mi didn't answer. She just followed the vehicle around. "He's . . . uh, familiar?"

Then I heard her suck in a breath.

She whispered, almost violently, "He lowered his window. I SEE him. I SEE him."

They were creepy sounds coming from her. Rasping as she coughed it out, "I SEE him . . ."

What was freaking her out? A man? A BlackStar executive? Nothing did that to her. What?

She blinked. Mi rubbed her watery eye with one finger and slammed it up against the scope again. She had to be sure, but we could tell whatever she saw just wasn't registering.

"I . . . SEE . . ." She kept choking on the words.

"What?" Dakota urged.

"I see him," she finally said with some clarity. I'd never really seen her lose it like that. Mi, she was as cool as dry-ice underwear.

"I saw him." She'd come back from wherever she'd gone. "Then he rolled up the car window again, but I saw him, clear as day. No mistakes."

"WHO?" York demanded. We were an elite unit. No time for babbling like that, and Mi of all people shouldn't get caught up in it.

"I saw YOU," Mi replied, pointing a finger right at my chest. "I saw you in the car, Phoenix."

We were all quiet for just a split second, but my mind clicked into gear. What a move. "It's fake. An illusion. Mind trick, using a hologram or something. Nice one too."

"Nope," she answered firmly. "I've got x-ray *and* infrared. Dude is *real,* honey. I've got no doubt in my mind that *you're* the one out there in that limousine, calling all the shots."

What? Like a twin?

"It's just a trick," I argued. "They're messing with you, sending that limo. To let us know we're not up against mall cops anymore."

"Nope. I know what I saw. Real life."

We all went quiet.

No one knew what to say. Maybe he was another tank body? A copy of my flesh, out here?

But wouldn't a copy be on *our* side? He'd be on Mi's for sure.

Or it was just a mistake. After all, Mi wasn't well. That cough. The teary eyes. She might be hallucinating. Time to get her to those pharmaceuticals.

And then the black stretch, speeding up, turned and rolled out of the XMart cordon zone.

Level 37

The hospital wing was basically a huge Plexiglas case for patients who could afford to pay. The bed racks were all motorized, delivering the patients to a treatment station where a human doctor would stitch or patch them up and punch in the code for how long they'd be warehoused before release.

That's where I found Reno, at the treatment station, sitting up on one of the hard particle-board slabs.

The doctor we'd kept was working quickly, but honestly, it was hard to make a guess at her real age. Maybe ninety. Maybe double that. Her hands, though, were strong enough and quite good with the tools. Reno only winced slightly as she used a laser to cauterize the insides of the bullet tunnels.

"He's lost a lot of blood," she said without looking up. I turned her tag in my fingers. It just had a last name.

"Please replace it, Dr. Winters," I said, and slumped into a chair.

"The good stuff?" She smiled, still not looking up.

"What do you mean good stuff?" I asked, but I thought I knew what was coming.

"We have different supplies," Doc Winters explained. "Cheap stuff for citizens. A private supply for corporate."

"Yeah, give him the corporate stock." Then I asked, "So all this, the blood, the medicine, it all comes in on those cross-country trucks?"

She nodded. "Everything. Can you imagine there's a city or colony out there in which the only way they could survive and stay on the XMart supply routes was to begin selling *blood?*"

I thought about that.

"Freaks me out," the old woman spat. "But we gotta have it. Every burg in the network has to chip in something or that town goes to the horde."

She was winding bandages now. Then replacing Reno's blood bag. It made me wonder what they put back in the poor people— red Kool-Aid? With just enough vitamins to get them back to work?

"Your eyes must see some interesting things from right there."

"Oh, it's all the same." She finally looked at me. "You look like yours have seen some things yourself, son."

She called me "son." I couldn't remember ever being addressed that way. It felt good.

Doc Winters pointed. "Those outlets in your heads are quite a piece of work."

"Yours?" I asked, motioning to the truck bay. Maybe right after the captives got off, they came over here for the drill press.

"Oh, no." She laughed. "You can't do *that* to a person." I felt someone walking up behind me, quiet, and knew from the pace it was Dakota. Mi and York were setting up defenses. She must have finished wiring the cameras to the electronics section.

"Why can't you?" Dakota asked for me. "*Some*one did it."

Doc Winters looked closely at Reno's port. It was red around the edges, kind of like mine, but not nearly as infected and gooey. I was here to get antibiotics too.

"See?" She tapped it with a nail and wiggled her fingers like jellyfish strands. "It goes in, then the tendrils are woven back into the brain. This is *way* beyond my capabilities. Plus, the orbital bone has grown in around it. Locked tight. Part of the temple now. So—best guess—they went in when you were all very, very young. Newborns. Possibly even *earlier*, while your skulls were still soft and they could muck around with the connections and not risk snipping the critical brain functions."

I wasn't too sure what all that meant, but Dakota was definitely interested.

Doc Winters motioned that she was done with Reno for now, then turned to us. She pulled a drop of blood from Dakota's finger and stuck it in a scanner, then did the same to me. A moment later she handed me a clutch of big pills.

"The private stock?" I asked. "Let me guess. Workers get something different to swallow?"

She nodded. "I'm just amazed at those sockets," she kept saying. "I don't think whoever took the trouble to implant them can be too happy you all got off the end of your extension cords."

"No, they're not happy."

Mi walked up, and I had her tested and asked for some meds for that cough. Doc Winters swung over a jug of syrup that Mi began gulping like she'd been lost in the Sahara and had just found water.

I asked, "Why'd you say that about my eyes?" I realized I had a lot of questions for this experienced woman.

"Oh, you know." She smiled again. "The corporate people I treat over at BlackStar, they have one kind of look. Lots of money stress, but at the same time, that attitude like no one in the world would have *anything* if it weren't for their brilliance. They stare at everyone below them like they deserve their place. Like anyone not smart enough to program games is just a tool for them to exploit."

"Just like the shot callers in a game." Mi slurped more syrup. She was already hooked on the stuff. So were her lungs.

"But the people out *here*"—Doc Winters waved to the racks —"they have another look. Defeat, but with that stray glimmer of hope. Like maybe, after the wall is built, they'll have it easier or they'll get more food or some time off or pleasant moments with their families."

"That gonna happen?" I asked, remembering what Screw had told us.

Winters shrugged. "But you, son, aren't like the corporate guys *or* the grunts. You're a fighter. You don't seem to blink, either. You've got a hard, hard stare for someone so young."

"We've all been through the grinder, ma'am."

"Stop calling me ma'am. Well, you couldn't have survived the wasteland, so what that tells me is these wanted criminals who've taken over my hospital came out of BlackStar's big R and D toy box up the hill."

"You got that right." Dakota was rubbing an ice pack on her neck. "But where did we come from *before?* I can't believe we were born up there. I have memories."

Now the woman smirked. "*Are* they memories? Or maybe dead ends or blind alleys or fake suggestions they tested when they started pouring things into that hole?"

"I don't know how to tell the difference."

"Ninety percent of brains are on their own program. They make changes, absorb random events and block out others. Many times they try to make the best of things so they can live with the hardships. You might just be holding on to a movie you saw or a game world you liked."

Dakota stared back. She looked angry. I think she was trying to connect the dots. She'd had those dreams about swim lessons, but then it turned out she was perpetually underwater in a slave tank.

And of falling. But we all have those.

My memories, well, what was the point? Maybe my hometown in Arizona was a closed-off city-state just like Redwood was about to become. Did it really make any difference? I had *here* problems. We had *now* problems. We were desperate. Sick. Hunted morning and night. That was the real world for me.

Doc Winters interrupted my thoughts. "The biggest danger for people like you, son, is in that stare of yours."

"My stare?"

"Your hard eyes. When people get that cold, they tend to forget what's really important. They neglect the things that make them decent. That make them kind or generous or sympathetic. I've seen it in men *and* women. Soldiers. Police. Homeless. The guys who scavenge the wasteland for metal. They're saturated with so much war and brutality that it drowns any sliver of kindness they've got left. And you're almost there. You're on the verge of forgetting."

"What makes me human?" I asked.

"What makes you happy," she replied.

Level 38

There were two ways BlackStar could play this. For one, they could send a test invasion, see how we responded, and adjust. I didn't think they cared much about the people in the sickbeds, but they risked destroying their own supplies and not having any until the next shipment arrived.

The other move was to wait. To play mind games. And I figured that was their plan. The twin in the limo was solid evidence. What a way to cause dissension in my team. To make Reno, York, Mi, and Dakota suspect that *I* was a mole. That *I'd* given Jevo our position.

Mi was still certain she'd seen my double. And I believed her.

York and I pulled bunks and couches from the furniture section and made a circle with them in the electronics department. We had a brand-new CO, and on the screens, this one gave us a 360-degree night-vision view of our entire perimeter. In our old CO, we'd had no idea what was on the outside.

But straight up, they were both prisons.

How long would BlackStar wait? No more than a day. They had to have this food. They had to regain control. The trade had to continue: scrap metal and game systems go out; food, supplies, and wall panels come in.

We had our pick of clothing, but everyone went after military-style gear. It's nice having extra pockets.

One section of the store was stocked with supplies for the troops. We also found heat guns and a stockpile of high-tensile plastic. Helmets were customized and weapons modded, and we began to look a lot more like my old crew and a lot less like escapees from a mental institution.

I'll tell you, though, my eye was just stabbing with pain. Mi saw me cringe once and walked over.

She pulled back my hair.

"Oh, Phoenix," she whispered, reaching for a tube of anticoagulant, her fingers red with my blood.

"It's worse?"

"Its . . . something," she muttered, and spread whatever she could on it. "It's swollen, and there are white pus balls all around just waiting to pop. I mean, it looks *revolting,* and I'm not the squeamish type. You took the penicillin?"

"Do I need more?"

"Buckets."

So I popped a pile of horse pills. The pain stayed, though.

Stupid port. Those holes in our heads were tough to deal with. Dust in the air was just one enemy. Imagine having metal running behind your eyes. Then it gets cold. Now it seemed to be infected. When I found the guy who'd drilled this thing, well, you can imagine, I was going to hold him down and drill a few holes of my own.

Jevo, though, he had some kind of plug. A safety cap. I guess that's one perk of being on BlackStar's side in this war.

With nothing happening, I set up sleep shifts. Just an hour at a time. It would help. We were sick and needed rest. Two would rack in the bunks while the other three watched the monitors and made rounds. Luckily, we could stay in the middle of our fortress in electronics. We had excellent vision and multiple firing positions if troopers breached a wall.

Reno and Mi were off to the sack first. Outside, clouds had covered the late-afternoon sun. Low light and fog are great if you're laying siege but major problems if you're trying to hold a position. Still, the cameras covered every inch. That ring of BlackStar trucks and troops just sat and waited.

Doc Winters was listening to a little kid's lungs through a stethoscope when I went by on one of my laps, and it seemed a good time to pry more information from her.

"You came in on one of those trucks as a captive, didn't you?" I asked her, watching the cold metal disc make the boy squirm.

She nodded, then pushed the kid down flat and hit a button on the rail. The bed slid back and rotated away.

"How'd you know I was born in another city?"

"Your education." I pointed to the charts. "I haven't seen *any* schools for the poor. And the rich all work for BlackStar making games. So you must have learned medicine somewhere else."

She frowned, nodding. "I was bought. Then shipped. XMart does good business in skills trade."

"You had no choice?"

"No one does. Work or starve. Go where there's work. I do all right. Better than most. Long hours, but that's the same for everyone, even up at BlackStar."

"Human trade? That's where they got the game programmers who live in the plush section of town?"

Another nod. "Their own kids will learn the skills and go to work for their parents. It's almost a monarchy now."

"But the people down here" — I was looking at the racks — "never get a chance to learn any kind of valuable skill that can bring them up out of the gutter, do they?"

Doc Winters signed some sheet and yawned for a long second. "How could that happen? The separation between rich and poor is always something the rich are very interested in keeping in place."

I looked at my hands, so comfortable around the molded grips of my gun. "And *they* own all the guns."

"I think that was the first thing corporations did after oil ran out," Winters said. "They had to disarm the poor. They're clever, too. It was a simple matter of changing calibers on new weapons . . . forty-fives to forty-sevens. Fifty-cal to fifty-five. They stopped making ammunition for the size of firearms that were still in the hands of the people. It took no time for the masses to expend all their bullets. After that their weapons were no more useful than cars with no wheels."

"So they got turned in for scrap?"

"Metal for food. That program continues. Now it's slave labor for food. Good people do anything they can to survive."

I thought of Screw. "Rumor is that once the wall's complete, BlackStar isn't going to have any more need for a working class."

Now the Doc just stared at me. She kept peering with those tired gray eyes. Finally, I had to break the silence and asked, "What's in that spray they coat the ghettos with? From the helicopter?"

A wrinkle appeared on the edges of those eyes, like a squint. Like she knew something she wasn't proud of knowing.

She answered, "BlackStar tells the people it's vitamin boosters to keep them free from horde diseases that blow in from the wasteland."

"Makes sense, but total BS, right?"

"Of course."

"What are they doing, poisoning everyone? Slowly?"

She shook her head. "That would affect labor productivity and increase health problems. Most people don't even realize that the rate they pay at this store for food or clothing doesn't fully cover the cost of the goods we get shipped in on those trucks."

"What?" That didn't make sense to me. How could they not be charged the cost, unless . . . "You mean BlackStar covers the rest of the expense? Out of gaming profits?"

She nodded again. "Corporate charges people every dime they can, but in the end it's not enough to pay XMart's rates. So eventually, when the wall is up and we don't need so many people, it makes sense that not everyone will be allowed to stay."

BlackStar. Can you believe that? So they weren't poisoning everyone slowly. No, they needed hard workers.

"The spray is a dopamine aerosol," Doc Winters said flatly. "I ran it through my scanner one day. A low-dose hallucinogen that's full of THC, LSD, and some tricky military compounds."

"What's it do?"

"It's their pacifier, like happy gas. A modern Soma. Makes the people work harder. Stops them from organizing or revolting. Tricks them into thinking they're happy and valuable and part of something bigger and more important."

"*We* breathed the stuff" — I lifted my gun a bit — "and we're not getting in line to work for their cause."

She looked at her hands, smiling. "Well, it takes a while to learn your place, Phoenix. Once you absorb a few more doses, you might even *like* living in the projects, hammering metal all day under a hot sun, then tuning out into fake game worlds all night."

I stared at her. "Do you like your life?"

She was still staring at her hands. How many people had those hands helped? Millions? What a remarkable use for ten frail fingers. Was *that* the feeling Dakota had been looking for that day she'd tried to reattach those limbs to our hostages?

"Do I like my life? Son, I accept my life. I do what I can. I have friends across the country in my chosen game world every night. So yes, Phoenix, this is enough for me. It has to be. I can't change a whole planet.

"But you," she continued, "I don't think you could ever make my life work. You don't have the . . . skill set."

"We didn't come in on that truck, did we?"

"I can't tell you for sure. They bring in babies all the time. The top brass trade wives and families more often than they trade programmers and designers. You just might have been some of those infants."

"Have you ever met Max Kode?"

She shook her head. "But he has masters too."

"Does he look like me?" I then asked, hoping she'd seen a picture or something.

Winters paused. "You're definitely products of the same environment. Always playing angles. Working your advantages." She took my hand and began tracing the tattoo. "And it's not like you or your team would ever be banished. You're company property. The chosen ones. After the full wall goes up, everyone inside will get these markings."

"One big happy commune?" I pulled my palm back. "What will everyone else get?"

"Overrun. Cornered right up against the outside of the fence they themselves built."

"What's to the north?" I asked, mentioning the other wall gap, which was less secure.

"Nothing," she answered quickly. "There's nothing up there. But I don't think the answers you seek are on the other side of the barricade," she finished, turning away. "I think if you're really interested in who you are, you need to go back to where this all started."

Level 39

I've never felt closer to death—to real death—than I did thirty seconds later, when I returned to our furniture fort in the middle of the store.

I saw Reno. And Mi. Lying together on one of the wide couches. He'd shucked all his weapons, over in a pile with hers, but it was the two of them that made my lungs seize up and my heart nearly stop.

No big deal, right? We were all friends.

But not so . . . *intimate*. Mi and I shared something special, and that made some lines the other guys were not allowed to cross.

Reno was stretched out on the deep cushions. His leg was elevated, and it looked better. At least it'd stopped gushing. Now it just oozed.

Mi was horizontal too. They were watching a movie on one of the TVs, some romantic story, I think. Her head was on his chest, just lying there, like he was her pillow. She was all snuggled in, as comfortable as she'd be with a stuffed animal or, straight up, with me.

Mi's hair spread out, soft, flowing, and Reno was absent-mindedly stroking it with his fingers.

They both giggled. The movie. One of the characters was being sensitive and funny.

When they laughed together, it felt like someone had stabbed me in the gut.

He squeezed her tight. His hand kept moving, brushing a stray lock out of her eyes so she could see. They were so cozy. Like old friends, and more, like lovers. Like two lost souls who'd finally found each other.

And who'd found a private, quiet, tender moment in the middle of the chaos that was our lives.

Betrayal.

I felt like throwing up.

Nausea flooded my throat, head went dizzy, knees felt crippled.

How *could* he? I felt like killing him. My hand reached for a shotgun. I'd just blow his backstabbing head off, the blood would soak Mi, served her right. That'd teach them. No one betrays Phoenix. Not if they want to live.

They had no idea I was watching. They had no clue they'd been discovered. Private moments like that are not made for three.

But my hand didn't grab the pistol grip. It wouldn't slay him. Why not? It should have. I wanted it to. Anger burned through every pore. Crazy how my brain calculated it in a military assessment kind of way, but . . . killing him would, unfortunately, deplete my forces by twenty percent. That would hurt the team.

Still, he deserved it.

Mi belonged to me. We were meant to be together.

And this, the snuggling, the laughter, the shared joy: it was the lowest form of treachery. As new as we all were to the flesh-and-blood world, this was as close to infidelity as any of us could get.

Mi was mine. Everyone knew it. Reno would die for stealing

her affection this way. There were plenty of pillows around. She didn't need him. She didn't need him for anything. I was supposed to be enough.

Enough? Even in this small body? Weak? Powerless? On the run? Scurrying around in a world where I was the very bottom rung of the ladder, instead of the very top?

Then he leaned over and softly, deliberately, kissed her on the side of her head. Right above the port. It was slow, it was tender, and it lasted forever. His other hand held her soft cheek so tenderly, with so much love. It was the kind of thing you only see between two people whose bond has long history and goes deeper than those around them can imagine.

I almost murdered him. I almost splattered his skull right there. But for some reason, as my brain swam with this new, ugly emotion, I slunk off, leaving the two of them to finish their movie.

To finish it together.

Level 40

How long had that taken to develop? A few hours? Our siege wasn't even one full day old. In the tank, everything moved at game speed. Out here, it was slow death, but the five of us must still have been on our NPC clocks. We couldn't settle in for long. We'd always be cursed with the need to make big moves and make them fast.

I waited. I didn't lash out. I found a way to back off and bide my time.

Mi went on patrol. York was checking the vehicle bay. Dakota was sacked out. I gave Reno an extra sleep shift and took his rounds. He was hurt bad; he needed more rest.

BlackStar *had* to be planning something. And it had to be big. What would their next move be? That helicopter, armed with guns instead of drugs? Explosives along a wall? A tunnel?

One surgical or tactical strike and they might just take this store back. I could just see the five of us — the ones who lived through the firefight — kicking and screaming as they plugged us back in, shoving our heads under, into the blue murk. Holding us there until we stopped squirming, until we drowned. Then we'd go back to work.

And with no meddling children allowed to find a way to bring us back out.

Reno, man, I hated him on a gut level, but he did not look good. The hollows under his eyes were darker. The skin around the bandages was blotched and pocked and turning white. How long does it take humans to heal from three large-caliber supersonic rifle bullets? In-game, it barely slowed us down. Out here? It'd been twenty-four hours. What was the problem?

Maybe I'd smother him in his sleep. It wasn't exactly a warrior's death, but he didn't deserve one. Never mess with another man's woman. It's part of the male code. It's the primary element in great stories, love and war: we *have* to defend our princesses.

I picked out a pillow. A square yellow sponge creature. Then I crept over to where Reno was napping and raised the weapon over his face.

I'd just press down. No one would know why he'd passed away. It wasn't like we would run an autopsy. Everyone would figure Reno finally died from the wounds . . .

But I knew immediately I couldn't finish him. I wanted to. I *had* to. In my mind, I could easily snuff him out. But there was no way my hands would push down. He was my brother. Mi was much more, but still, even if they *were* interested in each other now . . . even if that tenderness was genuine, I had to learn how a man handled these things, not how a gamer did it. The human Phoenix must prevail.

"What's the pillow for?" Mi asked, standing right behind me.

My heart almost stopped.

Tears flooded my eyes. But she couldn't see that.

I thought quick. "I wanted to elevate his leg more." I put the cushion under his mangled limb. "He doesn't look too good."

"No, he doesn't," she agreed.

Then I slunk away. I did shoot a backward glance. Yeah, she had tears in her eyes too.

I went back to the loading bay. I'd help York get the truck ready.

Level 41

"Phoenix, up front," York chirped into the mic. Daylight had just broken, and it sure wasn't a bluebird day. Clouds had packed in thicker, and everything was covered in a dense mist. Our cameras were having a hard time seeing the trucks, let alone what might be lining up beyond them.

"Rain is over the city wall," Mi told us as we assembled, "and moving our way. If making some kind of break under cloud cover is the plan, this might be our best chance."

"We've got enough food in here for centuries," Dakota reminded her.

"Yeah, but the people outside don't," Mi argued. "They'll never let us just hold out, no matter how valuable we are."

York again on the radio: *"Phoenix, get to the front of the store! You really want to see this."*

He was right. But something else came up before I'd see what it was.

I heard a painful hack. Mi was wheezing even more. Almost every few seconds now.

I kicked into the hospital again and pulled down the highest-price prescription bottle Winters had available. Mi was gulping all that stuff like soda pop. And it helped. It helped a lot. I might have been really angry with her for the Reno thing, but you just can't sit and watch a person cough so hard you can tell it hurts on a rib level.

Great. So I catch them together, and what does the mighty Phoenix *actually* do? I give Reno a pillow and Mi some medicine. What a tough guy.

Back to York and the front of the store.

Our enemy was right outside now. There he was, the hooded shadow from the limousine.

"He just strolled up, not a care in the world," York said, pointing his rifle center-mass even though his bullets would never get through the Plexiglas. "I'll open the door, you pretend like he gets to come in to talk, and then I cap him here on the inside floor so we can take his stuff. Then they'll know we mean business."

"No," I answered.

I couldn't see his face behind his tall collar, just the eyes, but immediately, I knew Mi was right.

Under that hood I was sure was someone who, at the least, *looked* a whole lot like me.

"Let him in. I want to hear what he has to say. We all do."

York stared at me, cold, as I gave the order. Not because he thought I was losing it, but because he knew about letting the enemy behind your lines. He knew about suicide bombs and tracking devices and surveillance gear that can be hidden in a freckle.

"He's wired for sure! They'll fix on our positions. They'll plot our weapons capabilities. They'll know our *health.* Phoenix, this is a *major* mistake."

"Let him in."

The gate slid up. York unbolted the main door, and then there was one more of us inside.

Our gun sights never left his head. All safeties were off. My heart, and it'd taken a beating lately, was hammering away.

Why? Because of one man? Maybe because this was *the* man. Just from his confident gaze, you knew he was a player.

We moved toward the electronics section. You couldn't even hear his feet touch the floor, and this was a big, empty echo chamber now.

His hood panned around, eyes taking in everything. A nod.

"Very impressive, Phoenix."

I nodded back. I didn't need his approval.

"My experts said we'd catch you trying to make a run into the wasteland. So in different spots, we left all our defenses down to bait you. Why didn't you run?"

"Is there a better life out there?"

A shake of his head under the hood. "No. There's no life out there, it's all fed out. Then we thought you'd try to take a truck and a squad, so we drove out a bunch of vehicles and fried some buildings. Didn't bite there, did you?"

"What good would one van do against hundreds?" I asked.

"But we found you eventually. Nice run. A great run. Sorry to see it end like this." His voice was so sure, so confident. Like he had the ultimate ace left to play.

The man said, "We really didn't expect this kind of offensive. Ingenious. You've got everything we need. People are already hungry. We need the new rivet and plate shipment down at the wall." Outside, lightning cracked, but I was sure the construction on the metal beast would go right on.

Then the cloak came off.

So there he was. The man was almost my perfect twin. Older, yes. Some gray hair on the sides, but he wasn't past his thirties. There was no port, of course, but he did have that beautiful tattoo around his palm. The BlackStar brand.

And those eyes of his, they burned with power. He was in charge. He *was* BlackStar.

"Hello, brother," he said.

"Not brother," I answered. "More like *spawn*."

"Spawn. Good choice of words."

"I assume you're BlackStar_1."

"That's right. Number one."

I stared at him. A lotta hate. In the back of my mind this guy's chances of leaving the store alive were about the same as my chances of sprouting wings.

"What *is* he?" asked Dakota, dying to know. "Your older brother? Young father?"

"No," I answered for him, "but we are related, aren't we?"

"Twins?" she guessed.

"No," he told her, "much more than that."

I got it now. Originally, he was the world's top player, right? He ran the most successful gaming company on the planet. Something in his DNA helped him rise right to the top.

So once we escaped, what should we have expected but a master strategy? We weren't going up against some novice. We'd been playing the guy who wrote all the mission code.

If there is a digital god, it's the guy who typed the *first* line of binary. The original 1010 himself.

"I'm going to win this, you know," he said to me.

"What do I call you?" I demanded, the old commander coming out.

"Max, you can call me Max. Or Mr. Kode, or just sir. Daddy? Master? God? What's it matter? I have a thousand gamer tags. You have even more copies yourselves. I've gone in there. I've tested you over and over. I've hung out at your CO sometimes. Just to see what kind of new edge you're working on."

Then he turned to my team. "But you, and Mi, Dakota, York, Reno, I want you to know before things get really out of hand, there's *no way* you can win this. You simply cannot walk away from us. There's only one end to this race, and that's for you *all* to go back in the tank."

"Oh, we'll play," York promised, itching to blast something. "And we'll win. We always win."

"You *sometimes* win," Kode replied harshly, "and you sometimes lose. The analog world out here is just as much a crapshoot as the digital one you escaped. What needs to happen now is for you to realize that in this environment, on this *frontier,* you, Phoenix, absolutely can*not* win no matter what. Your own bodies are already telling you why. The clock is ticking down. Your biological doomsday devices have no shutoff code."

"What doomsday devices?" Dakota asked.

At that moment, someone coughed. I thought it was Mi again, but when I looked up, I saw that she'd given the chest bug to Reno. He was wiping a spot of blood off his lip.

My lungs, to be honest, were also on fire. So was the skin around my eye.

Kode went on. "But if you come with me, then I'll give you a way where you can walk out with whatever you want. Or *think* you want. I offer you complete defeat and certain death . . . *or* . . . partial victory. No more, no less."

"*Whatever* we want?" asked Dakota.

"Name your price. Name any price, Dakota. I can build you a nice fairyland in there with a family and picnics and minivans. There are no limits, but to *really* win, you *have* to *choose* to go back in the tank."

"*What* is he talking about?" Mi rasped, her chest heaving as speaking got tougher. "In the tank? Or out?"

I told my team, "I think what the dark lord here is saying is that one way or another, this filthy world is eventually going to kill every one of us."

Max smiled as if my words made him happy, like he'd won a brief victory. "This world *will* kill you, Mi. Just like it'll kill me, and my friends, everyone in the company, my kids, their kids, and so on. For you, it's just a lot quicker."

"You're offering, what, tank immortality versus . . . what?"

Kode replied, "Being mortal and biological out here is not a winning strategy if you look at the long game. A tank life is predicted to be ten times the duration of a regular human life. Maybe more." Reaching into a pocket with two fingers, the BlackStar president pulled out a small metal device and dropped it on the table.

"Plus, we do still have a kill switch."

It was the size of a small flashlight and had a familiar hollow input on one end. On the other were batches of tiny optical fibers hanging loosely, just waiting for a neuro-connection.

I knew what it was. So did Dakota. The other three stared for a moment.

The outer surface was curled like a corkscrew blade. One that you drill sideways through eye sockets.

Then Kode pulled a detonator from another pocket. He hit a button, and the small device exploded. Bits flew everywhere. There was nothing left but dust and a smoldering burn mark.

He clicked another switch. "There. All your implant triggers are now live. You didn't think we could just allow you to run around free, did you?" He grinned. "You're *very* expensive collateral. Worth *every*thing to this city. We'll go to any length to protect our investment. Our way of life depends on those supply trucks. And in turn, the trucks depend on your playing games as the villain. From in the tank."

Brilliant. He was so cold. Decisive. A true gamer. I hated him and loved his moves. Apples don't fall too far from the tree, do they?

"*That's* the fail-safe?" I asked, pointing to the debris, already knowing the answer. "A brain bomb?"

"When we first came up with your NPC program, I demanded we install a foolproof termination device. I couldn't very well allow you to fall into a competitor's hands, could I? Seattle still makes games. San Diego. But they're so far behind. Redwood needs commerce. Superior game enemies are our sole market advantage."

My hand was rubbing the side of my head. Blisters popped. Everyone on my team was also fingering the device in their skull.

I could feel the throb around my input. Dark bands had begun crawling under the skin, north toward my brain, south toward my heart.

But now, of course, a little pus and some swelling were the least of my worries. How much C4 was behind my eye sockets? Enough.

"So why haven't you blown us up already?" Mi demanded. "Why let us run around out here? You could just terminate the runaways and drill more baby skulls."

Kode's face gave away nothing. It was stone.

"Yeah, why?" I repeated. "Let me guess. We weren't your average gamer villains, were we? Too valuable to detonate? Or too hard to build?"

Kode nodded. "Both."

"I get it." I looked at Mi. "I'm not his son or his brother. I'm a slice off the top gamer's brain stem."

"A big slice," Kode confirmed. "And a very painful one. The extraction procedure's incredibly difficult." He turned his neck and pulled aside the hood so we could see his spine. There were multiple scars across the vertebrae, deep and jagged.

I turned to Kode. "So tell me, is Mi, in real life, your wife? A girlfriend? Secretary?"

Kode's face was flat. "Mi's donor is our best research physicist, named Morgan. Her tag is BlackStar_4."

"Dakota?"

"Our open-world environmental artist. A rock climber. We bought her contract very recently, from the Black Hills refinery."

"York? Reno?"

"Reno's original brain stem tissue came from my first partner at BlackStar, a programmer named Cooper. He was number two at the company, and also, so you know, in this life, he was Morgan's brother."

"Brother?" Mi asked, looking over at Reno.

"Unfortunately," admitted Kode, "Cooper died last year in a horde infiltration. It was big, and bad. He shouldn't have left our neighborhood, should have let the citizens take the hit, but he was always too soft. Before that we wanted to order the materials for a wall, and losing a key guy like that pushed the order along."

I saw Mi put her arms around Reno's neck, but now it didn't hurt me at all. They were family.

Evidently, Kode liked to spout backstory. "Morgan and Cooper were close. She's still pretty upset about all that, and all this, too. She misses him badly.

"York," he continued, "was grown from BlackStar_3. He runs the company finance department."

"I'm a numbers nerd in real life?" York sounded shocked.

"You're a nerd in *this* life too," Mi reminded him, now putting the pieces together. "So we're all just copies of the company's big brass?"

"Yeah," barked Dakota, angry. Hyperventilating a bit too. "How could you *do* that to your own offspring? Or selves or whatever? Toss them in a tank for eternity? That is some sick, twisted shi—"

"Grow up, Dakota." Kode cut her off. "The real world isn't all garden parties for the people who have to make the tough decisions. You don't have the nerve to make the calls I have to make."

He waved to the store around him. "XMart ships us what they decide we get to have. Ten years ago, we couldn't even get bullets. We were losing families three at a time, every night, dragged off into that desert. Then my team starts making good games and cheap controllers. Plugging in became the best way for any city, anywhere, to control the rabble and give them something better than the horrible lives they were all cursed with."

"Don't forget to mention your bottom-line profits," I snarled, thinking of his enormous mansion on the hill.

"Right, profits. With which we train and equip our troops. Who protect those poor slobs and their families. Give them roofs over their heads. Heat. Work. Clothing. Which is a whole lot more than they'd get out beyond the city limits."

"You act like they should be grateful for the pitiful existence you force on them," Dakota growled.

"Not just them." He pointed right in her face. "*You* might try showing a little more gratitude too, Dakota."

"I don't owe you anything."

"You owe me everything, sweetie. Without our tank program, you wouldn't even be alive. You wouldn't be two cells, let alone billions of them. I *made* you. We *gave* you life. We give you a purpose. We *allow* you to exist. So now how about saying 'Thank you, sir' and scooting your skinny little butt back up the hill so we can get our top game engines back online?"

I thought Dakota might put a hole in his head right that second.

Little did I know she had even more twisted plans.

But I needed to try to defuse this. Maybe get my hands on that detonator.

"So," I said to Max, diverting his attention. "What gave you the balls to try and clone human game engines to run your servers?"

I'd fed his ego. Like I said, he clearly loved to tell his story.

Level 42

"How could we *not* try clones?" Kode began. "And it's not like we started out thinking that we'd end up with a basement full of experimental bodies. Plus, the cost for day-old babies? Brilliant ones? And a lot of them? Too steep."

"You're a sick—" spat Dakota.

"Oh, yeah, I'm a lot of things," the man admitted. "But you don't know what it was like. We launched those first games, mostly just to see if we could pull it off, and a month later we had more sales than we could count. Redwood went from a dying border town to an XMart prize. No going backward then. And those of us who got it there? Rewards, baby. We get the perks."

"What do average people get?"

"*Jobs*. To live. To have a security force that keeps them safe from the animals. Food on the table. Redwood's standard of living is assured as long as we continue to deliver. *Everyone everywhere* plays games. They go in there to shoot or race or just socialize and run their mouths. Now, with the tiara controller, we can make you *feel* the action, or the pain, or the love."

"But we have human rights." Dakota still didn't want to accept all this.

Kode spouted, "I'm not going to have this argument with you. You *don't* have rights. Technically, you don't exist, and neither did any of your previous versions, and, bad news, Dakota, we had to put them down too."

"Put other versions . . . ?"

"It isn't easy keeping you all alive, you know. Very tricky stuff. Very expensive. The first manipulation begins in an embryonic state. Then we fit the full-size port into a tiny skull so it grows around it. Feed it life experiences and data—well, that's top-secret big-league tech. We have to bring in biomed and neuroprogrammers constantly. Plus, there's a high failure rate. The mutations are unpredictable. I think you'd puke if you saw those pictures."

"I'm not the first Dakota?"

Kode snickered. "But you, now, are a *great* generation, this time around. The best yet. Man, all of you even got *out.* Wow, what a *move!* Major props there. But you're sick, so go back in the tank. I'm willing to deal."

Dakota had tears in her eyes. So much for the family who missed her or the manicured hedge around the house in the suburbs. "Having grown us in a dish still doesn't give you the right to play life and death . . ."

"Doesn't it? Of course it does. You're my property. My creative assets. You guys never played the old games. Eight soldiers *always* attacked from the *same* bunker *every* single time anyone tried that level. The cars always came in the same order. The enemy army was always packing the same weapons, every time through, and shooting from predictable places. It took one or two run-throughs before players knew the game tendencies, and then they'd really seen all the tricks the designers could come up with."

"So you wanted to plug human unpredictability into the NPC?" I guessed.

"Precisely. Nothing performs randomly or creatively like actual human neurons."

"Then why clone yourselves? That part I don't get," Reno interjected.

"Where else were we going to get enough of the *right* stem cells? We needed DNA that simply *rocks* at games. *We're* the best stuff out here. Which is why *you're* the best stuff in there. Every one of my people makes the sacrifice. Over and over. We grew mutated freak after pile of cellular jelly. There were a lot of failures. But finally, wow, it's so worth it."

"But your own clone, locking it in that tank . . ."

"Quit whining. You've had it way easier and safer than I ever did. Plus, you might live a thousand years if we keep changing the oil and rotating your tires."

I was doing the math, we all were. The ages didn't add up. How could we be so old already?

Kode was still ranting. "Was it hard? Oh, baby. Clones fall apart constantly. You need hypersterile conditions and a big vat of preservative. We buy steroids by the gallon. That's how to do it right. Then, once the input hasn't been rejected, we inject serious doses of growth hormone. You fill out fast. After all, we needed gamer brains quickly. We couldn't very well sit around and wait for you guys to mature naturally. That'd take a generation."

"So how old am I, actually?" asked Dakota.

"Sixteen months for you. The rest are almost four years."

"Oh God, I'm a toddler."

"But what years they've been! You've changed the whole world.

You've saved a city. Now, though, time is short. You're sick. We need you back online. No more field trips, OK?"

"So if we don't go back in the tank you're going to pop our heads off?" York inquired, not quite expecting the answer he got.

"There are people on my board who thought we should have popped your tops as soon as you were found to be missing. Hell, a few even wanted you erased when Dakota first acted erratically. But then we would have to go under the knife again. Now, I think, they understand *my* strategy was best. "

"Which was?" York prodded him.

"Wait it out. Use other clones to help us think like you would think. Play angles. You guys didn't know what you were yet. And we always could detonate the ports. But let's get to the health issue. You're all dying pretty quickly, so maybe that's what you *really* want to talk about."

Now Kode was looking around the room, slowly, like he had bad news.

"Give it to us straight," I told him.

"Yeah, well," answered Kode, "Doc Winters's console is online. We use it to determine which workers have more good labor in them and which ones we can fool by giving salt pills instead of real medicine."

Dakota cocked her weapon.

"Chill out, Dakota. Don't give me the *they're people too* speech. They are an expendable resource. At least I give them all some joy and relief through my games."

He nodded back to the medical wing. "The old hack scanned you. We had a good idea what was in your systems. There's a massive database of case history about what clones face when exposed to a polluted world. It's not like you have a sturdy defense system yet. There are multiple issues that, even now, you have to deal with."

"What kind of issues?" Mi coughed, which was itself part of the answer.

"From the scans, Mi, you have a really bad respiratory infection. It's like you have every pneumonia out there, which, of course, you do. You're going to need hospitalization soon. Your lungs are filling with fluid. You will drown in your own phlegm, and no simple store-bought antibiotic can battle that on its own."

To Reno he said, "That wound in your leg is already getting gangrenous. Gangrene is fatal. I'm not even sure we can save you if you do come back, but we'll try. One way or another, though, the leg is probably gone. It won't matter. Back in the tank, plugged in, you'll have no idea it's missing."

He turned. "York, like your donor, sorry to say, you were born with a congenital heart defect. It was part of the DNA code, but when you were in our care, it was never an issue, as your vital signs were all controlled and monitored twenty-four-seven. Now it looks like you caught Mi's chest virus too. You're a massive coronary looking for a place to happen.

"Dakota, I suspect under the gloves, and from your yellow color, you're starting to lose your nails. If the tips of your fingers have also gone black, you're screwed. It's a form of malaria that normal humans have a resistance to. Not you. You must have picked up a mosquito bite recently. You'll continue to deteriorate, and you can expect mental breakdown to be a big part of that."

"I'm not having a mental breakdown," she slurred. "I'm just being fed a boatload of BS. You claim we're not engineered to handle the natural world? We can't even survive a mosquito bite? Yeah, right. Doesn't everyone get sick? I'll heal."

But Kode was shaking his head. "I hate to break it to you, but look at the history. Clones—any clones, so far—unless they're kept in strict sterile conditions, *always* succumb to an infection of some kind. Frogs. Mice. Sheep. All the same. Real, natural human people, the ones not born in a tube, have a *lifetime* to build up the immunities that keep them walking and breathing. You five, and the others back at BlackStar, have none of those immunities. You simply can't live in a filthy, viral world."

"You must have worked on a cure. You *must* have . . ." Dakota was growling again.

"Like I said, you *have* to go back in the sterile preservative. But we'll take care of you. We *all* have everything at stake."

I looked around at my team. Solemn, somber, afraid . . . the wind had just been taken out of their sails.

But we still had the guns, right?

"So what are you going to *do?*" Kode asked me directly. "I mean, Phoenix, you're sort of my offspring. I don't want you or any of these friends of yours to die. We'd have to make more. It'd cost a lot of money. And we'd be offline for a long time. Worse, I'd have to go under the knife again. And who knows what the next version of you would try to pull? *You* won't know. The bottom line is you'll be dead. You won't have any clue how new Phoenix plays his hand."

"Gee, thanks for the warmth," I replied sarcastically.

"Honestly. I want you to live a long, satisfying life. And you can. Just come home. You'll have nothing to worry about other than new toys and guns and games and friends to hang out with."

Mi interrupted, "You're saying we could just walk out of here and go back to BlackStar, and you'll cure us?"

"Our top physician is waiting there right now," he assured us.

"But so is the cable for the sides of our skulls," Dakota added.

"Right. But, Dakota, be honest—do you *really* want to live out here? Think about what you've seen so far. Average people aren't really happy, they're mostly miserable and barely surviving. It's always been that way. They take every moment they can to escape into a world where *you* rule and have fun and don't have to worry a single minute about where your next meal's coming from. In games, you pay no rent. You never get sick. You're kings and queens of every world. You have the best buddies and the most exciting days imaginable. I bet that given the opportunity—"

"And given the implant," I tossed out there to make sure it was heard.

"—right, given the opportunity *and* the implant, ninety-nine percent of the world would absolutely love to have your life. They'd swap places in a heartbeat. Play games all day. Loaf. Never worry about starving or losing their work or getting killed or eaten or traded to a far-off city. They spend half their waking moments getting sick and abused and used and cheated on by their loved ones. You five have none of their problems. Plus, you have the *most* fun in there. You're *Team Phoenix*. You get to shoot and battle and race for a living. There are days *I* want to be you, in that tank, floating blissfully from mission to mission and world to world with my very best friends."

A long pause. I remember that pause so well.

No one said a word. They just let Kode's pitch sink in.

"You don't really get it yet, Phoenix. You've been playing against me all along. You think I didn't find out how you got out? What a great use of vulnerable resources. Then you gathered intel through the work detail. Trying to blend in. The excursion past the wall was a surprise. But I knew you'd come back for the other three. Then I chose to flush you out. I'm going to use this whole thing, Phoenix. I'm designing a new game as we speak: GAME SLAVES. It'll rock the world. Say you're the player. You're an invincible killing machine dominating every one of the top titles, but only as a villain. Then a member of your own team disrupts everything and wants out. Wants to be a free human. Where do you go? How do you get weapons? Do you kill innocents if you have to? Do you fight authority? Is it a sneak game or a shooter? Is it role playing or strategy? Each gamer can play it any way they want, and play it over and over with different turning points. I'll sell millions of this thing. It's *brilliant*."

Dakota was looking my way. So was Mi. Reno pulled his bandage up to look at some bubbling skin that was peeling off his wounds.

York rubbed his chest. Did he really have a time bomb in there? A heart defect? I could see him, with rattling lungs, trying to steady his breathing.

And Mi, well, it really didn't matter at that moment that I'd caught her with Reno at all. On a cellular level, they were siblings, so what was the big deal with a little hugging and sharing a movie? Maybe the DNA link explained why they'd always been so close.

Fine by me.

I wasn't going to hold it against her.

The only thing I was thinking—and this was so clear in my mind, even after all the time that had passed and the choices we'd made—was that *I didn't want Mi to die.*

Not here in this store.

Not out in the wasteland.

Not during some insane climb over deadly mountain peaks.

Not because of a bullet, or pneumonia, or even as she grew older and older and it naturally became her time.

No, it was clear to me. I wanted Mi to *live*. I wanted my whole team to see tomorrow.

That was always my objective. In a game or not.

Now I had to find an angle to make that happen.

Unfortunately, I was one step behind.

Someone else was ready to play her own angle, and I wasn't prepared.

Maybe it was because she was the newer generation. Perhaps that gave her one additional hit point or perspective or cheat or whatever, but in the end, it would change all our paths.

To save Mi, I *might* have made a deal with Max Kode—but I wasn't going to get a chance. See, I think Dakota *knew* I might have made that deal with him.

In any case, Dakota was smart. She always knew I cared for Mi's safety more than I cared about her quest for liberation.

I turned to Max, not positive what I'd say, when Dakota yelled in a loud voice, "I'm not quite done with him!"

When I turned, she was pointing a fire extinguisher at all of us. And I knew there was no fire.

Dakota squeezed the lever. Sweet on our tongues, a white mist stung our eyes and closed our throats. She gassed us. As we began to lose our bearings and fell like sacks of grain, I clearly remembered a stack of chloroform bottles in the medical office.

I bet they were empty now.

Dakota strode up, gas mask on her face, and pocketed Max Kode's detonator. She hoisted BlackStar_1 in her arms.

When I woke, the scene looked all too familiar.

Level 43

Max Kode was strapped to a table, reclined at about sixty degrees. A bright light burned in his face. Dakota stood in front of him with an array of sharp instruments on a small side table. On top of the cutting tools was a heavy semiautomatic handgun.

I tried to move. No luck. We were all bound like packages and piled on the floor. She'd made quick work with tie-downs from the home furnishings department.

"Dakota!" I barked. "Let me loose."

"I'm going to cut on him a bit." She leered at Kode.

"Cut my straps first."

She came over and knelt down. Her gloves were off, and I saw what our visitor had been talking about. Her nails were gone, replaced by blackened sores and peeling flesh. I wondered how the original skeeter bite looked by now. Not pretty, I bet. She was rotting away. It had gotten to her brain. You could see it in her glassy, bloodshot eyes.

"Phoenix, brother," she began, "I hate to play this way. You had my back this whole time. And I know we wouldn't be out here if not for me, but you gotta know you're not in charge anymore." She held up that little remote control. The one Max had brought in. The one that blew up brain implants.

Her thumb was on the trigger.

"Don't do that," I told her. It was an order, but a soft one.

"I won't. Not yet. Not if you go along, OK?"

"Go along with what?"

"He knows *more*," she insisted, pointing at the man who was bound, fittingly, exactly the way he'd strapped down both me and Dakota back in that interrogation chamber so long ago.

"What's to know?" I asked. "Survival is the key to winning. If we die out here, Dakota, we lose."

"There's more," she repeated. "I can tell. You needed to listen to him a little more closely, Phoenix. You needed to ask harder questions."

She stood again, walked over, took a pair of sheers, and cut the man's long coat. Then she sliced his shirt and ripped it open, exposing his chest. Her blade ran smoothly over his throat, his nipples, then down toward his groin.

I remembered what she'd done to Jevo, and it made me cringe to think what we might witness now.

Suddenly, she dropped the blade and picked up the pistol. A gnarled, experienced thumb cocked the hammer, and she jammed the heavy barrel into his forehead.

"Do you care if I shoot you?" she asked Max.

He nodded. His eyes were stretched so wide I feared they might pop out and dangle there, still staring at the gun.

"Why do you care?"

"I don't want to die," he whimpered. "Think of my kids. Think of Jimmy. You like Charlotte, right? Don't leave her without a father."

Dakota smirked. "Nice try." She mimicked him, "Leave her without a father? You left me without anything! No mother, no father, no family!"

"*They're* your family." Max twitched toward the four of us, all tied up tighter than crazy-bin lunatics.

"They're illusions, aren't they?"

"Illusions? Of what?"

Dakota smirked again. "Of your twisted programming, right, Max?"

"What do you mean?" He was almost crying now.

"Yeah," I joined in, "what do you mean?"

Dakota turned to me now but didn't take the gun off Kode's brainpan. "I overheard, Phoenix. I was listening to what Jevo told you before you busted his face."

The memory came back. Oh, yeah. I knew exactly where this was coming from.

Now she was back focused on Max Kode. "Is this all a game?" she howled. "Are we still in one of your environments? Another one of your twisted system tests?"

She was really screaming, all worked up. I had a hard time believing that with the emotion letting loose, she hadn't accidentally budged that hair trigger.

"What?" Max asked. "No!"

"What if I blow your brains out? You'll just take off your game controller wherever you really are? Back at your house or whatever!"

Then, a smell. Pure urine. The bright yellow kind, and we were all breathing the stench. Dakota looked down.

Max Kode had wet his pants. He might have even soiled them.

The man who was in charge of the world's biggest gaming corporation was sobbing. Uncontrollably. It came in heaps as he tried to explain, to try to save his own life. "Dakota, *please* don't pull the trigger. PLEASE. No, you are *not* in anything but here with me now. Jevo is a moron."

"Jevo *is* a moron." Mi had also woken up.

"You're flesh and blood, Dakota," Kode assured her. "We told him the game thing because we didn't want him knowing any more than a goon of his limited capabilities needs to know."

"Prove it." Dakota pressed the gun again.

"How can I?" Kode asked.

"Tell me about cloning. You can't make me believe that if you've tried duping us before, all those times, and failed, that you haven't *also* worked on a *real* cure for our immune system."

BlackStar_1 went silent. The sobbing stopped. He narrowed his eyes at Dakota. As if, even though he was emotionally broken, she'd punched through a wall to something he did not want revealed.

"There's *nothing* to know," he insisted. "None of our tests ever worked. In polluted air, you *all* die. All clones get infections. Do you have a clue what version you guys are? Do you know how many Phoenixes and Miamis and Yorks I've buried? Dozens. And they all died. One after another. Sometimes as babies, or toddlers, or children the same ages as my own. Sprouting third arms, hunchbacks, gills, vestigial tails. You think this is easy? Or fun? I have a city to take care of."

"But you tried to cure them."

"We tried. The serums never worked. Only the tank solution keeps out the bugs. So you should thank your lucky stars you're not six feet under, Dakota. Or a pile of ash in the basement incinerator."

"So the *basement?*" Dakota grinned. "*That's* where you're working on some kind of master cure? A way for us to live outside the tank without risk of infection?"

Kode was still staring at her with such fury. "*You* are the infection, Dakota. We took your independence genetics too far. Now it's spreading. *You're* killing your team. They were healthier without you. And way better off."

"I want to be free."

"So what? Free will should only go so far."

Then she did the cruelest thing I've ever seen. And remember, I've seen it all.

It's just that this was real.

"You're about to tell me where to find the latest version of your cure," she said flatly. "You're going to tell me which room, in which of those big buildings up on the hill, me and my team have to go break into."

"There is no cure. At least, not . . ."

"*Aha!*" she screamed, and then picked up a small chain saw.

"You wouldn't have a chance of getting in there, past our security," he cried.

"I'm out of patience with your games. You're lying. It's *all* lies! I may be trapped in this loop, but I can prove it's all fake!"

Then she spun the blade, narrowed her eyes, and cut his right hand off, just below the elbow. It was quick, but made a horrifying grinding noise as the metal teeth chewed bone. That sound was replaced by an even more horrifying scream.

Max Kode. In extreme agony.

I glanced up. It looked like a graffiti artist had laid a red stripe in a big semicircle across the ceiling. I remembered seeing similar stripes before. Twelve of them. But those had been special effects.

This stripe was dripping wet. And the smell of fresh blood was back. Kode was crying. Shaking. Going into shock. She gunned the motor again.

"He didn't log out of any game, Dakota," taunted York. "He's still right *here*."

However, Dakota was right. Kode did begin blabbering. He started telling her everything he could get out so she wouldn't go near him with the saw again. He was now a top programmer with a stump for one arm. Two would be a complete disaster.

He told her exactly where the lab was. He admitted to her they'd been developing a supercure, an *ultrabiotic*. Through his gasps, he gave detailed instructions on how to find the right room.

And Dakota, with that remote detonator in her hand, was giving the orders now. Because if there was some kind of miracle cure up there, well, she just had to have it.

Level 44

Dakota freed me first, pointing the remote at my head the whole time.

I went straight to Kode and used strapping tape to stop his bleeding. He looked so small and weak, and I just bet he *wished desperately* that he could have pressed to escape that five minutes.

Dakota cut the rest of the team's bonds and began issuing orders for us to saddle up. She told York we were on our way back to Black-Star. To the same research center where we'd first emerged from the tank.

"No one knows if the biotic will work," Kode moaned to me as I tried to make him more comfortable. Doc Winters appeared from behind an aisle and was already injecting morphine directly into the wound.

I found his detached hand. The old woman began lining up her surgical tools.

He was slurring his words as he kept trying to speak. "Really, it might just kill you outright," he warned. "The core ingredient is radioactive RNA. It could change your whole physical structure. It might leave you insane, or a vegetable, we really don't know. We were going to test it on other . . ."

But some dream cure was the least of my worries. We'd all die out here anyway.

"My deal was your best deal." He was losing focus. "The last time we tried the serum there were . . . unfortunate . . . results . . ."

"Maybe," I said. "But I'm going where Mi goes."

Mi, York, and Reno were now collecting gear for the truck. I had only a minute or two before Dakota ordered us to start up the rig.

"You and me, we're so alike." Kode grabbed my arm with his remaining hand. "It's *amazing*."

"It's immoral," I replied.

"You don't get to make that call. You're just a product of a gaming environment where everything *has* to be either good or evil. Out here, nothing's *all* good or *all* bad. Everything's a shade of gray."

"Everyone still has to play by certain rules, Max."

"You haven't got the street cred to make the rules. You don't even have a street. *I'm* from Arizona, not you. None of you is from anywhere except my lab."

"So *you* were brought in on a shipment?"

"And I rose to the top right through BlackStar. I force-retired the former president, and he didn't like that one little bit. I *won*. And it was better for everyone. My innovations changed this whole city. Without my work, everyone would already be dead and eaten. Phoenix, you had no life. Other than what I gave you through the cable."

He just looked pitiful to me. A mean, greedy bastard with no internal code. No loyalties. Sure, he had two kids—who, remember, he sent into game worlds rather than playing with them himself —but he was far more alone than I had ever been.

Maybe he knew that.

"We're completely different," I said, pulling his fingers off my arm.

"Huh-uh." He shook his head. "You're my clone on every level. After a series of unjust events I couldn't control, I was given responsibility for an entire city. You, Phoenix, are the same as me. Simply because of events not of your making, you *have* to care for a group of men and women who look to you for everything."

"There are differences."

"It's a heavy weight we carry, isn't it? I can never make everyone happy. Sometimes we gotta sacrifice the weak so the strong get to keep playing."

"You mean with the wall out there?" I replied. "You're going to banish everyone who built it, aren't you?"

"What purpose could those bums serve afterward? They don't program. They can't design. Without tech skills, they're too expensive to keep alive. They are of no use to me other than labor. Our city will flourish once we have to stop subsidizing their food and shelter and clothing. It'll be a utopia after they're gone and they've stopped draining our supplies."

"You're just the typical boss, aren't you? Sending your minions to their death by the busload."

"Give me a break. We *both* make tough decisions about who lives and who dies. Who to send to their death. We're practically identical."

I didn't say anything.

"We're both at war, Phoenix. All true leaders are. Whether it's corporate or with guns."

"You're wrong, Kode. We're completely different. Want to know how? I *care* about my people. I care about them more than I ever cared about myself."

"Well"—Kode shrugged—"I'll just have to make sure we fix that flaw when we build the next one of you."

Then he passed out.

At the very least, *now* we had a clear objective. Out here, few people did.

And ours led back to the beginning.

The truck was huge, plenty of space for gear, and York and Mi were making the most of it. I helped, grabbing things off the shelves left and right. This assault was not going to be easy, so it was worth taking a few minutes to prepare.

We had to get to the bottom floor, the lowest basement. Down there, in their most secure area, BlackStar housed the keys to their success: the clones, their tanks, and a risky cure.

Needless to say, we took every gun and bullet we could lay our hands on. And a lot of other things too. This wasn't our first rodeo. I had an idea what kinds of state-of-the-art defensive technology we might face.

Finally, twin motors roared. Turbines spun, superchargers pumped, and long streams of black smoke bellowed out chrome pipes.

Giant moon-tires bounced as we loaded the last of our heavy ammo. Outside, along the perimeter, as troopers watched, the building started to rumble.

Explosive locks detonated and the bay doors slid up. Rubber

began to roll. Through a mist of dark smoke, Reno gunned the gas and dropped the clutch, and we lurched into open air.

From the front cannon turret, Mi reported that the troops were taking aim.

These rigs were made to haul multiple trailers at high speed across hostile desert. They were the only things that could still cross a thousand miles of barren landscape, following old highway or railroad grades, fording rivers that had swallowed the bridges, navigating rocky outcroppings and fallen trees. These rigs gulped fuel. They could take a hit. And they were heavily armed.

We tore a straight line across the lot, shopping carts and barrier fence bouncing in all directions.

The enemy vehicles stayed in place, a tiny ring of men and metal trying to keep us contained.

So be it. Turbochargers roared as all-wheel-drive trannies clanked into gear.

We crushed a half dozen of their security patrollers on the way out of the lot while men dove and shot wildly at our gun placements. Mi began unleashing short bursts, but not at the troops. She was aiming for gas tanks or engine blocks. The more of them she could disable now, the fewer we'd have on our tail once we hit open streets.

Then we were past the barricade. Just like that. For the first time since we'd launched out of the store, I noticed the steady rain. A faint mist swirled around hot gun barrels. Wet streets caused twin roosters to spray off the back tires.

Additional vehicles rode up on our tail. A few more stretched out in front. A motorcycle appeared. Then five more. But they were all outsized and outgunned.

"So this is your plan?" I leveled the question at Dakota through the mic. "A bum rush on a highly fortified industrial complex just so you can pump your veins full of a toxic supercure?"

She grinned at me across the top of the truck. Blood was on her teeth. "*And* I'm going to free all the other clones and pump them full of the stuff!"

"You better ask them first if they really want out."

"It's not like I'll be giving them a choice."

That gory smile again. I'd never realized she was both devious *and* crazy. Dangerous mix, huh?

Level 45

We were making good time, and even with the rain it was easy to pick out the destination. Just keep going uphill. Reno raced toward the huge complex of BlackStar buildings. Every passing block, the city got nicer and nicer. From ghetto to suburb to estates.

And still security rigs chased on. The motorcycles thought they were nimble, right up until they got within range and Mi showed what she did best.

One, two, three, four. The bikes exploded as bullets ripped open their gas tanks. I wondered what was more valuable to BlackStar, the hurtling riders or the three gallons of low octane that exploded between their legs?

The closest patrol car was a hundred feet back. The roof un-folded, bouncing along, one mile down. Two to go. Then a missile launcher poked up.

"They've got bottle rockets!" York announced.

"Take out the front tires first," I suggested. If we disabled that rig, it'd block the rest of them from overtaking us before we reached BlackStar.

KABOOOOM! York was a good shot too, but the explosion was

unexpected. Must have hit batteries. The front half of BlackStar's armored peacekeeper became a fireball, tires popping, whole thing grinding and rolling to rest across the road.

Good idea, but it didn't work. The three others jumped right through the burning metal, bursting out of flame and smoke, not losing more than a few seconds in the pursuit.

Reno hit his nitrous boosters, shooting us ahead. Under the next overpass we began blasting round after round of explosive armor-tipped shells into the roof cement. We made a pair of dotted lines in the top of the tunnel.

The ceiling began to buckle and quiver. Their three vans had to line up single file to enter. And just as we cleared the far end, the whole thing gave way, falling in a *SPLAT* of dusty debris. Two more of the enemy vehicles were gone, squashed flat.

One was left, but it wasn't a major concern. For the next mile or so we were pelted with lead. Mi was now loading rocket shells and firing as fast, if not faster, than she ever had in a game environment.

Up ahead, BlackStar's massive towers, walkways, and smoked-glass windows loomed dark and cold. All that stood between us and the front doors were the wall, a stadium-sized stretch of open grass, guard dogs, sentries, and three rows of cyclone fencing topped with razor wire.

Electric fencing, to be sure. Thousands of volts. That stuff doesn't just shock you, it welds you to the ground.

Reno's foot clanked the pedal to the cab floor.

And then we hit. Doing a hundred, probably a bit more. Concrete debris exploded into the air, everything turned gray, but the outer wall crumbled. We raced through the gap, the drenching rain washing pale streaks of dust off the crumpled nose of the truck.

Grass zoomed underneath, squishing, the tires' weight making a sucking noise.

"If we hit that electrical field . . . !" Dakota was warning, her voice up an octave, the adrenaline really flowing. She fired off a hundred quick rounds, trying to slow our pursuer, but the shells bounced harmlessly off thick hood plate.

"I know, I know," I answered. "Reno, stomp on the brakes, let the last police truck get in front of us."

"What?"

"Do it, quick!"

He did. We were all thrown around, but it caught the enemy driver unaware. Suddenly, he was in our path . . .

"T-bone him and continue on!" I ordered.

Reno grinned. He understood my solution to the power-fence.

Our front bumper caught the BlackStar vehicle dead center. Reno punched the nitrous and it almost lifted their whole truck off the ground.

Strike that. Across our bow like that, it was no longer a truck. Now it and the men inside were just a big steel bulldozer. We'd become a nine-thousand-horsepower plow, aimed straight for high-voltage wire.

Impact. The crackle of grounded electricity sounded like dropping frozen fries in a tub of boiling fat. Their troopers up front, completely exposed, screamed as the surge danced through their bones, but still we pressed on. Reno had the gas to the floor, metal grinding, sparks everywhere. Up the steps we went, dogs and sentries diving, until we collided abruptly with the BlackStar entrance.

Then, after the chaos and gunfire, in an instant, it all stopped. It was dead quiet. Dust began to settle. A Doberman whimpered. My eyes cleared. Up ahead, I could see the shattered windows of Black-Star's second floor. Down below, I knew, the fried jeep had been shoved through the first-floor lobby like cheese through a grater.

"Hello, Dad, I'm *home!*" Dakota yelled to no one.

The place looked deserted. It probably was. From here, it was likely we'd be up against their automated defense system. Human guards would be few and far between.

Dakota still held her little detonator, and as long as she could push Mi toward her magic cure, I'd be along for the ride.

All five of us piled out and jumped the gap over to the second floor, heavily armed, very determined, and playing for keeps.

And, OK, I have to admit . . . after all that time out there, un-sure of my purpose, I finally felt like I was back on top of my game again.

York and Mi unloaded the truck. We each had a pack with the gear we'd brought. Dakota quickly found a map, and when Max Kode had said "lowest level," well, he meant it.

We were going all the way to the bottom.

What I'd have given for a functioning elevator right then, but all the shafts had been shut off when the front alarms sounded. York pried open a door to one, and I leaned over to look down. Security barriers had slid across it. We couldn't drop that way. Not without cutting torches and ten hours to slowly descend floor by floor.

"The stairs." Mi pointed. Fire doors still open. We'd be on foot.

Floor after floor, level after level, through everything they could dream up.

In the first sub-basement, we ran into mechanized kill-bots armed with laser-sighted machine pistols. Mi blinded them with a chaff grenade (shredded aluminum foil wrapped around a thermite charge) and the rest of us ran through the sector, kicking the bots harshly off their wheeled bottoms, leaving them helpless, unable to get back upright.

The next two floors were filled with unguarded office cubicles, each section marked off by game title. We knew most of the titles very well. So this was where they designed and programmed HIGH PLAINS KILLER and SLAUGHTER RACE EXTREME! and the rest.

Below that was a floor with pressure plates everywhere we could step. Along the walls, shutters hid heavy weaponry. From the propane smell, I guessed flamethrowers.

"Let's rope," I decided. Reno was carrying a modified spear gun we'd taken from a scuba mannequin back in the XMart, you know, just in case. He zipped a line to the far wall. Mi crawled across first, since she was the lightest, then secured the cable when she made it past the sensors. It only took a minute for the rest of us to pulley over.

As we entered the next stairwell, out of curiosity, York tossed the expended weapon backward onto the floor. Shutters dropped. The room behind us was immediately toasted to a crisp.

We found a level that had infrared body sensors. It looked like the test floor for the console head straps everyone used. Mi had rolls of chemical ice packets. We gave them quick snaps of their internal bladders, shook them up, and wrapped them around our arms and legs. Walked right through.

The following sub-basement had a spider-web laser security system. It also had gas canisters placed in each corner. If we broke a single red laser beam, the entire floor would flood with toxic gas.

It's funny. In a game or movie, there's always a way through. Why is that? Players can contort and jump and wiggle their way to a solution. Not out here. Expert security leaves no safe path.

Did we use mirrors to reroute the web? That too would have taken hours. Fool the receptors by shining our own lasers into them? That might have worked for one receptor, but good security has hundreds of strands.

Everyone looked at me. I took great pleasure in pulling a big roll from my pack. I plugged in a pump. Air began to fill a giant plastic globe.

"What's *that?*" Mi begged to know.

"Reno isn't the only one who brought the right tool for the job." I smiled at them.

"Frosty the Snowman" music filled the room. Thank you, Christmas department.

My solution: a giant snow globe. So common for the rich. Too expensive for the poor. But if it held air, well, that meant it was airtight.

We crowded into the orb, sealed it up, then rolled all the way to the next stairwell, tripping the alarms one after another. Outside our globe, the room was doused with heavy green gas.

Inside, we had fake flakes, a snowman mascot, and happy theme music.

When we got to the stairs, we climbed out of the orb and continued down. And then, just like that, the stairwell came to an end.

This was it. The very bottom level. As deep as they had dug.

The end of the line, and if you looked at our situation, it was the beginning of the line too.

I put a rifle barrel up against the door. Slowly, pushing it open just an inch, I waited for bullets or flames or . . . something.

But the vault was so quiet. Sterile. And exactly as it had been when we were here before.

The tanks were just as blue. The umbilicals were just as active. Information surged into and out of the bodies. Deke, Rio, Syd, Dub—they were all in there somewhere, with no clue we were staring through glass at their liquid tomb.

I saw one girl twitch slightly, roll, turn, and mime the motions she was going through in some game world.

"It's hideous," Dakota spat, still holding the detonator.

"But *we* were taken out by couple of *kids*," Mi coughed at her. "Look what it's gotten us."

She was right. Dakota's skin was past yellow, Reno might lose his leg, my eyeball was festering, and York was waiting on a massive coronary.

At least Jevo had had the right procedure, plus a dust cover to manage his skull port.

Mi asked, "Do you really want to do this to Dub or Lima? I like Rio a lot. You might scramble their brains if you just jump in there and start pulling plugs."

Dakota began to weigh that information. What was she going to do now?

"Let's find the serum first," she decided. Her hand came up, pointing to a set of double doors marked LABS. "It's right where Kode said they kept it. Behind those doors. Look for a big bubbling neon-green rig. LED lights, the whole shooting match. He said it's in some kind of tricked-out coolant case to keep it stable."

I took up position on one side of the door, Dakota the other. York, Reno, and Mi hobbled into place as our backup.

Then I kicked the left one.

Dakota kicked the right.

And machine-gun bullets sprayed out as if we'd burst a high-pressure hose.

I got about five steps into the cavernous room and dove behind a heavy laboratory counter. Dakota had done the same, so at least we had two positions from which to return fire while Mi, Reno, and York found safe spots.

I provided cover, and Dakota moved up a row.

Her turn, allowing me to advance. York and Mi somehow got into the room.

We worked like that, not sure how many men were out there. Lots, it seemed, since every time we showed some body, we got pelted by enemy fire.

Row by row, we were making progress.

Behind the troopers, through bulletproof glass, stood a huge container. It had to be the ultrabiotic: a viscous, speckled slew with slow bubbles wrapped by hoses dripping liquid nitrogen to keep it from melting down.

But the troopers had better position. Dakota, to make sure we remembered, waved the detonator again and motioned for us to continue our advance.

I figured I could either take a bullet or get my noggin popped. No choice in the matter except to fight.

That's when Mi came up beside me and whispered, "Notice something?"

"What, Mi?"

"Well, I've been watching the enemy, up behind those front barricades. There's five of them."

"Only five left?"

"Yeah, but one isn't shooting."

"Why not? Five on five's a fair fight. Plus, they have better angles."

"Shhh," Mi ordered. York came up next to us now, and he went quiet too.

We listened.

We could hear the enemy whispering on the other side of the room.

It went like this:

A BlackStar guard, a woman's voice, hissed, *"But I don't wanna die!"*

And one of her buddies ordered, *"It's your job to die! Now get out there, expose yourself, fire off a few random shots, and let the enemy—"*

"OH!" York yelped over everyone. "You've *GOT* to be kidding!"

"Kidding about what?" I asked him.

York quickly began fumbling with his pack, trying to find something, all freaked out. He was still moaning, "No way. No way. No way."

Suddenly, one of the dark-clad BlackStar guards stood up. Hands in the air. Weapon tossed to one side.

She started walking toward us, saying, *"I'm not going to hurt you!"* Her helmet came off. Blond locks tumbled out. *"Really! Trust me! I just want to talk. You look like a reasonable person . . ."*

York was panicked. I'd never seen him so frantic. Scrambling through his arsenal to find the right items . . .

Ever weirder . . . Dakota stood up. In plain sight?

"I totally *hear* you," she answered. Then lowered *her* weapon. What was she thinking? What a trick for the enemy to pull! And someone on my team fell for it!

The woman stepped forward.

Dakota mirrored the move. "All we want is the serum. You can walk away."

York was blabbering, "NO WAY NO WAY NO WAY!" and wrapping a grenade in double-sided supertape.

The woman rambled on, *"So have you ever stopped to ask yourself why we have to fight and why we have to die and what's the point of—"*

Dakota bellowed, "Exactly my original point!"

"You don't have to kill me! And we don't have to kill you either! There can be peace between our species!"

Then, York stood, yelling, "Not again! Not *again*. Die, crazy witch! Die!" He tossed his charge right at the BlackStar woman. It stuck square to her forehead and she turned, helpless, to look at the other four BlackStar troops.

My team? Well, a plasma grenade has a *really* short fuse. We all sprinted and dove back out of the room as fast as feet can move.

After that blast, there was nothing left of any of their guards. The whole area was clear.

"Anyone get the idea we're stuck in some kind of loop?" York said, but we were being too cautious to make small talk now.

Slowly, we advanced.

Was that it? *All* the traps? We were at the very bottom of the BlackStar hole now. What else could there be? They'd never flood the whole complex with water, as that would affect the tank clones.

That must be it, then. We'd made it.

In front of us, the ultrabiotic boiled in its chamber. The liquid was so dense the bubbles moved at lava-lamp speed, combining, recombining, splitting, like it was alive.

Maybe it *was*.

I wasn't so sure I wanted that stuff coursing through my veins. It sparked, it churned, it just didn't seem safe . . .

But Dakota, maybe because of the virus coursing through her own veins, was not apprehensive.

The troopers had given their lives to protect it. Therefore, this must be the goal.

She took urgent, hurried steps forward across the rest of the cement floor. Closer and closer.

She was almost to the container, reaching out, when we heard a loud *CLANK!* Her foot stopped dead.

It just *couldn't* be. Not after everything we'd beaten. From infrared to lasers to gas to fire to troops to . . . Plus, we were on the *bottom* level now. There was nothing beneath us.

However, that *CLANK* was something you just know when you hear it.

Dakota had stepped on a trapdoor. The oldest and lamest of all traps, right?

But she'd walked right onto it. It sprang. She turned as a swath of the concrete began to open below her feet.

It wasn't slow motion—more like everything just sped up and no one could do a thing to help, not reach out a hand or toss a line or even shoot her with that harpoon gun . . .

But there was one thing that did happen. It took no more than a hundredth of a second. Her eyes, as she fell, locked on mine. We shared the deepest gaze. And I've peered into *millions* of faces at that exact moment, the moment of certain death.

No one—not a single person in a game or in reality—*welcomes* it.

But Dakota . . . I might be wrong . . . she almost looked like she was about to smile . . .

. . . and then she tumbled straight down through the floor as if she'd been sucked right to hell. We heard her scream, "AHHHHH-HHHhhhh . . . ," until we could hear her no more.

I jumped to the edge and looked down, hoping to see her still alive. It was amazing how well it had been hidden in the smooth concrete, but there it was, a square opening just big enough to drop a body through.

And down the hole? Absolute blackness. None of us mentioned that it was so deep we hadn't even heard her hit. No pit is truly bottomless, but this one seemed close.

Just that quick, the door swung back up and sealed shut.

You can bet the rest of us four went up on our toes as quick as possible.

We shuffled to find a safe path, reached the container, and pulled the serum out.

The syringe was dark chrome with blood-red and radioactive-green LEDs along one side. No one bothered to read the warning labels.

It was heavy in my hand.

Reno limped forward. He looked three shades past death. These might be the last steps he'd take on that gangrenous leg. York was holding his chest, hoping that big seizure could wait a little longer.

And Mi, well, the way she coughed made me think breathing

for her was even more painful than having an arm buzzed off. My girl never showed pain. Now she was hiding agony.

We were all sick as dogs. And we had no real place in this world. My skull was on fire as the bacteria from the port infection played war games in my brain.

"Hit me with it," Reno offered. "I'm worst off. See if it helps."

"I'll be the guinea pig," York argued. "My ticker's a death sentence."

"We're *all* dying," Mi reminded them. "But this may have just been a ray of hope Max dangled in front of Dakota."

"Dakota would have taken it."

"She was just steps away. Nasty trick to fall for," York spat. "I'm gonna do it," he said, grabbing the needle. He got it right up to his arm, but the glittering tip of the syringe didn't pierce his skin. He wouldn't quite inject it. There was still a lot of doubt.

"How do we know we could trust that Kode guy?" Reno suddenly asked. "It might just knock us out so they can tank us again."

Mi glanced at him, then offered, "Well, he is the exact same DNA as Phoenix, right?"

Everyone nodded.

She turned to me and asked, "And we trust Phoenix, right?"

"Always have."

Mi stared my way. "So, P, if you were him, would you have lied to you right then? Or would you have told yourself the truth? What would you have said?"

The question hit me like a knee in the gut.

Talk about a twist. Would I lie to me? Even for my own good? Now, there's a puzzle that has no solution.

Still, one thing remained.

Mi.

And the rest, but mostly Mi.

I wanted her to live. So I'd do whatever it took.

"I'll take the injection first," I said, reaching out.

York slapped the device in my hand. It burned at the grip. Whatever was in there was just teeming with nuclear material.

I slipped the needle into my arm, then began a slow, nervous squeeze on the plunger.

⊕ ⊕ ⊕

My eyes opened, and I could tell something was wrong. All four of us were lying on the floor of the lab. An empty syringe, shared by me and then the rest of my team, rocked to a stop against a wall.

The pain was a new kind of pain. Excruciating. Like I was being burned from inside one vein at a time.

"You fool," a voice said. "Now you can never win."

I looked up. Saw a shoe. Pants. Then far, far above, like I was falling or he was growing taller and taller, Max Kode stared down at me.

His arm was in a sling. His head was shaking. "With that serum in your system, you can never be put back in the tank environment. It nullifies all the sedatives. You blew it."

I wanted to speak, but no words would come. My lungs were molten, my throat a pipe full of flame.

"You might have just killed us all," he said, almost sadly. "Me. Jimmy. Charlotte. The people you met. The crank who reattached my arm. Mi, York. Reno. So was it worth it? What if the whole city starves? Or gets overrun?"

I was dying to remind him that a short time ago, he had guaranteed that he would win and I would lose.

The words, I wanted them to come out of my mouth, but maybe he knew what I was thinking.

Level 46

It was comforting to be out in space again. Sure, your planet has some interesting perks, but if you ever get the chance to pilot a fully loaded Z-class interstellar attack bomber, take it. These things will do warp ninety-three and have an arsenal that can split your average moon.

Imagine being able to enter orbit, sweep in over France, and decimate everything between Paris and Rome. Yeah, it leaves a mess, but it's pretty darn fun.

I angled toward a pair of ringed planets. This, I assumed, was where the enemy would come out of warp. Little did they know, we'd be waiting.

Mi was on my left, Reno over to my right. York made a quick lap around a few of the closer asteroids to make sure the quadrant was clear. We didn't want anyone getting the drop on us while we were planning to get the drop on them.

Space battles are just *great*. So many variables. And everything is three-dimensional, so when the attack came not from our front or rear but from straight overhead, out of the sun, we barely had time to react.

The gamers were flying the double-Z-class, but while faster, they had limited range with their nukes. We used this advantage for as long as we could, but soon enough all of us were zipping around in close-quarter dogfights. *BAM! Bam-BAM!* Explosions. Go back home, PTA moms . . .

I had another one lined up. Then a third was on my six. I shook him, went over and picked a pursuer off Mi's tail, then rolled onto my back and skimmed off the atmosphere of a rogue meteor.

The sudden flames from my high-speed skip into its thin air blinded my scanners, and just for a moment I was engulfed. I left its gravity seconds later, but it was too late.

During that instant when I couldn't see, two enemy ships set up a nice little bottleneck on the other side. I came out and spotted them, and no more than a half second later a bolt of plasma ripped the primary engine off the rear of my fighter.

The next blast cut my cockpit in half. I ejected, but to where? I was in deep space.

So there I was, floating along, powerless, shipless, through an intergalactic dogfight the likes of which no human had ever really seen. What the heck? I unholstered my puny little hand-blaster and began firing off random shots at the gamer ships. They were still moving at light speeds, so it wasn't like I was hitting much, but it was fun target practice.

Practice that might serve me well someday.

And it gave me an idea. Next time, in case this happened, I'd give each of my team a mini-nuke as a cockpit weapon. One they could ride. Then, if they ever had to eject and were floating into a star like I was about to, they could still help put up a fight.

Down below, between my feet, I saw Mi's craft explode as three fighters surrounded her. They pumped shot after shot into the glowing fireball.

Reno had just lost guidance and slammed into another of those random asteroids. Bummer for him.

York, as usual, was battling to the very last gasp. His ship had lost everything: both engines, most of the armaments, even a majority of the hull itself. All that remained was his seat, a bubble over his head, and one huge laser cannon. Still, he was putting up one heck of a fight. The gamers just couldn't finish him, and he was knocking their numbers down one by one with shot after well-placed shot.

"That-a-boy!" I chirped into the mic. He whittled them down to four. Then to three. He fired as his gun reached overheat temps, and another enemy ship mushroomed into white light.

I was trying to help, with my tiny little pistol, shooting from like a million miles away, but why not? We might have been losing this skirmish, but I'd learned a lot about the way these gamers played. Do you think, for a second, that attacking out of the sun was going to work for them next time?

Nope.

We'd set a better trap.

The last two gamers maneuvered to a place where York had no chance of getting them both, then caught him in a crossfire.

He went out with a bang, that's for sure.

Team Phoenix does not whimper.

Now you might expect us to move to the Re-Sim table.

Buzzer sound.

I sat up slowly, the battle still ringing in my ears. It took a few seconds to clear my head. I rubbed my hair, moving one hand down to where the port was located. Very gingerly, I felt around the large connection cord coming out of my temple. It hurt. That horrible redness was still shrinking. The infection was dissipating. Good thing. According to the BlackStar docs, I'd been hours away from it spreading to my brain.

If not for the serum, I'd be some kind of vegetable now.

I sat up, not in a tank of course, but in a comfortable gaming chair. It stood in a line with three others, each of them holding one of my teammates. All were still plugged in, but I'd come out of the digi-verse first. That's my role. I still lead Team Phoenix.

Slowly, like the doc had shown me, I pulled the connection tab and very gently removed the long spike that ran behind my eyes. Immediately, the glow from my hand tattoo died to a normal ink shade.

My shift was over. I glanced at the clock. It'd been sixteen straight hours. A long one, but now I had time off. Plus, it was Friday. Yippee, here came the weekend.

I glanced to the right. Mi was in the next seat, and I could see her beginning to stir. She also had a respiration mask over her face. She's taking daily treatments for the pneumonia that ravaged her system.

She still wasn't out of the woods yet. Doc had shown me her chest scans. It might be years before the bugs finally cleared out. So, every time we came to work, she also had to wear the mask. It was, according to the same BlackStar physicians who'd made the ultrabiotic, slowly feeding her disinfected air that'd help her lungs rebuild.

So, for us at least, work was actually good for our health.

York and Reno were on the other side of Mi, but I didn't need to wait for them. We'd planned a barbecue the next day and we'd get to catch up.

Plus, I had a little surprise for Mi that I planned to give her at the cookout. One of those surprises that involves a way-too-expensive ring and a date and some kind of bells or something.

Yeah, don't judge me too harshly. I was going to take the plunge. Why not? We were like four years old or something. Can't wait around forever.

I checked Mi's readout. Accuracy stats through the roof again. More kills than York and Reno combined.

She had another hour on the chest meds, so I wandered down the corridor and stopped by the doc's office. He was out, but the assistant took a look at the side of my head. She rubbed in some more antiseptic butter and gave me an ice pack to cool the area. It's a slow recovery.

And—in case you want to know—part of the deal I had to make to get a real life with weekends off was that I didn't complain about them leaving the explosive device in my head. BlackStar would always have me on a leash. I gave that up in the deal.

But I got something, too. Don't doubt that. I played my best game, and it's up to history to decide if I won or not.

Level 47

They couldn't tank us again. With the ultrabiotic in our system, any attempt to drown us in a preservative would lead to the serum counteracting the tank fluid.

But that ultrabiotic did work. To a point. Call it a partial cure.

There were still details that were being hammered out. Mi wanted to have kids one day. I was all for that. But that's down the road. Kode promised his physicians would work on making it safer for her.

And I wanted something too. My demand was even harder to convince him of than Mi's. We argued about it constantly.

"All the people, Max. You'll make room for them all."

"I can't support that many," Kode negotiated. "They cost too much. But we may be able to make room for, say, twenty percent of the workforce."

"All of them."

"We can go to twenty-one percent, but mostly women and children who don't eat much."

"All of them, or I stop my team from playing so well."

"BlackStar profits cannot support them all. Maybe if you played better, worked longer hours, we could add some."

I pointed, "Or, you could give up some of *your* share." Like that's going to happen.

They'd sold me a small house near the center of the suburbs. Certainly not in the mansion district, but it was plenty. It had a yard I had to mow. A place to park the car Mi and I shared. And a few other things that make for a normal life.

Kode had arrived early for the barbecue, he'd probably leave early too. He was griping as usual, "Phoenix, what if you'd tried to *negotiate* and *reason* with me from the beginning? We could have saved all that trouble." But we both knew that wasn't in my programming back then. Or in his.

Jimmy and Charlotte, however, were always here. They'd really taken to our backyard. We didn't have a pool or anything. They probably just liked it because Mi and I would stay out there with them, playing like kids until it was time for them to go home.

Plus, I liked to build forts. They stretched throughout the trees.

The kids were back there now, hanging a rope swing.

Max and I watched through the window while we continued our same conversation.

"Why don't you," he said, "stop pumping your share of your profits into building that school?"

"Those are my people, too," I told him.

"You butcher millions of them in games every day you work!"

"Not out here. Out here, I take care of them."

He reminded me, "You could have a house as big as mine. Sports cars, motorcycles, even your own helicopter if you budget it right."

But I shook my head. No. Mi and I wanted to be good for a while.

York and Reno? Well, that was a different matter.

York took his share, his pay, and bought a house right on the lake. Spent millions buying custom boats he had shipped in from XMart. Sailed the waters, romancing the ladies, and for some reason thought he was this century's greatest pirate-slash-playboy.

Reno. He *did* take the helicopter. Cost him a fortune and a fortune more to run. He told me he'd been dropping in on the powder fields in the northern mountains, actually skiing up there beyond the wall.

He kept trying to get me to go up there with him. And this from a guy who almost lost his leg six months ago. Sure, he still limped. But it was getting better.

It was all getting better, little by little, every day we were free.

The party was great. The neighbors were all decent people, even though their kids constantly asked to play the newest video games. We still didn't have any consoles in the house.

Yeah, sure, at work, we'd be chained to our desks—strike that —chained to our BlackStar gamechairs and the meds for a long, long time. But aren't we all shackled? A job is a job, it's just that we still had the best one on the planet.

I'd cooked up some burgers and brats on the grill. Mind you, I'd also burned over half of them. I'll get it. Some life skills are hands-on.

Reno arrived wearing his ski clothes. What a show-off. York had been diving at the lake, and it occurred to me that of everyone left on the planet, we might be the *only* four who don't spend a single minute of free time playing video games. Not one.

Mi was laughing. Some of our other neighbors had come over and one guy's wife was a real kook. Tons of makeup, huge hair, and her clothing was 90 percent sequin, but Mi really seemed to like her. The hubby worked on BlackStar satellite feeds or something. Boring. But he gamed in his off time, too. Everyone needs escape.

So that ultrabiotic had done its work. Maybe not all the way, but I wasn't going crazy and had exactly the right number of arms and legs. No second head, no sprouting gills or webbed toes.

I was getting healthier all the time. Bigger and stronger than Max Kode. Slowly, very slowly, my body was morphing into the one from the games. I knew I would never be as huge and heroic as game-Phoenix, but at least I wasn't so sickly anymore. Had been lifting weights. I could run a couple miles without collapsing. I may not have been a real-world gladiator, but I was turning into a nice mix between digital-dweeb and digital-abomination.

So that's about it. Happily ever after.

For everyone except Dakota. What a way to go. At least it had been quick. And she went out fighting for something she believed in to her very soul. I respected that. We all did. But I bet they wouldn't grow any more of that model anytime soon.

I reached in my pocket. The ring was there. Good thing; it cost a lot. Took weeks to get shipped. BlackStar may own Redwood, but XMart owns BlackStar. If not for supplies, there'd be no gaming company. And without Kode's revenue and worth to the planet, every poor soul in the city would be doomed.

Like Kode said, everything out here was a lighter or darker shade of gray. I wanted to be a really light one for a while.

So, it was time. All our friends were here. Work was far away.

How would I do it? Something like, "Mi, my love, with whom I've killed and slaughtered billions, taken over galaxies, ruled the universe, enslaved worlds, fought bloody wars and crushed all opposition . . ."

No, maybe I would leave the mundane day-to-day stuff out of it.

I'll just tell her I love her. That should be enough.

And then the doorbell rang.

I don't know why I answered it. I should have just let whoever it was wander in.

But I was close, so I opened the door. And there was Dakota.

How did she look? Sick? Dying?

Not really. Certainly not as healthy as those of us who'd taken the ultrabiotic, but her skin was almost a normal shade again. Her eyes were bulging less.

"Dakota? No *way*. I saw you die!"

"I didn't die."

"You fell . . . ?"

"Is that what you think?"

"That impact must have broken every bone in your. . . ."

"Phoenix, man, shut up! Time's short! It was *so* hard to get to you."

I just stared back. Hard to get to me? Just walk up and ring the bell. Like she did. I don't have guards stationed anywhere.

I stepped back to let her in, wondering how she got some of the serum. She was a climber—did she climb out later? Was there water at the bottom of that pit? "What are you doing here, Dakota? You don't look so good . . ."

"I don't have time," she urged. "I think they're right on my tail. Really, listen, this is *huge*, Phoenix."

"Huge?"

"Look around," she told me, pointing left and right. "Do you think this is real? It's not! You're still in the game! BlackStar tricked you! The ultrabiotic was a re-slavery drug! So they could drown you back in the tank!"

I looked at her blankly. Behind me, I could hear the music, the party, Mi laughing at another of that crazy neighbor woman's jokes.

Dakota continued, "Max told you what he knew you'd react to. That you could never get to the serum. So *of course* you'd try. You're so objective-based, he counted on that."

"I did it because you had a detonator and were threatening . . ."

"I pulled the batteries out of that even before we left the store," she admitted. "I would never blow you guys up . . . I wasn't *sure*. Just wasn't positive it was another test. Not until I saw the trapdoor. And I heard the woman say my lines."

Behind us, Reno was asking some kids whose parents also worked at BlackStar if they all wanted to go powder skiing. Out in the wilderness. Beyond the wall. No takers there.

And I could smell the grill; I'd left something cooking way, way too long. Again.

"You're nuts, Dakota, but let me help." I showed her my port, now covered with a nice cap. "Let's get you in and fitted and on the payroll and heck, I'll buy the place next door for you, and . . ."

"Really!" she stressed. "I'm not insane. I didn't fall into a pit. I jumped that environment because I figured out it was all fake!"

"All fake?"

"You thought I wanted to try to escape through the north wall gap? To climb? That wasn't what I meant. What was weird was the way the people would only edge their toes to the very limit of the wall border. Because *that* was the edge of the environment BlackStar had built! Fake rabbits! It was *all* another trick. To make us *choose* to be in the tank. So we'd be satisfied and happy with our place as slaves and keep gaming!"

I shook my head. "Reno's been skiing up there for weeks, way past that wall."

"So they added it on. What do I care? Phoenix, this is all an illusion created by BlackStar to keep you happy! Oh, my God, here they come!" She waved behind her, at an empty street. "They're going to pull me out of here!"

Dakota pointed to my front drive like there were a bunch of cars or agents or something on her heels.

She was nuts. It was all empty. Nothing was out there but the commuter vehicles driven by our friends.

"I've been trying for weeks to track you down! I met a wasteland hacker. He knew about Kode building a duplicate reality environment. Then he turned me onto some backdoors through the servers . . ."

I didn't know what to say. Not really.

I knocked the door for effect. A nice, wooden clunk. I knocked it again in a another spot. There it made a different sound.

"Look," she urged, "I gotta go or they'll trace my router, then they'll finish the job! Phoenix, you can still be free! You can still escape! Just give the word and . . ."

Then, suddenly, as if she thought someone or something was right behind her, she spun and ran as fast as she could toward the driveway, jumping through a small hedge.

I didn't know what to do, I was so worried. She was all cracked up. The malaria was wreaking havoc on her brain. But I had to follow. Once I got to the bushes, though, I couldn't find a trace of her.

It was as if she just disappeared.

Regular footprints in the dirt, then none.

Not even an indentation where she landed on the other side.

For a second, the hedge gave me the creeps. What if it *was* some kind of portal? What if I reached out my hand and it completely vanished into the other side? What if it hit an invisible wall, like back there in the desert . . . ?

Where had Dakota gone?

My fingers came up, stretching, expecting some kind of tingle or shock. After all, where could she have disappeared to? She was always fast, but not that fast.

I reached out.

Fingers stretching through the air to . . .

Nothing. My hand didn't vanish. It didn't hit an invisible door.

There was no portal. She was out there in the woods, or I was cracking up.

And I wasn't cracking up.

Listening, I could hear her footsteps retreating. Running far away now.

I'd tell Kode about this as soon as I could. That poor girl. She really has bad luck. The bacteria must have been eating away at her brain. We had to get her some help.

I went back into the party, ring in my hand.

It was time. Time to build a life. Time to just be human and frail for a while.

Mi said yes. There was a lot of clapping and hugging, and I saw genuine tears in her eyes. As I held her and kissed those soft, cool lips, my fingers came up, brushing the embedded port on the side of her forehead, knowing we had a bond no normal humans could match.

And that port, that explosive shackle, was really the bottom line.

In games, we didn't have them. Out here, we did. So we *were* here. Our world was real.

In a game, that port wouldn't have still been tucked into the side of her head. Dakota just didn't ever make that connection.

. . .

. . .

. . . **STILL LOADING** . . .

. . .

. . .

Level 48

What a beautiful day that turned out to be. Mi was beaming, my buddies were slapping me on the back, and the afternoon just rolled on and on.

I liked it in the real world, though. We heard you citizens complain so many times about the endless grind of real life. We picked up constant crosstalk about how hard it is. How relentless the pressure can be. The dangers you face are more terrifying than any games can create.

It's not fair how, without money or resources or education, all you really have for an escape is the same place my team made its living.

Reality is brutal. It's cold, hard and merciless. I feel for you, I really do. So I'll give you our best fight—that's my guarantee—when you come online and we're on duty. You can count on Team Phoenix to continue to deliver the very best in digital entertainment. We'll make it so real, so bloody, and so graphic that your everyday life will be a lot less frightening.

That's our BlackStar promise.

I was standing with Reno over by the Ping-Pong table. Not

exactly a bloodlust type of game, but you have to have *actual physical skills*. If you don't, even little kids rough you up.

And Reno and I both sucked at it. It was a fair fight.

The door opened again. No knock. I didn't expect it to be Dakota.

It wasn't. In fact, it was Jevo, although I sure didn't remember inviting him. The big guy wasn't limping, even after the jagged hole Dakota had put through his nethers. Maybe she'd missed because the target was too small.

First to greet him was Max. They seemed to be tight now, especially after Jevo had been chosen as bounty hunter and sent on our trail. And though they'd both been carved up a bit by Dakota, they were now on their way to full health. Max's arm worked fine. I hoped Jevo's injury was more trouble.

And that, right then, was when something twitched. It was right at the side of my eye. Exactly where the port was located.

It burned. Then it subsided. Then it came back again. It felt a lot like when the infection was raging. Oh, *no*. Was *that* coming back? Maybe the ultrabiotic hadn't been strong enough, maybe the . . .

Then something else. It was something Jevo had said as we left him bleeding and dying on that strip mall floor.

What was it?

"If this was a game, you hadn't . . .?"

Wait a minute.

" . . . we hadn't seen the last of him."

Hold on.

Of course he'd be out now too. Right?

What about Max? What about all these people? What about the neighbors? What about this house?

The memories washed over me, a flood of clues. A torrent of stray facts. What had I missed? What had been said?

This was my house, right? We lived in Redwood and worked for BlackStar, right?

But what if . . . from the beginning . . .

No. *This* was real now. Back when we lived in Central Ops, every sound was recorded and the same. Every time a gun shot or a table clanked, it was programmed. That was digital. All created by BlackStar.

Out here, the sounds were individual. The smells were unique. The people were unpredictable. There's no way BlackStar could write software around that. You could always tell. There's always a little glitch.

My love for Mi. My pain. The throb in my neck. All because *I was human* now. I was not something else. I was not . . .

Then, one of those stray facts planted itself right square in the middle of my mind.

It was something Max Kode had said. He'd stressed it more than once: *"To really win, you have to choose to go back in the tank."*

Were we now back in . . . ?

No way.

He'd been lying. Dakota had tortured an alternative out of him. We'd won on our own terms. This was not fake.

Right?

I panned the room. There were so many random events—the laughter, the television, the interaction between York and Jevo and Max and Reno and Mi and everyone and . . .

A ringing phone. The juice stain on the carpet, the small crack in some plaster near the door. One of the hall pictures wasn't hung exactly straight. My keys had fallen off the entryway table and lay in a corner — they'd even picked up stray lint.

That's when my eyes narrowed past them all, focusing on the back wall, on the giant window that overlooked the yard.

Jimmy and Charlotte. They were out there, having a blast. Water balloon fights. Giggling. Laughing.

I looked at their father, Max.

I stared at them.

Such a close resemblance. The same hair. The same faces, just younger.

And then I looked at myself in the wall mirror.

Bigger than Max. Stronger than Max. But still, I *was* Max. I was his clone.

And, the pain in my skull pointed me to this . . . I'd spent *weeks* in his guest house. Where Jimmy and Charlotte had seen me every single day. Growing my hair back. Becoming my human self . . .

Two thoughts suddenly became clear. Each of them made the side of my brain sear like the port had caught fire. I reached up, was it bleeding? Would it explode? Was my mind going somewhere it shouldn't?

First, *how* had Jevo even found us at that strip mall? And silently closed that gate? That was always eating at me. But there just wasn't an answer.

Still, the second thing — how could I have missed it?

Sure, when we'd been floating in the clone soup for years, we didn't look all that good. No hair, no muscles. We were just growth-accelerator pieces of BlackStar property.

Then we'd come out. Jimmy and Charlotte, to be precise, had pulled us out.

And we'd become human. We'd begun using our physical bodies.

It should have occurred to me before. I should have figured this out. Maybe this wasn't a shooter game. Maybe it was a puzzle all along. The whole damn thing.

Because . . . I was Max Kode's clone, right? So, if I was his exact duplicate, living in that guest house . . . *why hadn't Jimmy and Charlotte recognized their own father?*

My eye stopped pulsing. The pain went away.

I solved it, didn't I?

But if I did, that meant . . .

In a burst I dropped my drink and ran full speed toward the front door. Crashing through, onto the porch, I scanned left, right, up, down, everywhere.

Scrambling, crawling, poking with my hands, I scoured the yard. The hedge. The driveway. The grass and gutter and street.

Where was it? Where was the door?

"Dakota!" I screamed. "Dakota! Come back! Come back . . . You were right . . . *You* solved it . . . *You're* the one who won . . ."

Silence.

The wind whistled slightly. Leaves rustled. Bugs crawled. Trees creaked.

But I got no answer.

Other than from Max, who came up behind me and said, "Phoenix, you're missing the party. Mi needs you for something. Time to come back inside."

. . .   . .

🕐

. . .   . .

. . . **GAME SLAVES LOADED** . . .

. . . **PREPARE TO PLAY** . . .

. . .   . .

🕐

. . .   . .

Acknowledgments

Big thanks to Andrew Stuart, Julia Richardson, and Jon Cassir, who moved so quickly and purposefully to bring this book to you. Overdue thanks to all those editors at all those papers and magazines who let me do things in ways they hadn't been done before.

Creative thanks go to Buck, Flash, James T., Zap, Deckard, Logan, Overman, Lara, Marcus, John Marston, and whoever that guy was in Liberty City. Cranial thanks go to Vonnegut, Thompson, Asimov, and PKD. Occupational thanks go to Mark McG., who let me store all those arcade games in the rugby house. It was quite a 1-up on anyone who still played Atari.

Also, to Mom and Dad. You put up with a lot. Dad, you once told me that society, throughout history, reserved a special place for its storytellers. Whether around a campfire or scrawling shapes on a cave wall, the exploration of our humanity is critical to learning the truth about who we are as a race and as individuals.

We've barely begun to reserve that same place for our digital designers. Just like writers, directors, and musicians, developers are weaving incredible tales filled with startling game characters and brilliant observation. But now we get to stand side by side with protagonists and choose our own paths based on personal morality, goals, and experience.

The best part is that we've *barely* scratched the surface of those environments. This decade is a straight throwback to one century ago. The world was just discovering science fiction. *Everything* was possible. Look where we are today. I can't wait to see tomorrow.